one story

Introducing
One Story

One great short story
mailed to you
every three weeks.

For a free trial subscription visit
www.one-story.com

GRANTA

GRANTA 78, SUMMER 2002
www.granta.com

EDITOR   *Ian Jack*
DEPUTY EDITORS   *Liz Jobey, Sophie Harrison*
EDITORIAL ASSISTANT   *Fatema Ahmed*

CONTRIBUTING EDITORS   *Neil Belton, Pete de Bolla, Ursula Doyle,*
Will Hobson, Gail Lynch, Blake Morrison, Andrew O'Hagan, Lucretia Stewart

FINANCE   *Margarette Devlin*
ASSOCIATE PUBLISHER   *Sally Lewis*
CIRCULATION DIRECTOR   *Stephen W. Soule*
TO ADVERTISE CONTACT   *Lara Frohlich* (212) 293 1646
PUBLICITY   *Jenie Hederman*
FULFILLMENT MANAGER   *Richard Sang*
SUBSCRIPTIONS   *Dwayne Jones*
LIST MANAGER   *Diane Seltzer*

PUBLISHER   *Rea S. Hederman*

GRANTA PUBLICATIONS, 2-3 Hanover Yard, Noel Road, London N1 8BE
Tel 020 7704 9776 Fax 020 7704 0474
e-mail for editorial: editorial@granta.com
Granta is published in the United Kingdom by Granta Publications.

GRANTA USA LLC, 1755 Broadway, 5th Floor, New York, NY 10019-3780
Tel (212) 246 1313 Fax (212) 586 8003

Granta is published in the United States by Granta USA LLC and distributed in the United States by
PGW and Granta Direct Sales, 1755 Broadway, 5th Floor, New York, NY 10019-3780.

TO SUBSCRIBE call toll-free in the US (800) 829 5093 or 601 354 3850 or e-mail:
granta@nybooks.com or fax 601 353 0176
A one-year subscription (four issues) costs $37 (US), $48 (Canada, includes GST), $45 (Mexico and
South America), and $56 (rest of the world).

Granta, USPS 000-508, ISSN 0017-3231, is published quarterly in the US by Granta USA LLC,
a Delaware limited liability company. Periodical Rate postage paid at New York, NY, and additional
mailing offices. POSTMASTER: send address changes to Granta, PO Box 23152, Jackson, MS 39225-
3152. US Canada Post Corp. Sales Agreement #40031906.

Printed and bound in Italy by Legoprint on acid-free paper.
Copyright © 2002 Granta Publications.
Design: Random Design.
Cover photographs: Deirdre O'Callaghan

ISBN 1-929001-08-8

GRANTA 78

Bad Company

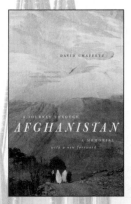
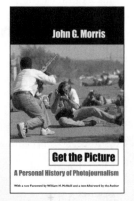

INTRODUCTION

Does writing do any good? Does documentary photography do any good? More specifically, does the kind of writing and photography that examines the lives of people less fortunate than the writer or photographer change those lives for the better?

Anyone with an ordinary share of fellow feeling who has ever interviewed or taken a picture of, say, a beggar in London or a flood victim in Bangladesh has asked this question of him or herself, and sometimes the moral answer that marches uprightly back—oh yes, I am doing good—is no more than a desperate attempt at conscience-salving, there to excuse the original intrusion and the essay, the book, or the exhibition that might profitably follow, usually at some distance, socially and/or geographically, from the intruded-upon, the people who are portrayed. Documentarists like to describe their role using the dignified word 'witness', but, tilting your wine glass at a launch party in a publishing house or a gallery and tut-tutting half-heartedly at pictures from a refugee camp, you may be forgiven for wondering if there is any real difference between witnesses and voyeurs. People rarely become writers or photographers to 'do good'—that instinct is fulfilled by other and more humanly useful vocations. Nor, these days, do many of them have much truck with Marx's dictum of 1845: 'The philosophers have merely interpreted the world in various ways; the point, however, is to change it.'

The name George Orwell often crops up in this argument. Orwell was a documentary writer—there to describe—but also a highly political and polemical writer—there to change what he described. Moreover, he was or tried to be a participant in the different worlds he entered: as a volunteer in the Spanish Civil War, as a lodger in the worst lodging house in Wigan, as a temporary tramp in London and a restaurant scullion in Paris. To understand people and situations more fully and sympathetically, and at a time when social class was a far bigger barrier between people (Orwell was an old Etonian, though not a rich one), he felt he had to go beyond detached observation and into disguise and involvement. Or that at least is how his history is often written. In fact, as Bernard Crick shows in Orwell's fullest biography, his initial motivation was nowhere near as clear. When Orwell wrote his first published book, *Down and Out in Paris and London*, did he intend a political effect, a call to action? Orwell himself later wrote that he then 'knew nothing about working-class conditions... What I profoundly wanted, at that time, was to find some way of getting out of the respectable world altogether.' What he also wanted was to be a writer, a poet or a novelist or a journalist (he wasn't sure which). As Crick concludes, he went among the 'lowest of the low' in London and Paris for literary reasons; the political, conscience-tugging interpretation of the book is retrospective and arises from looking back over this time in the writer's life 'in a more political manner' because of the subsequent books that established his name.

Orwell's exploration of the London underworld in the late 1920s was not some kind of martyrdom in a good cause. He could escape from the East End streets to his parents' house on the Suffolk coast, or to the offices of the *Adelphi* magazine where he wrote reviews and sat in Katherine Mansfield's chair. What drove him was a sympathetic curiosity. Sometimes this now seems comic in its innocent deliberation. (He wanted to know about life in jail. How would he find out? By getting himself arrested. How would he get himself arrested? By getting incapably drunk. What happened? The police court recognized a gentleman down on his luck and 'shot me into the street forthwith'.) But his accounts of drinkers, tramps and dosshouses can never be forgotten; without them, our ideas of British poverty would be very incomplete. He gave drunk, damaged and homeless people a specific, human reality which a visiting reporter with a notebook could never have achieved.

In this issue of *Granta* Deirdre O'Callaghan's photographs are of men who still live in what would once have been called a dosshouse (though of a superior kind), but now goes under the name of hostel. Orwell might easily have stayed here on one of his several journeys. Conditions—beds, cleanliness, care—have improved a lot since his day. Will the pictures 'do good'? It's the wrong question to ask, but they may do—partly because, paradoxically, they don't set out with that intention; these aren't pictures of a 'problem' but of people who, though less lucky, are as funny, various and sad as the rest of us. That thought in itself will at least do no harm.

Ian Jack

GRANTA

I GAVE THE NAMES
Adrian Leftwich

Adrian Leftwich, April 2002

One

In July 1964, when I was twenty-four, my life in South Africa came to a sudden end. The events which brought this about were of my own making. No one else was to blame. In the gulf that opened up between my reach and my limits, between my knowledge and my self-ignorance, between my fantasies and my capacities, I crashed. It did not happen privately, but publicly and in full view of everyone who knew me. The events which took place wrecked a pattern of life which up until then had been active, promising and committed. For reasons which I still do not fully understand, I tried to do things which were far beyond me, and I failed. I tried to help change the world around me but in the process I destroyed my own, I betrayed my friends and colleagues and I damaged the cause which I believed in and had worked for. Most of the people who until then had trusted and respected me now regarded me with contempt. Others, in the government and security services, who had seen me as a radical and troublemaker, knew me to be broken and finished. When I left the country six months later, nothing remained of the life I had led at the start of that year.

It has taken me a long time to be able to look at what happened and try to come to terms with it. But now that the obscenity of official apartheid has been formally buried, perhaps it is time to do so. What follows is as much an essay in the personal politics of fear as it is an essay in the politics of failure and betrayal.

Two

At the Cape of Good Hope, in the Western Province of South Africa, it rains in winter. Winter days are not much shorter than summer ones, but they seem so, because it is colder. People spend less time out of doors. There can be clear, blue spells but it is often overcast and damp. The soil is dark and moist, the trunks of the Cape oaks are wet and black. I do not remember frost. Now and again the mountains which rim the Cape Peninsula were topped with snow and sometimes even Table Mountain had a white fringe on it, but the snow never fell on the town or suburbs.

With its beautiful mountains, its mild climate and its long coasts, the Cape was a wonderful, almost innocent place to grow up during the 1940s and 50s. I came from a liberal, Jewish, professional family.

11

Adrian Leftwich

My father was a quiet but much-loved doctor; my mother taught the piano occasionally, did charity work and played bridge. I did the things that most boys did. I went to the equivalent of a good grammar school (an all-white school in those days), played rugby and cricket in an undistinguished way, climbed the mountains of the Cape at weekends, swam and surfed my way through the hot and often windy summers, and rode around barefoot on my bike. I enjoyed drama at school, and loved being in plays.

It was a wonderful childhood, especially so because the Cape seemed to be exempt from the extremes of climate and politics that characterized much of the rest of the country. Travelling north to Johannesburg in the winter holidays to stay with cousins, I was always struck by the contrasts there: the dry, frost-hardened brown veld, the ugly squatting mine-dumps, the violent city, the relentless segregation. But even as I was entering my teens the political forces whose origins lay in those northern provinces of the Transvaal and Orange Free State had already begun their southward march, and I developed a sense of outrage at the way my fellow South Africans were being treated under apartheid. By the time I reached late adolescence I was writing angry political poetry. It was inevitable, I suppose, that as soon as I entered university I became involved in student and national politics.

Cape winters are driven by a north-westerly wind. The swell of the ocean is grey and thick. Storms batter the sea and it lashes the coast. When it was foggy and the wind was in the right direction, you could sometimes hear the mournful, repetitive thud of the Moullie Point foghorn many miles away, around the arm of Signal Hill, as it warned ships of the dangers at the entrance to Table Bay. Unlike the warmth and windy openness of summer, winters seemed enclosed and dangerous and I felt trapped in them. Summer always came as an escape.

It was in the middle of just such a winter, on July 4, 1964, that I was woken by the security police at dawn. My girlfriend was in the flat at the time. It was a sudden, threatening invasion. One minute I was asleep, the next there was banging on the front door and then the small flat seemed to bulge with security men. They opened drawers and cupboards, pulled books off shelves, fingered their way through files, rifled through papers, read letters, checked address books, clambered on to the veranda and prodded under boxes.

The raid turned out to be one of many that were conducted across the country that morning. The security police had come to search for incriminating material which might connect me with any proscribed political organization or illegal political activity. So far as I knew, the flat was 'clean', apart from a few academic journals and books that were probably banned. But I was wrong. I had made a fundamental error which was to set in motion the events that followed.

About two years previously, I had been recruited into a small organization which came to be known as the African Resistance Movement (ARM), though it had originally been named the National Committee for Liberation (NCL). I did not know everyone who was in it as it was organized in a series of supposedly insulated regions and cells, but its active membership probably consisted of about forty people across the country, plus a wider group of local supporters, and a handful abroad. Its main purpose was to sabotage public installations such as electricity pylons and cables as a means of protest against the apartheid regime. It was careful not to endanger human life. The cause was right, and politically it seemed to me to be the next inevitable step. Small as it was, the organization had in many respects been very successful in what it did. Its activities provided an outlet for the frustration and hopelessness I had increasingly come to feel about conventional forms of resistance to the regime. But I now have the uneasy sense that perhaps it was my personal needs that found expression in those activities, needs that had only a tenuous relationship to the politics of the country. There was excitement in the secret danger of the work, and I was flattered to have been asked to join the organization. Maybe membership of it gave me a sense of self-importance, even of worth. It certainly served to ease the guilt that I had come to feel about growing up white and privileged in South Africa. Perhaps, in striving to be ever more radical, more daring and more risk-taking, I was trying to appear superior to other young men with whom I felt myself to be in competition.

I cannot give a clear profile of my motives except to say that, looking back now, I detect a fatal mixture in them which I was not able to explore. Without really realizing what I was doing, I slipped into a kind of danger for which I was neither suited nor prepared.

Months before that morning's raid, I had been given a document to read by the man who had been training us in the use of explosives. If I remember correctly, it was no more than two or three pages in length. It set out in very general terms the kind of steps one should take when identifying and assessing a target, and how to attack it. It might well have come from an elementary military handbook. In its generality, it was both innocent and incriminating. I had concealed it in a book on one of the shelves and then forgotten about it. There were a lot of books in the flat and it was pure chance that a security man pulled out that particular one. He paged through it, came across the document and handed it to Lieutenant van Dyk, who was in charge. Van Dyk was a well-known and feared member of the Cape Town Special Branch. I had seen him on a few occasions observing demonstrations and protest meetings, always taking notes. A lean man, he stared at one through black-rimmed glasses and could switch rapidly from mild, perceptive questioning to fury. He and his more violent sidekick, 'Spyker' van Wyk, whom I was to meet later, were a formidable pair.

He flipped through the document and seemed uninterested. From where I sat, waiting for the search to finish, I could not see what it was and I tried to appear unconcerned. The men collected a pile of papers, reports, books and an LP which they were going to take away for further examination. Then van Dyk handed me the document, and asked me quietly what it was. When I saw what it was, a wave of fear washed through me and then receded. There was a moment when I felt that my world was about to come to an end. I cannot remember precisely what I said. I probably tried to convey nonchalance, mumbling that it was something I had found or been given, but could not remember where or when, it had hardly seemed important.

I suddenly became aware of the cold. There was cold without and cold within. I began to shiver and moved closer to the one-bar electric fire. 'Cold, hey? I see you feel it,' said van Dyk. There was both menace and understanding in his words. Men like that, hunters of other men, seem to be able to smell fear. I had been involved in importing plastic explosive, blowing up electricity pylons and railway signalling cables and attempting to topple a radio transmitter. To be convicted of such sabotage meant a minimum mandatory prison sentence of at least five years, more likely ten or twenty, possibly life, and conceivably death by hanging. I was in serious trouble.

The security men took the name and address of my girlfriend and then allowed her to go home. They appeared to have no interest in her. Although she was also a member of the organization, she was unknown to them. She kept explosives and other incriminating materials at her flat and in a nearby lock-up. She knew it was important to move them.

Collecting their findings, the security men suddenly left. Still shaken by what they had discovered, I was now confused by their departure. I was unable to think clearly about what had happened or what I should do. Yet what did happen, in the hours, days, weeks and months that followed, was to devastate all our lives. But there was not the slightest premonition of this, in the few empty minutes that followed. I didn't even consider making a run for it, nor think about where I might go. Although I was frightened, a rational adult awareness of the reality of the danger I was facing had not yet displaced the illusion—the illusion of a child—that nothing especially terrible could occur. Something would change the situation. This was not supposed to be happening. It would go away. Time seemed to be suspended. Almost ritually, I washed and dressed. I'm not sure what I intended to do next. A friend and I had planned a day's climbing on the mountain. It was a Saturday morning. It was still early, perhaps seven or seven-thirty. It was very quiet. And it was cold.

Within ten or fifteen minutes, perhaps less, there was a thundering of feet on the stairs and the security men were back. Van Dyk seemed breathless and excited, almost aroused. It was as if he thrived in these sorts of moments, and I saw this in him again, later, during interrogations, when a junior brought him a bit of news from somewhere else. It was almost as if his self-control intensified under excitement and stress. He re-entered the flat and told me that he was placing me under arrest and would be applying to detain me under the (then) ninety-day detention provision whereby people could be held, for interrogation, in solitary confinement without charge for up to ninety days (this could be repeated again and again). Weeks later, I asked him why he had not done this as soon as he found the document. He said he wanted to wait and see what I would do or where I might go. I don't know if this is true, or whether he had in fact not assimilated the implications of the document until he had got back to his car and begun to read it properly.

In the event it did not matter. I was taken to the central police station at Caledon Square and allowed to phone a lawyer (a privilege that was quite usual for whites, if not always for blacks) to tell him that I was going to be detained in solitary confinement under the ninety-day law. They took me over to the cells, above the charge office, and steered me into one that was about five feet by eight. Then they slammed the door and left.

Three

I had spent weekends in the cells before—indeed, in the very same cell on one occasion—after having been arrested on demonstrations or sit-ins. But this was different. I can remember little now about the first two days except that I swayed between hope and terror.

I tried to believe that they would not be able to make much of a single document. I began to make up a story to account for it having been in my flat. I remember saying to myself: 'Well, boy, now you have to sit tight and sweat it out.' If I could stick to my story about the document for long enough, maybe it would be all right.

But my confidence about this began to flap backwards and forwards like a curtain in a breeze, letting in waves of fear. For I was also certain that there was no way out of the cell. There would be no heroic escape from the situation, and I knew that I was guilty, if that is the right word, of what they suspected. I hoped that the lawyer I had phoned would make public the news of my arrest so that others in the organization would be able to go underground or get out of the country immediately, as was our policy if any one of us were to be arrested.

Most of my Cape Town associates heard about my arrest over that weekend or shortly afterwards. Three of them went into hiding and then made daring escapes out of the country by land, sea and air. As they went, some were able to warn people in Johannesburg and a few more managed to escape. I am very glad they did. But others did not. They waited, going about their normal business, in some cases for nearly a month. Why did they wait? I don't know, although I think I should have done exactly the same. After all, I had remained in my flat for that critical fifteen minutes between the departure of the security men and their return to arrest me. Why did I wait? Could I have escaped? Did I want to be caught? Did I not believe that what was happening was real? I don't know.

Four

I am ashamed to write about the events that followed my arrest. Whenever I think about them, there is a side of me that simply wants to die, and always will. But the bare bones can be stated quite plainly. The suddenness, speed and near-comprehensiveness of the disintegration of my will and ability to resist interrogation in solitary confinement took me totally by surprise. It took others by surprise, too. I just caved in.

The security men had shadowed my girlfriend back to her flat and had observed her moving suitcases and boxes. They tracked the equipment to where she had taken it, and arrested her. At midnight on the third day of my detention—it was the Monday after the dawn Saturday arrest—they marched me from my cell and confronted me with what they'd found. It was all there in the suitcases: explosives, detonators, wire, tools and documents. They wanted to know about everything and, especially, everyone involved.

I have two clear memories from that night. First, as I waited for the interrogation to start, I remember seeing balloons of eerie blue light outside the window of Colonel Rossouw's second-floor office. It was the winter fog wrapping itself around the street lights. Beyond loomed the dark shape of the deserted City Hall, its Victorian trimmings glistening black from the damp of the night. Second, I remember seeing Rossouw, the chief interrogator, taking a pair of red rubber gloves from his desk drawer and putting them on as he approached me. Whenever I see gloves like that now, I remember that night.

Rossouw waved the other security men out of his office, shoved me against a wall and started to punch me in the stomach. He roughed me up with his fists, but it was nothing, absolutely nothing, in comparison to what other people in South Africa and elsewhere have been subjected to at the hands of political police. Moments later the other security men burst through the door, wanting (or pretending to want) to have a go as well, screaming at me. But they didn't touch me. I slid to the floor by the wall, more in shock than in pain. At that moment I knew for certain that the roughing up would continue until I eventually cracked. It was then that I started to talk.

Over the following days and weeks, they played the good-guy-bad-guy routine in their interrogations; and I knew and yet did not know that they were doing it. Slowly but surely I spilled the beans. I gave the names of colleagues who had been members of the Cape Town wing of ARM—at first a few, hoping others would go to ground and escape, then a few more and then more. Randolph Vigne, Eddie Daniels, Spike de Keller, Stephanie Kemp, Tony Trew, Mike Schneider and Alan Brooks. Then I gave the names of people in the Johannesburg wing whom I knew, including that of one of my dearest friends, Hugh Lewin. Though some were fortunately able to escape, arrests followed quickly, first in Cape Town, then in Johannesburg. As the organization unravelled, the security police pursued links and connections, making further arrests in the provinces of Natal and the Eastern Cape.

Then, about three weeks after I had been detained, John Harris, one of the Johannesburg members of the organization who had not been arrested, planted a bomb in the city's main railway station. Although a warning was given, the bomb went off before it could be found. An elderly woman was killed, a child mutilated, and twenty-three people were injured. Late that night, my cell door swung open to reveal van Dyk, white with rage, his eyes bulging behind his glasses. He screamed, 'Twenty people have been killed in Johannesburg by one of your bombs. You fucking Jew. Now you'll hang.' He believed that I had concealed John Harris's name from him, so allowing the bombing to happen. In fact, although I had once met John in a different context, I had no idea that he was a member of ARM. And it had been our policy never to endanger human life. I remember the look on van Dyk's face as he drew his finger across his throat, first slowly and then with a final, quick jerk, pointed at me, and slammed the cell door shut.

For the rest of that night I could barely control a muscle in my body, and I shivered in terror until dawn. If I had been cracked by the interrogations of the first week, now I was split wide open. More or less (though not quite) everything that I still knew about the organization poured out. I was to remain in solitary confinement for five months, but I was undone in the first two months, perhaps even the first two minutes, of detention. Any remaining ability to resist the urge to do anything to get out of there—to crawl, to beg, to trade—dissolved that night. Whatever remaining determination I had to stand by my colleagues, whatever commitment I had to doing the right thing—and whatever fear I had of what people would say or think of me if I did not—simply evaporated.

Afterwards I realized that I had learned something else that night. I learned that at the root of every fear I had ever had, and every fear I would ever have, was the impossible thought, the horror, of my own extinction. That terminal terror was at the core of all my fear and it has fed every fear I have had since, however unimportant, and each has seemed like a small reminder and expression of it. Today, when trivial things give me a fright or when I am apprehensive about something relatively minor, I am aware how quickly and directly those superficial fears can connect with that deeper, final fear.

As a child, I did dangerous and stupid things—all children do. I climbed rock faces without ropes, swam in treacherous currents and rode bicycles without brakes on busy roads. In early adulthood, I blew up pylons and dodged police patrols, and I felt tense and excited when doing such things. But none of this implied bravery. Instead it was the false childish courage that comes from self-ignorance. Nothing ever felt life-threatening, and so I don't think I ever really understood fear. I had certainly never known real fear. But now I understood it: now I really understood it.

Three or four weeks after the main interrogations were complete, I was moved from the police station to the local Roeland Street prison. For a while I was held in one of the former death cells, used for condemned prisoners when hangings were still carried out in Cape Town (by the 1960s all hangings were carried out in Pretoria, at the rate of some sixty or seventy executions per year). It was a contradictory place, given its function. Though it had been a kind of death row, it was a large, sunny, airy cell, in a separate block from the rest of the prison. The top half of the door was covered in heavy mesh through which the twenty-four-hour guard could keep watch in case the prisoner tried to take his own life. Final messages by condemned men (I assumed they were men) were scored deeply into the walls. The messages were still visible despite many coats of institutional paint. One, in a corner near the door, read: 'Why does man fear death but death fears no man?'

How many men had been through that cell before being finally led away to the gallows I did not know. Nothing in my life had prepared me for such a place. And the weeks spent in it only strengthened my longing to escape, whatever the cost. For some of the time I was there I believed I might be hanged myself, until it became clear that the authorities were going to try the station bombing separately from other ARM affairs. Which they did: John Harris was found guilty and executed in Pretoria on April 1, 1965. He went to the gallows singing 'We Shall Overcome'.

Looking back, it would be easy to blame my collapse on the roughing up, or the detention in solitary, or the interrogations and the fear they generated, or on my short stay in the former death cell. But it wouldn't really be true. It was much less what was done to me in detention, and much more the encounter with myself that brewed the acid that stripped me. I very quickly realized—almost as soon as I was arrested—that what lay ahead was the probability of twenty years or more in prison, perhaps something even more terrible and final, and that I could not take it. I felt the uncontrollable inner hiss of a deflating capacity to resist. By and by, I was exposed: shameless, self-ignorant, terrified and miserable. I gave names. I betrayed comrades.

Many people in detention and under pressure make statements and many can be made to talk. But I was to do worse: I gave evidence against my friends and colleagues at the trials of the Cape Town and Johannesburg groups. Some eight or nine other members also agreed to give evidence and a few of them went on to do so (the others were not called and were released). But my responsibility for the face-to-face betrayal was by far the greatest. Having been at the centre of the organization, the evidence I gave was the most damaging. Though I was able to protect some members, and some other people who had helped the organization, I told the court in the November 1964 trial of our Cape Town group (Eddie Daniels, Spike de Keller, Stephanie Kemp, Tony Trew and Alan Brooks) about recruitment, about training, about meetings and about attacks on targets, about who did what and where and when. Towards the end of this evidence, I broke down in the box and wept. But it was not over, not yet. I was flown north in a creaking military plane, to be a witness in the Johannesburg trial of Baruch Hirson, Raymond Eisenstein, Fred Prager and my friend, Hugh Lewin.

Though there was one acquittal (Fred Prager) everyone else went to prison. Eddie Daniels served fifteen years on Robben Island; Baruch Hirson served nine years; Hugh Lewin served seven years; Raymond Eisenstein, Tony Trew, Alan Brooks and Spike de Keller each served two years and Stephanie Kemp served one year. Finally, after five months, when there was virtually nothing left to betray and the court cases were completed, the authorities kept their side of the filthy bargain I had struck, removing me from detention, and from South Africa, forever.

Five

I left South Africa on January 1, 1965, at the height of the southern summer, when I was twenty-four. I have never returned. It is where I come from, it is where I grew up. There are some things about it that I miss more than I can bear to think about: the pluralism of the cultures and the colours; the sea and the sun and the oaks and the grapevines below the mountains, and (now) the few people I know personally who are still there or who have gone back. But I miss little else: certainly not the brutality of its history, certainly not the ugliness of its still-enduring social distortions and crudities, certainly not the offensiveness of its staggering inequalities, certainly not its endemic cruelty, and certainly not the continuing violence of its uncertain future. Now with official apartheid dead, I hope that the immensity of the country's optimism will overcome the problems of its new democracy. But I do not feel easy about going back, apart, perhaps, from now and again wishing I could visit some of the places of my childhood.

What had started as a successful late teenage and early adult life was now, in 1965, a wasteland. Nothing remained. I had been an able student at university, president of the university students' union and the national union of students, active in a wide range of causes and committees. I was seen as a good speaker, energetic, courageous and respected. It was thought I would go far. I had spoken out, marched, demonstrated and campaigned against apartheid in all its forms. I had helped to raise scholarship funds for black and brown students. I had made illegal visits to black townships and colleges to forge links with the much more courageous students and activists at those institutions. I had been invited abroad to conferences. I had criticized people for not standing up to be counted. In an article (embarrassingly entitled 'Courage of Conviction') published shortly before my arrest I had even written that 'those who are not for us are against us'. I had called for sacrifice and I had led people to expect things from me, and they did. As I became increasingly involved in ARM, I had urged action and more action. Though I had them, I suppressed my fears about what we were doing and why we were doing it, put aside my doubts about our usefulness and entirely failed to examine not only the sources of my energy, but also the way it was expressed in political activism. I had actively helped to draw people into the organization. They trusted and depended on me.

When arrested and interrogated, I simply collapsed like a house of cards. Giving his verdict in the Cape Town trial, a judge said that to refer to me as a rat was hard on rats.

In the years that followed it is unsurprising that, apart from some family members and a few extraordinary friends, most South African radicals disowned, excommunicated or avoided me. The national student movement which I had led for two years wrote to tell me that I had been struck off its list of life members. I had been a member of the South African Liberal Party, but had grown disillusioned with its policies and practices. Now the party sent me a crisp letter of expulsion. After I arrived in Britain, people advised me not to try to study at this university or that, as there would be much hostility, or it would be very awkward as other South African exiles were there. An old friend advised that I should not study politics and should certainly never try to teach it. People wrote with more or less controlled venom, suggesting I return to the woodwork from which I had crawled. A friend from university days, the distinguished South African poet, C. J. Driver, wrote a novel in which the weakly disguised main character—obviously me—ends up being executed. An acquaintance wrote to say that when he had heard about what happened he had sworn to kill me. People pointedly avoided me. Occasionally in London I would catch sight of a South African exile whom I knew, and I would turn and flee. On the whole I avoided the city and I still sometimes feel uneasy in it. Of course it was not London that I was uneasy with, but myself.

Six

This is only a summary of the outer history of my betrayal. It took a long time for me even to be able to acknowledge what I had done. I doubt I will ever really understand the inner history of my actions. We are all capable of self-deceit, especially when seeking to tell the truth.

When people have spoken to me since about what I did then they tend to express themselves in one of two ways. The charitable way says: No one really knows how he or she will react when faced with those kinds of pressures, however severe or slight, and it is prudent therefore not to judge others. But I have often wondered why we do not know how we will react. Is it because we do not know ourselves sufficiently well? Is that why we may sometimes act in a fog of self-ignorance and so get ourselves into situations which we should not be in and to which we turn out not to be equal? Or is it that we can never anticipate what those situations will be anyway, and that we can never know ourselves until we are in them? I honestly do not know.

The other way says: How could you do it? Why on earth did you behave like that? Why did you collapse so quickly and betray so completely? It is almost incomprehensible how someone like you could do that. Cracking in solitary is understandable, most people do, but going on to give evidence for that bloody state against your colleagues? Why? How could you face yourself while doing it, let alone afterwards?

The simplest and most obvious explanation would be to say that I was yellow: straightforward cowardice explains a lot. But why? My behaviour and outlook before detention and confinement was not cowardly, at least I don't think it was. I did things and risked things that most of my companions did not. In no way did I foresee or plan what happened in detention: I cannot actually imagine anyone planning such a thing. So if it was cowardice, what explains it in those circumstances? I have come to think that not all of the choices we make are as rational as we might want them to be, especially the fateful ones. Perhaps they are more like lunges, propelled by deeper currents of animal fear, survival urges, aggression, insecurity, pain, hate, lust or hunger which surface unpredictably and which can have the power to push aside all values, beliefs, morals, culture, restraint, reason and self-dignity. They don't always do this, but they can. I think something like that was going on when I came to choose what

I was going to do. It was a choice, and it was mine: for although there was pressure and fear and disorientation, no one forced me. I can remember making some elementary calculations of costs and benefits, of what might happen if I did or did not give evidence against my friends and colleagues, searching for justifications and let-outs. But I also have the sense that the choice was actually driven forward on the powerful tide of another kind of energy, one which was prior to rational calculation and assessment. One current in that tide was fear, terrible fear. But it was more complicated than that, and deeper. It was almost as if I had found myself in a situation of my own making but one that I had never intended, never understood, never anticipated. It was as if I had woken up to find myself in someone else's nightmare, or perhaps someone else's life. But it was not a nightmare. It was my own life. It was real, it was horrible, and I had to get out.

I see now that part of the life I had been leading up until my arrest was a lie. Not a calculated lie—but a lie all the same. I must have had some awareness at the time about the tension between the kind of person I was and the kind of work I was doing, but I couldn't have understood it. The fact is that the outer shell of my image and behaviour was false: it was a construction, a sustained act, that arose out of a feeling of inadequacy, a fear of being small or unnoticed or unloved, and a corresponding need to impress people. I'm sure, looking back, that I got involved with political action because political action brought with it certainties and status that I felt I lacked. But by getting involved, I had got into something that started to take on a life of its own. It took me further and further away from being able either to understand my own limits or to accept them. The personal, social and political life I built for myself, although apparently successful, had flimsy foundations. When I was really tested as the person I had constructed and played, the make-up melted away, the false beard fell off, the belt snapped and the borrowed trousers slithered to the floor. The naked little actor, finding that what he thought he had entered as a play had in fact become real life, fled from the stage and begged to be let out of the theatre.

Maybe I allowed myself to become too involved in a struggle whose demands were beyond my capacities.

Seven

I'll try to explain what I mean by this. It was not that I did not believe in the values we stood for against those of apartheid and oppression: it was a detestable regime. However, there were many other white South African radicals who also genuinely loathed apartheid, but who either left the country to live abroad, or stayed without getting dangerously involved. Having decided against committing their lives to the struggle, they seemed to know where and how to draw the line between courageous but prudent opposition, and danger, and to be able to live with that line. Many of them were scattered throughout the universities and professions of Britain, North America and Australia. Some even travelled to South Africa occasionally for research or family reasons and some have gone back to live there permanently since the end of apartheid.

But why did they not cross that threshold into the danger zone? What stopped them committing their lives to the cause, at home or abroad? Why as dedicated anti-apartheiders did they not throw their entire lot in with the struggle? Some did, of course, but they were a handful of extraordinary people. The majority did not and were honest enough to know that the struggle was not their struggle, not really, not personally, and not exclusively, at least not in the sense that they wanted to commit themselves completely to it, to the exclusion of their careers, families and ordinary lives. Where they had the self-discipline, self-knowledge and honesty to match their involvement with their capacities, or to leave the country, I made the error of crossing the threshold into danger. Through genuine detestation of the regime and sympathy and solidarity with those who suffered under it, but without the necessary level of real personal understanding and commitment. But why? Why did I come to feel responsible for all that was going on in South Africa and seek to change it without first taking responsibility for myself? Was this not my real crime, my original one, the crime of self-ignorance, and did my other crimes not follow directly from that?

I can't really answer my own question. This line of thinking might help to explain why I behaved as I did: but perhaps it doesn't. Perhaps it only raises more questions than it answers.

And perhaps it is enough, quite simply, morally and politically, to know that my behaviour was shameful, harmful and wrong. There can be no other starting point than that, whatever the cause or context. Any attempt to explain how these things came to happen will also carry with it the whining implication of justification of some kind, by shifting responsibility to some other place, persons or situation. I have no wish to do that. It was me. I chose to get involved. I acted. I am responsible for what I did in slithering out of it all. I deeply regret how I behaved. If I could change the past, I would. But I cannot. So there it must rest. There it must stay. And some would say that it would therefore be best for me to shut up, say no more about anything and crawl away.

But I do have something to say.

Eight

Those events were for me and others a turning point: both an ending and a beginning. I do not think that any of us had ever seriously anticipated that such a thing would happen and certainly not how it would happen. Afterwards, all the people involved went in completely different directions. The lives we had led in South Africa before that quiet July morning in 1964 simply disintegrated. Friendships dissolved when they seemed healthiest; working relationships collapsed when they seemed bound by hoops of steel; careers ceased abruptly; memberships were ruptured when they appeared lifelong; belongings vanished. Quite suddenly, everyone was ripped from the daily structures of which he or she had been a part and their previous ways of life, having been snuffed out by the events of that year, were seldom given a decent burial.

After being arrested and taken away in the police car that morning, I never again saw the street in which I had lived, nor the neighbourhood in which I grew up. I still visualize it all, frozen as it was in July 1964. Snatched out of the ordinary textures of daily life, I was absorbed by the system, first in Cape Town, then in Pretoria. Having ingested and processed me, it finally spat me out in Johannesburg, five months on, from where I left the country for good. A year later, some books and a few personal possessions followed me to Britain, artefacts from a different time and place. They arrived in a wooden crate when I was living in a freezing stone cottage on the Welsh border and teaching nearby at a school in Oswestry. I found the crate one evening when I came home from work; it had been dumped outside the cottage door, in the snow, as if rejected and abandoned there.

Those who went to prison, and their families, suffered terribly. Although some were released early, others served the full terms. Only one, Eddie Daniels, remained in South Africa after being released, the rest went abroad. They all endured with courage and dignity what I had run away from, and whenever I think of it, I am overwhelmed by shame. Over the years I tried to contact them all, by letter or through intermediaries, to try and say sorry for my weakness, failure and betrayal. Some, with extraordinary generosity (like Eddie Daniels and Stephanie Kemp), responded directly or made contact with me— by letter, sometimes through messages relayed by others, once by phone and occasionally by email. Others, understandably, never have. The kind of apology that I owe them all can never be expressed in words, or in any other way I know. Those who were not arrested, who managed to escape, all went into exile, and had to build new lives of one kind or another outside South Africa, though some have gone back since the collapse of apartheid.

Nine

When I look back, the time since I left South Africa and came to live in Britain seems both compressed and distended: sometimes it flew, at other times it crawled. At first nothing happened, and yet a lot happened. For about fifteen years I lived as if I were half-awake, half-dead. On the surface, I functioned more or less competently. I slowly began to establish some activities and connections that tied me into daily existence in this new place. Initially, trying to find my bearings, I went away: I worked on a kibbutz and then as a farmhand in the southern United States. Then I came back to Britain and taught at a school in Shropshire for a year. More indecision and wandering followed, but eventually I completed my postgraduate studies, took some temporary university jobs and then was lucky to be offered a permanent one in York.

But there was not much else to me, and it was a half life. How could it have been otherwise? For while you can rebuild the outer framework of daily existence quite quickly, you cannot so easily re-establish your integrity, and especially some elementary sense of self-worth. Rebuilding takes time. As when dealing with a rotten tooth or a suppurating wound, you must first find and clear out the muck before healing can commence, otherwise it will spread. And you must be willing to look at that muck.

At first, I did not. Perhaps I could not. I certainly would not have been able to write as I have done here. I thrashed around, hoping to find some justification or even explanation for what had happened which would somehow exonerate me of my own behaviour. That a few good friends even tolerated me during this phase strikes me now as close to miraculous. For as long as I did not really accept and confront my own responsibility, I would never be able to stand on anything that was secure and sure: pretence would go on, weakness would remain, healthy roots would never form. Without embracing some truth, one embraces illusions, hopes, fantasies.

I married and divorced, twice, in quick succession, in the late 1960s and early 1970s, and caused more pain and disruption. I suppose I hoped to find in those relationships the kind of approval and acceptance that would allow me to approve of and accept myself. But you cannot sustain that kind of relationship—or any kind of relationship, perhaps—without some core of self-respect. Now I had even less. I began to rely on sleeping pills, and panicked when they ran low. My sense of fear, and powerlessness in the hands of the security police, stayed with me and I had two recurring dreams which reflected this. In one, I kept imagining that not all the explosives we had accumulated had been found and that some were sweating away in a decaying suitcase in a lock-up somewhere, about to blow up and injure people. In the other dream, I was swimming to Britain. In various versions of the dream I would sometimes see the white cliffs of Dover, or the Houses of Parliament transposed to the coast, or some other physical symbol of the country, appearing over the horizon, and would swim on, feeling relief that I was nearly there. But then a small dinghy with an outboard motor attached would putter up, parallel with me. In it were van Dyk and van Wyk, sometimes Rossouw, and they would wave, laughing at me, saying: 'Swim, man, swim, we'll pick you up before you get there.' I saw a psychiatrist for a while. He was a kindly man who reminded me of Beaker from the Muppet Show. I visited him weekly in his echoing Victorian house outside York. A large clock ticked, slowly, in the hall. A gas fire burbled in the grate in his consulting room. We talked.

There were long silences. Nothing changed. I kept thinking that I needed to change jobs, go somewhere else, take a new name or leave the country. At my lowest times during that period there seemed to be no point in going on, but my will to live appeared to be undefeatably strong. Extinction was terrifying, self-extinction even more so.

Ten

It is not necessary to go on here about this half-life period. But two things did happen, round about the same time, which produced a change.

First, some time in 1980 an important relationship came to an end. The woman had meant a great deal to me, and now she was moving on. I felt desolated by this. And that seemed to be an old feeling which called up and was engulfed by a wider sense of worthlessness, just as a yell into an amphitheatre of mountains will moan and rumble back all around you as if from everywhere.

About the same time, or shortly afterwards, I was visiting two friends in London, Jill and Tony Hall (both psychotherapists), and we started talking about the events of 1964. The last member of the group, Eddie Daniels, had recently been released from jail. We had talked about the events of that year countless times before. But then Jill, a person I knew and trusted completely, suddenly said: 'No. It was not okay at all. Whatever the pressures were, it was not okay to behave like that.'

I know it seems unbelievable, but I had never previously allowed myself to admit this simple truth.

A sense of worthlessness settled on me like a fog which would not lift. All my work, all my activities felt pointless and void, like a facade behind which I crouched in secret shame and fear, terrified of discovery but unable to come out. I realized that I had somehow avoided the truth about myself and what had happened in 1964, and now I was discovering the consequences of that avoidance.

I started going to a therapist called Robin Shohet, whom I saw regularly for some time. It is hard to describe what happened in those sessions. There was nothing dramatic. We sat on big cushions in a small flat, with the sounds of a west London street market wafting up, and at first I thought how silly it was. What could happen in here that would make any difference to anything? 'I have nothing to say to you,' he told me, early on, when I showed my ignorant disdain for the process. But we got past that and I soon found that he wouldn't let me get away with anything. Where I twisted, he challenged. When I tried to explain and dodge he cut me off and brought me back to what I'd done and what I felt about it. I learned what was, for me, a simple lesson of immense importance: to take responsibility for what I had done. Not why I had done it, or the circumstances of my doing it, but that I had done it. That I had betrayed my colleagues. Whatever the circumstances I was nonetheless an agent, not a victim. I had chosen, I had acted. I had behaved disgracefully, appallingly. I could not change what I had done: I would have to live with it. However much I regretted it, the past could not be altered. Unlike many betrayals, mine was public and known, not private and concealed. I could not duck it or suppress it or avoid it. Some people would always hate me. And I had to accept that. But I need not remain sleepless and incapacitated, I could find some way to move on.

Eleven

In early 1984 I threw away my sleeping pills. I was on research leave in Australia at the time. For a while, sleep was intermittent and shallow, like an outgoing tide running fast and thin over the sand of a flat beach, leaving a rippling film of water. But then it began to deepen, as a new tide came in. Slowly, over many, many months, normal sleep returned and with it a feeling of life.

In the years that followed, the recurring dreams became less frequent and then almost disappeared. I began to see the importance of the relationship between the personal and the political in a way I had never considered before. Energy slowly began to return and I devoted myself to my teaching and students. I worked hard at my research and writing, hoping to be able to contribute to the field I work in. And I began to feel more positively that I could settle and put down roots, here in Britain, and came to feel more at ease with my colleagues. Whereas before, raising a family had seemed either impossible or undesirable, I came to see it as a challenge, a plan for the future which did not concern the past. Now, as a parent with two young children, not yet even halfway through their school days,

I have the practical and ordinary responsibilities, commitments and worries which are centred on the children and their needs. The past cannot be changed, of course, nor can it be forgotten, but the future is always open.

Although the events that I have described will always be a part of my present, I now feel a lot further away from that cold morning in July 1964, when it all began, or ended. There are still times when waves of self-disgust and shame well up uncontrollably and I feel they will drown me. The sense of hopelessness returns and I want to run and hide. But I have come to believe not only that it is possible to go on and to keep going, but that we should and we must. There is simply no other way to be: to remember and take responsibility for the past in order to live in the present and contribute to the future; to learn from that past so as never to be like that again; to pass it on. □

TRANSITION

**Winner of
the 2001 *Utne Reader*
Alternative Press Award for
International Coverage**

Congratulations to *Transition*, winner of
the 2001 *Utne Reader* Alternative Press
Award for International Coverage.

The Alternative Press Awards showcase
the best of the independent press.
Transition has won the award for its
international reporting three years in a row.

Read more about this year's awards at
http://www.utne.com/apa/index.tmpl

TRANSITION
We get around.
Visit us at www.TransitionMagazine.com

GRANTA

WHAT THE SKY SEES
Jon McGregor

In the summer the sky is most times blue. A blue so pure and bright that it hurts to look into it. A blue so deep that if you tip your head back and lose the land from the edges of your vision then you become dizzy and have to hold something to steady yourself, for fear of slipping and falling in. The light which pours from out of this blueness sears everything it reaches, grants beauty where there was none. Anonymous fields of wheat become crowds of ears of grain, stagnant canals and drains become millions of glittering waterdrops, tarmac roads become shattered diamonds placed gently into soft black felt. In the summer, the sky is blue and lifted high, transforming the landscape and the actions of the people who live in it, a shimmering blue silence from which there is no hiding place save beneath the surface of the land.

In the autumn the sky is most times white, a ragged dirty white, and you wonder how this could be the same sky but it is. As the earth turns thick and hard beneath it, the sky seems to be struggling to remain unbroken. Cutting winds come from beyond the horizon, slicing across the land, ripping the sheeted clouds which protect the sky. Slashes of light emerge through these tears, running across the fields like searchlights before vanishing over the horizon and leaving the land as sullen as before. The colours of the earth change, and both landscape and lives turn faces away from the sky in preparation for the cold to come. Fields and ditches prepare coats of fallen leaves for themselves, rivers swell. People who grew up in other places claim they can smell the changing of the seasons, but that means nothing here. All we can smell is the richness of the earth. We know the seasons are changing only by the shape and the colour of the sky, stretched over us from horizon to horizon, the length and breadth of a day.

In the winter the sky is most times grey. A dark and bruising grey. The days shorten, the distance between the horizons shrivels, and what little light seeps down is thick and lifeless. There is no danger of falling into the sky at these times, our bodies and our lives anchored to the ground by the weight of the colour of the light. The earth hides secrets at these times, and the land is silent, save for the shriek of winds which the old people will tell you come all the way from Siberia. Sometimes the drains and the canals will freeze, and be covered in snow, and sometimes these snows will come fast in the night and block the roads so that the landscape is nothing but whiteness, all lines and textures concealed. At times it seems as though the land is giving back light to the sky, begging it to lessen the weight of its greyness and trying to hold off the load.

In the spring the sky is all of these colours, and more. Spring comes gradually here, clusters of bright flowers breaking through the surface of the soil and buds of palest green squeezing out of dry branches while the sky fades to light grey, then white, and finally a faint blue. The air cleanses itself then, with a warm wind from the south and sudden bursts of fresh sparkling rain. The sky lifts away from the ground, the horizons drawing apart to stretch it taut and let space and light flood back into our lives. This is the time when change is a daily force, woodlands smeared green overnight, fields purpled with lavender behind your back. This is the time when the floods come, and the ditches and the barriers have to be built a little deeper and a little higher, and the crops have to be replanted. But still, with all this life bursting up towards the sky, still the earth holds secrets. And still the sky watches.

People who grow up in other places talk about the hills having eyes, but that means nothing here. The land is level here and all we have watching over us is the sky, the ever-present, the always watching. People who grow up having hills to climb and valleys to shelter in think of the sky as neutral, as an emptiness sometimes covered over by clouds, but here the sky is all, arching over our lives.

I was seventeen the first time I kissed a girl. She had long dark hair and she took my face in her hands and pushed her mouth on to mine. She seemed to know what she was doing; I certainly didn't. She drew away just as I was beginning to understand what it was that I had been missing, and told me that she would like to see me again in the evening. That we should go somewhere, do something. She vanished inside her house, leaving me to walk away with the taste of her on my wind-cracked lips.

The bus from March, where she lived then, to my father's house in Upwell, where he still lives today, passes down through Wimblington and then swings around to follow the B1098 parallel to Sixteen Foot Drain. It was a journey I made every day, from the school where I was studying for A levels, to my father's house where I helped on the farm in the evenings. The road beside the Sixteen Foot is perfectly straight and lifted above the level of the fields, and looking out of the window on that newly kissed afternoon I felt like we were passing through the sky.

By the time the day had faded to black my father was asleep and ready for another early morning of work. With the taste of her on my lips and the spark she had put in my belly still dancing there, I slipped the car keys from the hook on the wall and took his car. I had driven before, pulling trailers of straw and silage along farm tracks, but I had no licence to be on the road and I knew my father would never give me permission. But she had said she wanted to see me, to go somewhere and do something, and I wasn't about to stay at home with those words in my head and wipe the salt taste of her away. Perhaps, now, I would. But I was seventeen then and things were different.

The drive to her house was easy enough, uneventful. The roads were empty and straight, and the sky was letting in enough moonlight to steer by. But the drive to her house was filled with my questions and her voice and my mouth and her hands and her face and her hair all at once in my head, one after the other, all at once. What had she meant when she said we should go somewhere? And why, when I'd been circling her for months, had she waited until now to show her interest? I didn't understand, but I had her taste and I wanted more.

I soon discovered that she didn't want to go somewhere at all, just to sit beside me in the car and drive through the flatness of the landscape, looking down across the fields from the raised-up road. We drove through Westry, over Twenty Foot Drain, past Whittlesey (and as we passed through Pondersbridge she put her hand on my thigh and kissed my ear). We crossed the Forty Foot Bridge, drove through Ticks and West Moor, the windows open to the damp rich smell of a summer night in the fens (and beside West Moor I put my hand into the length of her hair). We crossed Old Bedford and New Bedford rivers, drove through Ten Mile Bank, Salters Lode and Outwell (and on the edge of Friday Bridge she asked me to stop the car and we kissed for a very long time).

When we finally stopped we looked out across the fields and talked, about the things people talk about when they suddenly come together in that way. Home, and family, and dreams, and awkward silences. Then she turned to me and lifted my thin woollen jumper over my head, the wool snagging against my tingling skin and giving me tiny electric shocks. Starting from a point beneath my belly button she traced a line with her finger, around the edge of my ribcage and over my nipple, down under my chest cavity and up over my other nipple, around the other edge of my ribcage and back down to my belly button—a glorious heart shape burned on to my body by her fingernail. Sometimes, now, I redraw that shape myself, hoping to regain that moment. Sometimes, now, I think of her hair and wonder why I can no longer remember the way it smelled that night.

I remember the way she watched me as I undid the buttons of her shirt and looked at her breasts. I couldn't bring myself to touch them, not then, not so soon, and eventually she took my fingers and placed them there herself. I drew tiny heart shapes around the dark patches around her nipples, and then pulled her close to kiss her again, electrified by her skin on my skin. I can remember the touch of her whisper on my face as we told each other things we had never spoken before and asked for extravagant promises we believed we could keep. And I can remember the way she looked in the rear-view mirror of my father's car when I drove away from her house, knowing that life would be different now and terrified that it would be taken away from me. But I can't remember the way her hair smelled that night, it no longer smells that way.

This place that I have grown up in is a landscape of straight lines, a field of vision dominated by the parallel and the perpendicular. The straightest line of all is the hard blur of the horizon, a single unbending line which encircles the day. When I was a child I used to spin round with my eyes on the horizon, trying to spot the places where the line curved or turned or bent; but I never could, and the mystery of the encircling straight line stayed with me, troubled me, comforted me.

All other lines find their way to the horizon line, sooner or later. The high lines, the connecting lines: the railway tracks, telegraph wires, canals and drains and rivers, all banked and lifted up above the level of the fields and houses. Years ago, playing in the field while my father worked, I looked up to see a line of boats processing grandly through the sky. I think they must have been barges navigating the Sixteen Foot to Lynn, but at the time all I knew was these boats way above my head.

The other lines are the boundary lines, the low lines. There are no hedges between fields here, only ditches. Ditches mark boundaries, and suck the water off the fields, serve as the barriers which stop the sea coming back to reclaim what it rightfully owns; and you can never go far before you find somebody re-cutting the ditches of their land, making them a little deeper, a little wider, one eye on the sky, always wondering when the rains will come and swell the rivers by those few inches too far.

Floods. Sometimes the lines of this place are obliterated, and all that is left is flatness from horizon to horizon. This obliteration is always an act of nature, weather come from the sky to erase the man-made geometry and restore a resemblance to the sunken sea this place once was. Sometimes it will be rain, swelling the rivers until they break out of the embankments and sandbags and rush over the fields, ignoring the prayers of the farmers and settling across hundreds of acres for weeks at a time so that the sky can be seen from below as well as above, clouds and seabirds gliding across the land. Sometimes it will be snow, covering everything, blocking drains and roads, muffling sound as well as vision until mothers forbid children to leave their houses for fear of them losing their way.

I don't remember my mother telling me not to go out, but I suppose I would have been too young.

Sometimes it will be fog which obliterates our geometry, hiding even the horizon, veiling the sky. Sometimes the fog will come in with the floods, and our world will be utterly alien, unmappable, precarious.

The same floods that obliterate also bring life to the land, make our soil the richest in the country. At ploughing time the smell of the earth's nutrients seems to hang in the air, a smell like apple bruises and horse chestnut shells, a smell of pure energy. Sometimes, as a child, I would put my ear to the clodded ground and believe I could hear the richness of the soil, a richness my father claimed would grow five-pound notes if you planted a shilling. I suppose it must have been a similar sound to that which children hear when they listen to shells and hear the sea, but I didn't know that at the time. I had never been to the ocean. The sea regularly came to us, after all, since we lived on land which belonged to the sea.

Flatness, straight lines, a man-made geometry; this is the landscape

I grew up in, a landscape encircled by the unbroken straight line of the horizon.

A nd this is the journey that I never forget. It's a journey I make often, driving into town, but it's this journey I never forget, the night I returned to my father's house from hers, the night when I knew that things were going to be different.

I drove with my hand on my chest, feeling the burn of her finger there still, and I drove along the straight road with the moonlight shining off the Sixteen Foot. She had told me many things I thought I'd never hear, talking about us and we and our as if something had already been decided. Driving along that road I realized that something already had, that I would not after all be able to endure a life of solitude as my father had learned to do. I considered it to be an awakening, a welcoming to adulthood, and it felt right that it should take place out on the road with the sky taking up most of my field of vision and the land flat and dark on all sides.

It was sudden, it was so sudden.

First I was driving along the empty road thinking about her, and then there was a man in the road looking over his shoulder at me and I was driving into him. I don't know where he came from, I don't know why I didn't see him sooner. He was not there and then he was there and I didn't have time to do anything. I didn't have time to flinch, or to throw my hands up to my face, or to shout. I didn't even have time to take my fingers from inside my jumper, and as the car hit him I was flung forwards and crushed my hand against the steering wheel. As the car hit him his arms lifted up to the sky and his back arched over the bonnet and his legs slid under one of the wheels and his whole body was dragged down to the road and out of sight.

His arms lifted up to the sky, his arching back.

The sound his body made when my father's car struck him, it was too loud, too firm, it sounded as though I had driven into a fence rather than a man, it was a thump, it was a smack. And the sound he made, a sound which is always in the back of my throat now, a muffled split-second of a scream.

His arms lifted up to the sky, even his fingers pointing upwards, as if there was something he could reach up there to pull himself clear. His back arching over the bonnet of my father's car before being dragged down. The last I saw before my head hit my chest. The jolt and the lurch as he was lost beneath the wheels. His lifted arms, the sound he made, the lurch of the car, my hand crushed between my chest and the steering wheel.

Then stillness and quiet and me turning the engine off and my heart rattling inside me.

He lay on his back with his legs underneath him, looking up at the night. His legs were so far underneath him that I supposed they were most probably broken. I stood by the car looking at him for a long time before I moved towards him. He made no sound, there was no sound anywhere, the night was quiet and the moon bright and the air still and there was a man lying dead in the road a few yards from me. It didn't feel real, and there are times, now, when I wonder whether it really did happen at all; but then I remember the way his neck felt when I touched my fingers against the vein there. Not cold, but not warm either, not warm enough, the temperature of a stillborn calf. There was no pulse to feel, the man's eyes were seeing nothing. I looked at him some more, at his broken body on the tarmac, his eyes, his open mouth.

He was wearing a white shirt, and a red V-necked jumper, and a frayed tweed jacket. His arms were up beside his head, and his fists were tightly clenched. A broken half bottle of whisky was hanging from the pocket of his jacket. There didn't seem to be any blood anywhere; there were dirty black bruises on his face, but no blood. His clothes were ripped across the chest, but there was no blood. I didn't understand how a man could be dragged under the wheels of a car and not bleed. I didn't understand how he could not bleed and die so quickly.

The whites of his eyes looked yellow under the moonlight.

I didn't understand who he was, why he had been on the road in the middle of the night, how I had not seen him, why he was dead. I didn't know what to do. I knelt beside him, looking out across the fields, up at the sky, at my father's car, at my shaking hands, up to the sky.

The words we've been given by our ancestors to name these places have no poetry. There's no elegance or grandeur in our geographical vocabulary. Our waterways are called drains; not rivers or streams or becks or burns, but drains. And even then they are marked not by old legends but by civil engineering. The Thirty Foot Drain. The Sixteen Foot Drain. The closest our ancestors could bring themselves to come to grandeur was in the naming of the Hundred Foot Drain. Our farms are not named for fancy, but anonymity. Lower Field Farm. Middle Field Farm. Sixteen Foot Farm. Names that give no clue to map readers, outsiders. Names that will never find their way on to tourist maps or guidebooks. People don't come here because they've been drawn by the romantic sound of the place; people don't come here much at all, and so the landscape remains mostly empty and retains its beauty. The poetry of this place is not in the names but in the shapes, the flatness, the bigness, the completeness of the landscape. Only what is beneath the surface of the earth is hidden, everything else between you and the horizon is visible.

The poetry is in the hidden also. In the unseen movements taking place beneath the surface. The cycles of growth and decay which take place in these fields, the nitrates and minerals and salts which come from the sea and crackle life into the roots of the crops. It's the quietness of these hidden processes which so enthrals me, the stateliness of such magical things. This is not poetry which can be named, or fitted on to a picture postcard, this is non-poetry. A secret kept from all except those who have stood and watched the changing of the fields, the colours of the sky, the patterns of the land.

The girl I'd made my journey to that night taught me the words I now use about this place that I love. I think that is why I felt so strongly about her; that, and the promise she held in her fingertips. She talked about the land and the sky in a way that made what I'd always felt make sense. She told me that on a clear day the horizon is about ten miles away and that since the average adult can walk twice that in a day then our landscape is the size of the time from dawn until dusk. She said that ours is the only place so unceasingly flat for this to hold true and that this was a gift. She told me that the flood times are echoes of a past when our land was under salt water and that they're a reminder that we only remain here by the grace of the sea and the sky. She said we should always remember this.

She told me, and I can't remember her exact words because I had her breast pressing against my mouth at the time, but she told me that our sky was so much greater than in other places that it was our reference point in ways that other people could never understand. They say the hills have eyes she said, but we have no hills here and she smiled and I understood.

She said lots of things like this, and I was instantly in love with her language, with the connection she felt with this place, with the way she touched my skin. She made me love this place, and she made me realize why I loved this place, and she made me realize why people from other places do not.

People don't often come here to visit, because they don't understand all this; outsiders don't make their homes here by choice. And people who do stray into these flatlands often get lost, floundering along the roads and tracks from one side of the day to the other without ever reaching the place they're looking for.

(He was an outsider, the man I met that night. I can remember looking at him, into his face, thinking I don't know you, I don't know who you are, I've not seen your face before, you're not from this place, you don't belong here. And that almost took the edge off it, made what I'd done seem a little less terrible. I don't know this man I kept thinking, I don't owe him anything. If he hadn't been dead I think I would have been demanding an apology from him for spoiling my evening. What had he been doing, walking down this road, my road, half-drunk, not looking where he was going? Why should I feel bad for his stupidity? I remember I got it into my head that he was probably from Nazeby, and I remembered my father saying that nothing of worth could ever come out of Nazeby. And so although I felt bad that I had killed a man, and although it is something which keeps me awake in the dark hours, I didn't feel bad that it was this man. And I had my reasons for not doing the right thing that night, on that journey, for doing what I did.)

I had my reasons. Although I've often regretted it, and although I've often thought perhaps my reasons were not enough, I know I would do the same again. I was young then, and scared, and the sky hung so high over me that I couldn't look up until it was done. If I'd been older when I made that journey then perhaps I would have been stronger, perhaps my thoughts would have been clearer. But I was seventeen, and I had never knelt beside a dead man before. So

I drove away. I stood up, and turned away from the man, and walked back to my father's car, and drove away. I didn't look in the rear-view mirror, and I didn't turn around when I slowed for the junction. I suppose it was at that stage that I began to realize what had happened, what I had done. I had driven my father's car into a man, and then over him, and now he was dead. I felt a sort of sickness in me, a watery dread, starting somewhere down in my guts and rising to the back of my throat. My hands were locked on the wheel, I couldn't blink.

I knew before I reached my father's house that I would have to return to the man. The man, the body, the victim, the corpse, the man; whichever word I used made me flinch. But I knew I had to return, that I couldn't leave him laid out on the road like that with his legs neatly folded under his back. I knew that when he was found then somehow I would be found too, and the girl who'd drawn upon my bare chest would not even look me in the eye, and I knew that I couldn't let that happen.

So I fetched a spade from a shed at my father's farm and drove back to where I had hit the man. It sounds so terrible now, so mercenary, cowardly. Absurd. But it's what I did, and I had my reasons. I took the spade, and I walked down the embankment to the field below the road and I took off my thin jumper and began to dig.

I was used to digging. I knew how to strike an angle, break and shift, break and shift, pile the soil neatly so it can be replaced. The field had only recently been harvested, and the stubble was still in the ground. I laid sections of topsoil to one side. I was thinking clearly, working quickly but properly, ignoring the purpose of the hole I was digging. Once, when I was knee-deep in the ground, I looked up the bank and realized what I was doing. But I couldn't see the man, so I managed to swallow the sickness and dig some more. And all this time, the sound of metal on soil, the sky over me.

I dug a hole in the earth until I was in it up to my waist, breaking and shifting, breaking and shifting, metal on soil and soil on metal. My shoes and my trousers became heavy and dark with it, my face and my arms and my chest creased with sweat and dirt. And all the while the sickness rising in my throat, the dead man on the road, the sound of metal on soil, the sky above me.

It was deep enough, it was done. So long as it was further into the ground than the blades of ploughs could reach then it was deep enough, most probably. I walked up the embankment to the road, wanting to hurry and get it done, but holding back from what I had to do. He was still there, he would always be still there, me stood over him under the sky, him lying still on the road, broken.

To touch him.

I would have to touch him. I would have to pick him up and carry him down the embankment and into the hole I had made in the ground. I could hardly bring myself to look at him, and I would have to touch him. Put him in the hole in the ground, the hole I had made, the death I had made in the hole I had made in the earth. I bent down to take his arms. I could smell whisky on his face. I stopped, unwilling to touch him, unwilling to follow my reasons. They were good reasons, but perhaps they were not enough. But then I remembered her skin on my skin and her eyes and I knew I could do anything not to lose that and gripped his elbows and lifted them up to my waist. I backed away towards the embankment and his legs unfolded from beneath him, his head rolling down into his armpit, his half bottle of whisky falling from his pocket and breaking on the road. I didn't stop, I kept dragging him away, away from the road, down the bank, into the field.

I laid him down, this man, beside the hole in the earth which I had made for him, and I rolled him over into it. He fell face down, and I felt bad about that, about his face in the mud.

I returned to the place on the road and picked up the pieces of glass, caught in the moonlight, and threw them down on to his back and then I took the spade and began to pile the earth on to him. This man.

I threw soil upon him until he was gone, until the soil pressed so hard on him that he was no longer a man or a body or a victim or an anything. Just an absence, hidden under the ground. It was only then that I looked up at the sky, dark and silent over me, the moon now hidden by a cloud. I clenched my eyes shut and bit my lip until it bled. And when I returned to my father's house, I showered for hours, long after the hot water tank had emptied and I was left standing beneath a trickle of icy water.

When the dawn comes, when the first light slides in from the east, the sky is the colour of marbles. Thinnest grey, glass, frozen. Behind you, everything is dark still, silhouettes and shadows clinging to the last of the night-time, but as you look to the eastern edge of the horizon there is light.

The sky first, unveiling its shape for the day, cloud formations, texture; then giving that first thin light down to the lines of the land. And if you have the time to stand and watch, you can trace the movement of the light into the morning, the lines of fields and roads creeping towards you and then away to the west until the whole geometry of the day is revealed and the water in the drains begins to steam and shine. And gradually, you will notice the workers arriving, stepping from minibuses and spreading out in long lines across the fields, shadows, crouching, shuffling along the crop lines.

When the mid-morning comes, the sky is the colour of flowering linseed, a pale-blue hint of the full colour to come. Sometimes there will be clouds, joining together to form arches from horizon to horizon, stretching, tearing, scattering patterns across the fields.

Sometimes these clouds bring rain, puddles falling from the air and sinking into the earth, and the sky will darken for a moment. But then the rain will pass and the sky will be brighter. Cleaner. And now the workers are more visible, returning to their trays and boxes after the rain, lifting food from the ground, sorting, trimming, laying down and moving along the line. Occasionally one will stand, stretching an aching back, arching his spine and lifting cramped arms to the sky before returning to the soil.

When lunch time comes, when there is a moment of stillness and silence, the sky is the colour of the summer noon. This blue has no comparison, it is just the pure deep blue of the summer noon in this place. There are no clouds, there is no movement, and you hold your breath and turn around and follow the circle of the unbending horizon line. The workers eat their lunch in silence, gathered beside the road, looking out across the fields the way fishermen watch the sea. The workers spend their days lifting food from the soil; celery, spring onions, leeks, lettuces, fragile growth which would be ruined by machinery. But at noon they pause, and the sky stares down at the earth as if challenging it to reveal its secrets, and gravity seems to be reversed for a moment.

When the late afternoon comes, when the light is only beginning to fade from the day, the sky is the colour of a freshly forming bruise.

The workers are slowing their pace, pausing more frequently to savour the warmth of the soil in their hands, aware now of the slight chill in the air, waiting for the word that the day is over. It was at a moment like this, sitting here as a child and watching the work of harvest, that an old farmer once told me the story about the whale. His father had discovered it, while leading the horses in ploughing; a whale's skeleton, with the jawbone intact and the entire ribcage in place. It was in such good condition, because of the peat in the soil, that they used it in place of timber when they built Upwell's church—the jaws for the door frame and the ribs for the beams in the roof. I'm not sure now if the story was true, but at the time the ghost of that great lost whale haunted my sleep, and kept me away from the church.

When the evening comes, before the embers of the closing of the day, the sky is the colour of my father's eyes. A darkening, muddied blue, hiding shadows and gradually turning away. Awake still, alive, just, but going. Going gently. The workers have left the field and collected their pay, measured by the weight of the food they have gathered, and the marks of their footprints are fading, dusted over with soil blown by a wind from the sea.

I married the first girl I kissed. Some people said that was the wrong thing to do, that I should have gone with other girls, that everyone falls in love with the first girl but that doesn't mean you should marry her. But they were wrong. Some people said they were jealous of us, of our romance, of our reckless commitment, but they were wrong as well. I was in love with her, and I think I still am, but I have never been convinced that she was The One or anything as dramatic as that. I was simply terrified that she would leave and I would never find another girl to draw shapes on my chest and kiss me in the dark hours. So I married her, and ever since I've been terrified that she would find out what I did that night, on my journey back from her house. Why I flinch at the sound of metal on soil, why I drive so slowly at night. She still doesn't know.

We married before we got the chance to go to university. I had to take over my father's farm, and it seemed to make sense for her to move in and help me, to become farmers and turn the soil of the fields where we grew up. My father could no longer work because he had a heart attack that summer. I heard the dogs barking at the tractor in the yard and went outside to see him clutching his chest and turning blue, so I dragged him from the cab into the mud and began to hammer on his chest. I was determined that he wouldn't be lost to the land as well, and I beat his heart with my fists and forced air into his lungs until the blue faded from his skin.

When I remember it now, it's always from a height, me kneeling over my father in the mud of the yard, as if I can see it the way the sky saw it, the dogs circling and barking and me shouting at my father until he could hear me again.

Now my father, the giant man who could pull down trees with his bare hands, the magician who could breathe life into a handful of seeds, now he sits in an armchair clutching a hot-water bottle and watching the sky change colour outside. He refuses to watch television, choosing instead to listen to the radio while he keeps his vigil on the land and sky. Sometimes when I take him his evening meal he will tell me something he's heard on the radio, a concert recording, a weather forecast, a news report, and I'm scared that one day he'll hear my secret coming from the radio.

But he never has done, yet. Often I just sit with him and listen to his short creaking breaths, thankful that he is not yet ready to lay beneath the ground.

My wife doesn't sit with us at these times. She reads, or does the accounts, waiting for me to reassure myself that my father is still well. We do most things together, planting the crops, harvesting, ploughing the soil, and when there is no work to be done we walk the paths beside the drains and talk and look at the sky fading. The evening is when the fields beside the drain smell richest, the warmth of the day evaporating from the soil into the air and bringing with it the smell of the fertility which produces such rich harvests year after year. We walk, and we look at our fields, and we watch the sky, and we hold each other.

We never had children, and although this is sad for us both it has meant that we have spent our evenings growing closer, talking our way into each other or resting in silences. We've moved together the way rail tracks move together as they approach the horizon, and I'm very glad I took my father's car that night and let her draw upon my body.

And yet.

And yet that same night, that same journey I made which took me to her is the same journey which keeps us from ever being one, for we are not so close at all; the secret I hid in the ground is as much between us as if he were lying in our bed.

Sometimes I've tried to tell her, convinced myself that she would understand, that she could forgive me. I imagine myself saying that I have to tell her something very important, that she might be shocked or upset but that she should try and understand. And I imagine her stopping what she is doing and turning to me, joining her small hands in the hollow of my back and saying I can tell her anything. In my head I'm then able to say that a long time ago I drove into a man and killed him and that because I was scared and because I didn't know what to do I dug a hole and buried him. And in my head she kisses my tears away. And in my head she throws cups and saucers at my feet and tells me to leave. I'm ashamed that I don't know her well enough to know how she would react; but I don't and so I've always stopped on the edge of speaking. I know what a danger my secret is and I think it is safer where it remains, buried.

One time I saw a man metal-detecting in the field where my secret is buried. I was driving past and I saw his car parked up on the verge and a faint line of footprints leading out across the soil. The light was clear and strong behind him and he was no more than a silhouette, his shadow rippled across the plough furrows. I sat in my car watching him, the sweeps of his scanner like a pendulum, moving towards the place. Twice I saw him stoop to the ground and dig with a small shovel. Twice I saw him stand and kick the earth back into place and continue his steady sweeping. I wanted to go and tell him to stop, but I couldn't think of a good way of doing so, it wasn't my land, I had no right. He would surely have asked permission, and anyway he was doing no damage so soon after ploughing. He was moving towards the near edge of the field. He must have walked out to the middle and begun there. I don't know what he thought he'd find in these fields, there's no history here, not the sort which gets into museums anyway. There have never been dramatic finds of Saxon villages here, no burial mounds or hidden treasures. The only artefacts our ploughs have ever dragged up are rusted iron anchors from when this flatness was the sea.

Jon McGregor

The effects of ploughing on the soil can be unpredictable. There are the intended effects, the ripping up of hardened ground, the replenishing of nutrients, the breaking of the soil to strengthen it like scar tissue, always in perfect lines. We pride ourselves on the absolute straightness of our plough lines, fixing our eyes with perfect concentration upon distant points for as long as the blade is in the earth. But you can never tell what happens to the earth beneath these lines. Those rusted anchors sometimes found, they've been sunk in this soil ever since it was drained, and sometimes the turning of the earth will bring them closer to the surface and sometimes it will send them further down.

And so it is with my secret, buried down there at the edge of the field. When I dream of him, it's with a sound of the plough metal on soil, the roar of stones and earth as he either tumbles further down or is thrust to the surface. Sometimes I dream that he's been dragged away from the edge of the field, or turned upright with his arms stretched out towards the sky. When I picture him being found it's always his hands, open-palmed, that break the flat surface of the land. And whenever I see him in those dark hours, his face is hidden, covered with mud, only the tufts of a still growing beard sticking through the mask.

I was thinking all this when I watched the man swinging his metal detector back and forth that day. And I was thinking all this when I watched him stop, close to the edge of the field, and dig. I felt that this was the moment I'd been fearing, storing up my dreams until now. I hadn't expected it to happen this way, I'd imagined it differently. Him being dragged into the air by the blades of a plough, scooped into the sky by a ditch-digger, a sudden brutal discovery, not a man with a metal detector easing clods of soil away from his face and hands.

I've long been scared watching ploughing, not just in this field but in all the fields around here. You can see from miles away when a farmer is ploughing, because the gulls rise up in a dense white cloud behind the blades, picking out the worms and insects thrown up by the turning earth, and you can follow them as they rise and fall back and forth across the field. Always in a perfectly straight line. Once I had to help the farmer plough this field, dragging the blades across the spot where my secret is hidden, and I was so scared that I thought

I might follow my father and have to have my chest beaten in the mud and be left to sit indoors. But nothing was revealed that time.

And this day, as I sat watching the man slowly digging, I realized that I wasn't scared. My father would disown me, but the truth would be spoken and there would be nothing hidden, everything would be above the surface beneath the sky.

I got out of my car to stand beneath the sky, lifting my arms and staring into the brightest part of it. It felt like an epiphany. The man in the field looked up at me, and I looked down at him, ready for what he was about to say, ready to make my confession at last. But he just looked at me, packed his tools into a bag, and began hurrying back to his car, stumbling slightly across the furrows. I walked over to him as he was putting his equipment into the boot of his car, and he looked at me nervously. Perhaps he hadn't asked permission from the farmer after all. Did you find anything I asked him, and he said no nothing and got straight into his car and drove away.

I stayed for a while, leaning against my car and looking out across the field, looking at the small pile of earth the man had dug out of the ground. I'd been surprised by my reaction, and I was almost disappointed now. I wondered if that meant the time was right to tell my wife, to sit her down and tell the truth, to hear her reaction and accept her reaction.

I wanted to do this, but I couldn't.

And now here I am again, driving down the road which flanks that field for the millionth time. And this time is no less anxious than the rest, my hands locked on the wheel, my eyes not blinking.

Except the field's not there today. The floods have come again, and this road is like a causeway across the sea. The water reaches as far as the horizon, interrupted only by the fixed points of telegraph poles like the masts of sunken boats. The horizon is close today, a vague boundary somewhere between here and the water and the sky, confused by the thick fog which hangs over the flooded fields.

The road is busy today, cars ahead of and behind me, piercing red lights suspended in a long line through the fog. People are driving very slowly, and I wonder if there are roadworks.

And then it happens, and my secret is revealed.

I'm driving, and I'm looking as always at the place where it happened. And I see bright lights and men in white overalls standing knee-deep in the water. The lights cut through the fog and I see police officers standing on the embankment and a small white tent on the verge. There are two police vans in the road, and it's these that have caused the traffic to slow; a policeman is waving cars past a few at a time, and everyone is looking down to the water where the men in white overalls are doing something with poles and tape. I can hardly breathe, there's a rushing sound in my ears.

The policeman waves at me to stop, and I think I recognize him. He walks over to my window and asks me to wind it down. He tells me we were at school together and I smile and say oh yes and there's a moment of silence. A funny do this isn't it he says then and I say oh yes and I know he's waiting for me to ask him what has happened but I say nothing. There's a generator somewhere, I can hear its muffled rattle.

Yes he says, they found a body, well a kind of body, in the water down there, floating, face down. They think it's been buried down there near twenty years he says, they think the flood water must have disturbed the soil and brought it out. Not much left of it now though he says. I don't think they'll find out who it is, and he straightens up and looks at the traffic. Best let you go on he says. How's the wife, how's your father he asks and I say fine they're both fine thanks I'll be seeing you I say and I press my foot gently down on the accelerator and drive slowly into the fog.

Behind me in my mirror I see him standing looking at the traffic, a line of white lights leading towards him. I see the police vehicles, I see the tent, I see the men wading in the water, and then they've faded into the fog and I am almost home.

And what will happen when I reach home? Everything has changed, but nothing has changed. My wife will still meet me in the hallway with a kiss and touch my thinning hair. I'll still take a meal to my father, and although he might tell me the news of the discovery it will be with a tone no different to what he normally uses. We'll still sit in silence and listen to his creaking breaths, the dogs will still bark when the daylight fades. My secret has been revealed, but it has not been revealed at all. Even if they find out who he was, they have no reason to connect him to me. And he was no one from here anyway, no one from here has gone missing for a long, long time.

So I am safe as I always was, my wife will still want to touch me, I will still wake in the morning and have fields to look out over.

But I'm not safe at all. Each year of holding this secret has eaten away at me, as each flood has carried layers of soil away from the grave I made. And the truth is now barely hidden at all, straining to break out of the thinness of me which holds it in. My wife has come to know something is wrong, and how very wrong it is, and she thinks less of me for it, I know. When she kisses me now she is always first to pull away. When she touches me she is searching, looking for the way in. And her knowledge of my hiding has made her bitter, I know, I can smell it in her hair at night, a worn out smell, a growing old smell.

I drive into the yard and the dogs come barking out to meet me. I sit in my car for a moment, fearful of what I know I must do, too weak to open the door of the car. The lights of my house are clear and warm, spilling into the foggy night. I feel tired, I feel so tired, I want to lie down and sleep and wake when all this has passed. The strength and the relief I felt that day I saw the man metal-detecting, that day I thought my secret would be unearthed to the sky, those feelings have evaporated now, and now all I feel is weak and old. I get out of the car and walk to the house, pushing the dogs away, and meet my wife in the hallway. I look at her, I say nothing. I serve the meal she has prepared for my father and take it through to him. They found a body in a field down the road he says. I know I heard I reply. I can't think it was anyone from round here he says. No I say, I shouldn't think so. He eats his food in small mouthfuls and asks if I'm okay and I look out of the window and say yes thanks I'm fine.

In the spring, when the dark fields turn a pale green, it's possible to watch the new shoots swing from east to west through the day. Later, as the crops become taller and thicker, this movement will become imperceptible; but while the shoots are still small you can watch them following the brightest part of the day. I think this is part of why I feel so old now, why my skin feels thin and grey, because I've forgotten to turn through the day, have stooped, wilted.

I'm not a religious man, but I know about sin. I know what it means to carry that load inside you, shielding it from the light of day, straining to hide it behind ever thinning defences. And I know now that eventually the defences must give way, the load break free, the earth give up its secrets to the sky. And I know that time has come. In the dark hours of last night, while my wife slept beside me, I made a discovery. The load inside me, the sin which has been growing with each moment of deceit, is not what I thought it was at all. It's not that I killed the man, nor even that I dug a hole and buried him face down and told nobody. My sin is in the reasons I had for digging that hole. Fear. Cowardice. But more than these the thinking of him as an outsider, as someone who didn't belong and so didn't matter. This is the weight I've been carrying, and I've not even known until now. Can a man be guilty of something he doesn't even realize he's done? Does a seed planted by mistake still grow?

The mists of yesterday have disappeared now, the sky is reflected clearly in the flooded fields. The day is so open and clear that the great ship of Ely Cathedral is just visible across the water, and I wonder whether that might be a place I could go to put down what I've been carrying and can carry no more. But it's like I said, I'm not a religious man.

The air has a chill to it, a dampness; the air tastes salty like I remember her lips tasted that first night. She is walking beside me now, we are walking the road beside what should be the Sixteen Foot Drain, keeping an eye on the flood levels. The dogs are running ahead, their barking crisp, their claws clicking on the tarmac.

I think of my father, watching this sky through the window, listening to the radio, tasting the burn from his weakened heart. I remember how he used to love walking these roads, when he had time, how he would hoist me up on to his shoulders so I could see further across the land than him. Can you see anything he'd say, what's there, what's there? And I'd make things up, dragons, castles, so as not to disappoint him or let him know that it was really more of the same, that our landscape just kept going.

It was only later I realized that that was what was magical about it, when the girl who is now my wife told me.

I think of my mother, of the story our family has which is never told, of where she might be now.

And I think of the man with his face turned to me and his arms reaching up into the sky, and I wonder who he was. Whether anyone still wonders where he might be now, whether he's been one of the missing persons cases they sometimes show after the local news.

I feel a warmth on my back, and I turn my face to the brightest part of the sky. I stop walking, and she stops and looks at me. I look out across the flooded fields towards the hard blur of the horizon, I look at her. I tell her there is something I have to tell her, that she might be upset or angry but that I have to tell her. She moves closer to me, she joins her small hands in the hollow of my back, she asks me to tell her what it is. And I tell her, in a strong clear voice, that the same night I kissed her in my father's car I drove into a man and killed him and buried him in a hole in these fields. I tell her this, and I tell her my reasons for doing this, and I tell her I am sorry but that I know sorry may not be enough. I speak these words and then I am silent and she looks at me.

And in that flat landscape, under the arch of the pure blue sky, I wait for her to speak. □

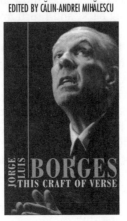

GRANTA

DERVISHES

Rory Stewart

'Dervish are an abomination,' said Navaid.
'What do you mean by a Dervish?' I asked.

'Dervish? Don't you know? It's a very old concept. Fakir? Pir-Baba? Sufi? Silsilah Malang—that beggar doing magic tricks...?' Navaid was staring at a man who was sitting cross-legged in the street with a ten foot black python wrapped round his neck. 'That beggar—medieval mystics like Shahbaz Qalander—the people who live and dance at his tomb. They are all Dervish.'

When I first met Navaid at the tomb of Datta Ganj Baksh a week earlier, he had been examining the same snake man. Now Navaid was standing very still, stroking his white beard. The python was asleep and so was its owner and no one except Navaid seemed to notice them. For the last ten years he had spent his days at the mosques of the old city of Lahore. He had neither a family nor a job. His voice was quick, anxious, slightly high-pitched, as though he were worried I would leave before he had finished his sentence.

'You foreigners love the idea of Dervish—whirling Dervish, wandering Dervish, howling Dervish—exotic—like belly dancers and dancing camels,' he insisted, '—surely you understand what I mean?'

'But what's that beggar there got in common with a medieval Sufi poet?'

'One thing anyway—they are both irrelevant,' replied Navaid. 'They have nothing to do with Islam or Pakistan. They barely exist any more and, if they do, they don't matter. Forget about Dervish.'

Two weeks later I was walking alone along a canal in the Southern Punjab. It had been five months since I started walking across Asia but I had only been in the Punjab for a few days. The arid mountains of Iran had been replaced by a flat, fertile land and I was struggling to turn my limited Persian into Urdu. I was also getting used to new clothes. I was trying to dress in a way that did not attract attention. I was, like everyone else, wearing a loose, thin Pakistani salwar kameez suit and because of the 120 degree heat, a turban. I had swapped my backpack for a small cheap shoulder bag and I carried a traditional iron-shod staff. In Iran I was frequently accused of being a smuggler, a resistance fighter or a grave robber. In the Punjab, because of my clothes, black hair, and fair skin I was often mistaken for one of the millions of Afghani refugees now living in Pakistan. Afghanis have a reputation as dangerous men and this may partly have explained why I had not (so far) felt threatened, walking alone along the Punjab canals.

A snake was swimming down the canal, its head held high over its own reflection, shedding bars of water thick with sunlight in its wake. In a hollow between the towpath and the wheat field was a stunted peepul tree draped with green cloth and beneath it the earth grave of a 'Dervish'. A thin bare-chested man dragged a bucket through the canal, staggered to the edge of the path and threw water on the dry track. I watched him weaving up and down the grass bank towards me. The history of his labour was laid across the path in thick bars of colour. In front of him, where I was walking, was pale sand; at his feet was a band of black mud. Behind him stripe after stripe, each slightly paler than its successor, faded through orange clay until, where he had worked an hour before, nothing remained but pale sand. This was his job in the Canal Department.

'Salaam alaikum.'

'Wa alaikum as-salaam,' he replied. 'Where are you going?'

'To the canal rest-house.'

'Respected one,' he smiled and his voice was nervous, 'most kind one. Give me a sacred charm.'

'I'm sorry, I don't have one.'

'Look at me. This work. This sun.' He was still smiling.

'I'm very sorry. Hoda Hafez, God be with you.'

I turned away and he grabbed me by the arm. I hit him with my stick. He backed off and we looked at each other. I hadn't hurt him but I was embarrassed.

Navaid had warned me I would be attacked walking across Pakistan. 'Violent? Pakistan is a very violent country—the Baluch caught a young Frenchman who was trying to walk here last year and killed him. Or look at today's newspaper—you can be killed by your father for sleeping around, you can be killed by other Muslims for being a Shi'a, you can be killed for being a policeman, you can be killed for being a tourist.'

But I could see that the man I'd hit wasn't dangerous.

He was now smiling apologetically, 'Please, sir, at least let me have some of your water.'

I poured some water from my bottle into his hands. He bowed to me, passed it in front of his lips and then brushed it through his hair.

'And now a charm: a short one will be enough...'

'No, I'm sorry. I can't.'

I couldn't. I wouldn't play the role of a holy man. *'Hoda hafez.'*
A hundred yards further on I looked back through the midday glare
and saw him still staring at me. He had, it seemed, perhaps because
I was walking in Pakistani clothes, mistaken me for what Navaid
would call a wandering Dervish.

An hour later, I turned off the tow-path down a tree-lined
avenue. There was a peepul, with its pointed leaves, trembling forty
feet above. This one had outgrown its pink bark but its trunk was
thin, its canopy small. It looked as though it had been planted when
the canal was completed in 1913, and it would probably outlast the
canal, since part of the peepul under which the Buddha achieved
enlightenment, 2,500 years ago, is still alive in Sri Lanka. Further
on, among the banyans, the ruby flowers of the Dak trees, and the
yellow of the laburnum, was the electric blue spray of a Brazilian
jacaranda imported I assumed by some extravagant engineer. Two
men and two boys were sitting on the lawn.

'Salaam alaikum.'

'Wa alaikum as-salaam. We had been told to expect someone.
Please sit down.' I sat on the charpoy string bed and we looked at
each other. They knew nothing about me and I knew nothing about
them. They were looking at a twenty-eight-year-old Briton, seated
on a colonial lawn, in a turban and a sweat-soaked salwar kameez
shirt. I was looking at a man, also in salwar kameez, but with a ball-
point pen in his breast pocket—an important symbol in an area
where less than half the men can write their own name. The other
man, standing on the balls of his bare feet, staring at me with his
hands forward like a wrestler, looked about sixty. He had shoulder
length grey, curly hair and a short beard. He was wearing an emerald
green kemis shirt and a dark green sarong, a silver ankle ring, four
long bead necklaces and an earring in his left ear. I asked if I could
boil some water.

'Acha, acha, boil water,' said the old man with the earring and
immediately loped off in a half-run, with his hands still held in front
of him, to the peepul tree. I watched him build a fire and shout to
a boy to bring a bucket of water from the canal. He and the column

of smoke seem small beneath the Buddha's tree. The man in green returned with the handleless pot of boiling water in his hands. When I took it from him, I burned my fingers and nearly dropped the pot. He asked if I'd like some honey and I said I would very much.

Ten minutes later, he returned breathless and sweating with part of a cone of dark wild honey in his hands.

'Where did you get it from?'

'From there,' he pointed to the peepul, 'I just climbed up there to get it.' I thought I could see where the cone must be—it was on a branch, some way out, about forty feet above the ground. It was a difficult climb for a sixty-year-old, even without the bees.

'What do you do?'

'Me?' He laughed and looked at the others, who laughed also. 'Why, I'm a Malang—a Dervish, a follower of Shahbaz Qalander of Sewhan Sharif.'

'And what does it mean to be a Dervish follower of Shahbaz Qalander of Sewhan Sharif?'

'Why, to dance and sing.' And he began to hop from foot to foot, clicking his fingers in the air, and singing in a high-pitched voice:

Shudam Badnam Dar Ishq,
Biya Paarsa Ikanoon,
The Tarsam Za Ruswaee,
Bi Har Bazaar Me Raqsam.

Come, behold how I am slandered for my love of God
But slander means nothing to me,
That's why I'll dance in the crowd, my friend
And prance throughout the bazaar.

'Who wrote that?'

'My sheikh, my master, Shahbaz Qalander, when he lived in the street of the whores.'

'And where are you from?'

'Me? Well my family is originally from Iran not Pakistan—we came like Shahbaz Qalander.'

Laal Shahbaz Qalander was a twelfth-century mystic, what Navaid would call a Dervish. He belonged to a monastic order, wandered from Iran to Pakistan preaching Islam, performed miracles, wrote poems like the one above, and was buried in a magnificent medieval tomb in Sewhan Sharif, a city founded by Alexander the Great. His name, Laal Shahbaz, they say records his brilliant red clothes and his spirit, free as the Shahbaz falcon. He is one of the most famous of a group of mystics who arrived in Pakistan between the eleventh and fourteenth centuries. Their poetry and teachings often celebrate an intoxication with and almost erotic love of God that appears at times to transcend all details of religious doctrine. Their mystical ideas seem to have passed, like the use of rosary beads and the repetition of a single phrase for meditation, from the sub-continent through the Islamic world, and from the crusaders into Christianity. It is they, not the Arab conquerors of the earlier centuries who are credited with peacefully converting the Hindus of Pakistan to Islam. Indeed, if the shirt of the man in front of me was like Shahbaz's red, not green, he would look, with his long hair and jewelry, exactly like a Hindu sadhu. And he is one of half a million Pakistanis who gather at Shahbaz's tomb once a year to celebrate with dancing and singing.

'Do you not have land?' I asked, 'Work as a farmer?'

'I used to but I gave it all away—I have nothing now.'

'Nothing?'

'I need nothing else. As the prophet says, "Poverty is my pride,"' he replied, smiling so broadly that I wasn't sure whether I believed him.

When it was time to go, the Dervish accompanied me to the gate hobbling slightly on his bare feet.

'Have you always been a Dervish?' I asked.

'No, I was a civil servant in the Customs Department. I worked in the baggage inspection hall of Lahore airport for fifteen years.'

At the canal bank, I took out some money to thank him for the cooking and the honey. But he was horrified.

'Please,' I said, employing a Persian euphemism, 'take it for the children.'

'There are no children here,' the Dervish said firmly. 'Good luck and goodbye.' He shook my hand and, bringing his palm up to his chest, added in a friendlier voice, 'God be with you—walking is a kind of dancing too.'

When I walked back into Lahore, I met a very different kind of Muslim civil servant. 'Umar is a most influential person,' said Navaid. 'He knows everyone in Lahore, parties all night—meets Imran Khan all the time. And you must see his library. He will explain to you about Islam.'

I was invited to Umar's house at ten at night because he had had three parties to attend earlier in the evening. As I arrived, I saw a heavily built, bearded man in his mid-thirties stepping down from a battered transit van. He was talking on his mobile and holding up his arms so his driver could wrap a baggy, brown pinstriped jacket round him but he managed to hold out a hand to greet me. Still clutching my hand, he led me into a government bungalow of a very similar age and style to the canal rest-house. We removed our shoes and entered a small room, with shelves of English-language books covering all the walls and no chairs. Umar put down the phone, sat on the floor and invited me to sit beside him.

'*Salaam alaikum*, good evening. Please make yourself comfortable. I will tell the servant to get a blanket for you. This is my son, Salman,' he added. The eight year old was playing a video game. He waved vaguely but his focus was on trying to persuade a miniature David Beckham to kick with his left foot.

Umar's eyes were bloodshot and he looked tired and anxious. He never smiled, but instead produced rhetorical questions and suggestions at a speed that was difficult to follow.

'*Multan*, but of course,' he said, 'you must meet the Gilanis, the Qureshis, the Gardezis—perhaps as you move up the Punjab—Shah Jeevna. I know them all. I can do it for you.' All these people were descendants of the famous medieval saints who had converted Pakistan—Navaid's Dervish or Pirs. It was said that they had inherited a great deal of their ancestors' spiritual charisma—villagers still touched them to be cured of illnesses or drank water they blessed to ensure the birth of a male son. They had certainly inherited a great deal of land and wealth from donations to their ancestors' shrines. But Umar, it seemed, was not interested in their Dervish connections. He was concerned with the fact that they were currently leading politicians. Thus the female descendant of a medieval mystic, who once stood in a Punjabi river for twelve years reciting the Qur'an, had just served as Pakistan's ambassador to Washington. Another

Dervish, who it is said entered Multan riding on a lion and whipping it with live snakes, and 600 years later is still supposed to stick his hand out of the tomb to greet pious pilgrims, has descendants who have served as ministers in both the federal and provincial governments. Umar knew them all and perhaps because he was rising fast in the interior ministry he was able to help them occasionally.

Umar's mobile rang again. He applauded one of his son's virtual goals, dragged off his shiny silver tie, dark brown shirt and brown pinstriped trousers for a servant to take away, pulled a copy of V. S. Naipaul's *Beyond Belief* off the shelves and pointed me to a chapter, which I slowly realized was about himself—all this while still talking on the phone.

I had seen Umar earlier in the evening at the large marble-floored house of a wealthy landowner and Dervish descendant. A group of clean-shaven young Pakistani men in casual Gucci shirts had been standing beside Umar drinking illegal whisky, smoking joints and talking about Manhattan. And there he had been, in his brown suit and brown shirt, bearded and with a glass of fruit juice in his hand, not only because he was not educated abroad but also, it seemed, because he had very different views about religion.

'My son,' said Umar proudly, putting down the phone, 'is studying at an Islamic school—his basic syllabus is that he must memorize the whole book of the Qur'an—more than 150,000 words by heart—I chose this school for him.' The boy concerned was trying to decide which members of the Swedish squad to include in his dream team. 'You know our relationship with our families is one of the strengths of Islamic culture. I am sorry it will not be possible for you to meet my wife—but she and my parents and children form such a close unit. When you think of the collapse of families in the West, the fact that there is (I am sorry to say it but I know because I have been to the West) no respect for parents—almost everyone is getting divorced, there is rape on the streets—suicide—you put your people in "Old People Homes" while we look after them in the family—in America and perhaps Britain as well I think, there is rape and free sex, divorce and drugs. Have you had a girlfriend? Are you a virgin?'

'No, I'm not.'

'My friend,' he said, leaning forward, 'I was in a car with a friend the other day, we stopped at the traffic lights and there was a beautiful girl in the car next to us. We wanted to gaze at her but I said, and my friend agreed—do not glance at her—for if you do not stare now you will be able to have that woman in heaven.' He paused for effect. 'That is what religion gives to me. It is very late, my friend, I suggest you sleep here tonight and I will drive you back in the morning.'

'Thank you very much.'

'No problem.' He shouted something. The servant entered, laid two mattresses and some sheets on the floor and led Umar's son out. Umar lay on his mattress, propping himself on one arm, looked at me with half-closed eyes and asked, yawning, 'What do you think of American policy in Iraq?'

His phone rang again and he switched on the TV.

I reopened Naipaul's *Beyond Belief*. Naipaul portrays Umar as a junior civil servant from a rural background with naive and narrow views about religion, living in a squalid house. He does not mention Umar's social ambitions, his library, his political connections, his 'close friends' in the Lahore elite. He implies that Umar's father had tracked down and murdered a female in his family for eloping without consent.

When Umar had finished on the phone I asked whether he was happy with this portrait.

'Yes, of course I am—I have great respect for Naipaul—he is a true gentleman—did so much research into my family. You know most people's perspectives are so limited on Pakistan. But I try to help many journalists. All of them say the same things about Pakistan. They only write about terrorism, about extremism, the Taliban, about feudalism, illiteracy, about Bin Laden, corruption and bear-baiting and about our military dictatorship. They have nothing positive to say about our future or our culture. Why, I want to know?'

He pointed to the television news which showed a Palestinian body being carried by an angry crowd. 'Three killed today by Israel— why is America supporting that? Why did they intervene so late in Bosnia and not in Chechnya? Can you defend the British giving Kashmir to the Hindus when the majority of the population is Muslim? Is it a coincidence that all these problems concern Muslims?'

I tried to say that the West had supported Muslims in Kosovo but he interrupted again.

'Let me tell you what it means to be a Muslim,' he said, lying on his back and looking at the ceiling. 'Look at me, I am a normal man, I have all your tastes, I like to go to parties. Two months ago, a friend of mine said to me, "Umar, you are a man who likes designer clothes, Ralph Lauren suits, Pierre Cardin ties, Italian shoes, Burberry socks—why don't you do something for Allah—he has done everything for you—why don't you do something for him—just one symbol—grow a beard."' He fingered his beard. 'This is why it is here—just a little something for Allah.'

He was now lying on his mattress in a white vest and Y-fronts. I didn't really remember his designer clothes. Perhaps he had been wearing Burberry socks. The new facial hair was, however, clearly an issue for him. I wondered whether as an ambitious civil servant he thought a beard might be useful in a more Islamic Pakistan. But I asked him instead about Dervish tombs. He immediately recommended five which I had not seen.

'What do you think of the Dervish tradition in Pakistan?' I asked.

'What do you mean?'

I repeated Navaid's definition.

'Oh I see—this kind of thing does not exist so much any more except in illiterate areas. But I could introduce you to a historian who could tell you more about it.'

'But what about their kind of Islam?'

'What do you mean? Islam is one faith with one God. There are no different types. You must have seen the common themes that bind Muslims together when you walked from Iran to Pakistan. For example the generosity of Muslims—our attitude to guests.'

'But my experience hasn't been the same everywhere. Iranians, for example, are happy to let me sleep in their mosques but I am never allowed to sleep in a mosque in Pakistan.'

'They let you sleep in mosques in Iran? That is very strange. The mosque is a very clean place and if you sleep in a mosque you might have impure thoughts during the night...'

'Anyway, basically,' I continued, 'villagers have been very relaxed and hospitable in Pakistan. Every night they take me in without question, give me food and a bed and never ask for payment. It's much easier walking here than in Iran. Iranians could be very suspicious and hostile, partly because they are all afraid of the government there. In some Iranian villages they even refused to sell me bread and water.'

'Really, I don't believe this—this is propaganda. I think the Iranian people are very happy with their government and are very generous people. I cannot believe they would refuse you bread and water.'

'Listen to me—they did.'

'Well, this may be because of the Iran–Iraq war which you and the Americans started and financed. Do you know how many were killed in that war? That is why Iranians are a little wary of foreigners. But look how the Iranians behaved...'

The phone rang again and he talked for perhaps ten minutes this time. I examined the bookcase while I waited. Many of the books were parts of boxed sets with new leather bindings and had names like *Masterpieces of the West, volumes 1–11.*

When he turned back to me again, Umar seemed much more animated. He sat cross-legged on the mattress and leaned towards me. 'My friend,' he said. 'There is one thing you will never understand. We Muslims, all of us—including me—are prepared to die for our faith—we know we will go immediately to heaven. That is why we are not afraid of you. We want to be martyrs. In Iran, twelve-year-old boys cleared minefields by stepping on the mines in front of the troops—tens of thousands died in this way. Such faith and courage does not exist in Britain. That is why you must pray there will never be a "Clash of Civilizations" because you cannot defeat a Muslim: one of us can defeat ten of your soldiers.'

'This is nonsense,' I interrupted uselessly. What was this overweight man in his Y-fronts, who boasted of his social life and foreign friends, doing presenting Islam in this way and posing as a holy warrior. It sounded as though he was reciting from some boxed set of leather books called *Diatribes against Your Foreign Guest.* And I think he sensed this too because his tone changed.

'We are educated, loving people,' he concluded. 'I am very active with a charity here, we educate the poor, help them, teach them about religion. If only we can both work together to destroy prejudice—that is why people like you and me are so important. All

I ask is that the West recognize that it too has its faults—that it lectures us on religious freedom and then the French prohibit Muslim girls from wearing headscarves in school.'

'Do you think Pakistan will become an Islamic state on the Iranian model?' I asked.

'My friend, things must change. There is so much corruption here. The state has almost collapsed. This is partly the fault of what you British did here. But it is also because of our politicians. That is why people like me want more Islam in our state. Islam is our only chance to root out corruption so we can finally have a chance to develop.'

I fell asleep wondering whether this is what he really believed and whether he said such things to his wealthy political friends.

When he dropped me off the next morning, Umar's phone rang again and as I walked away I heard him saying in English:

'Two months ago, a friend of mine said to me, "Umar, you are a man who likes designer clothes, Ralph Lauren suits, Pierre Cardin ties, Italian shoes, Burberry socks—why don't you do something for Allah..."'

'A beard?' said Navaid, stroking his own, when I went to meet him again that afternoon at the tomb of Datta Ganj Baksh. 'When people like Umar start growing beards, something is changing. But he must have enjoyed meeting you. His closest friends are foreigners.'

I told Navaid what Umar had said about a clash of civilizations and Navaid shook his head. 'Forget it—don't pay any attention. He was only trying to impress you. He doesn't mean it. People should spend less time worrying about non-Muslims and more time making Muslims into real Muslims. Look at this tomb for example. It is a scandal. They should dynamite this tomb. That would be more useful than fighting Americans.'

Behind us were the tomb gates which Navaid swore were solid gold and which had been erected in the saint's honour by the secular leftist prime minister Zulfiqar Ali Bhutto, Benazir's father. He gave gold gates to the tomb of Shahbaz Qalander in Sewhan Sharif as well. 'That beautiful glass and marble mosque in front of us,' continued Navaid, 'was built by General Zia after he executed Bhutto and took power. Then the CIA killed Zia by making his airplane crash. So the marble courtyard we are standing on was built by our last elected prime minister Nawaz Sharif. It hasn't been finished because of the military coup.'

'But,' he reflected, 'this Dervish of Shahbaz Qalander is all nonsense. This tomb of Datta Ganj Baksh is nonsense. It has nothing to do with Islam, nothing at all. There is nothing in Islam about it. Islam is a very simple religion, the simplest in the world.'

Beside us a man was forcing his goat to perform a full prostration to the tomb of the saint, before dragging it off to be sacrificed.

'But what do people want from these saints' tombs?' I asked.

'Babies, money—but the Prophet, peace be upon him, teaches that we should not build tombs. They tempt us to worship men not God.'

'And the Dervish?'

'They are cheaters, beggars and tricksters, who sit at the tombs becoming rich by selling stupid medicines.' He led me to the balustrade. 'Look at him, for example.' There was a half-naked man in the dust below the courtyard, where the snake-charmer usually sat. His upper body was tattooed with the ninety-nine names of Allah. 'He's probably got a snake in that box, and,' Navaid dropped his voice prudishly, 'has intercourse with his clients.'

'And the history of these saints, their local traditions?'

'I think looking too much at history is like worshipping a man's tomb. Allah exists outside time. And we should not look at local things too much because Allah does not have a nationality.'

'People say there are seventy-four forms of Islam in Pakistan, what do they mean?'

'Nonsense.' Navaid was being very patient with me. 'Islam is one—one God—one book—one faith.'

'But what do they mean? Are they referring to Qadianis?'

'Of course not...Qadianis are heretics, they are not Muslims. General Zia has confirmed this in law.'

'Or are they talking about differences between Naqshbandiyah, Wahhibis, Shi'as...?'

'Pakistani Shi'as are not true Muslims—they are terrorists and extremists—worshipping tombs—they are responsible for these Dervish. But in fact there is only one Islam. We are all the same.' He turned away from the beggar. 'There are no real differences because our God is one.'

The politicians had spent millions on this tomb to win the support of the saint or his followers. But it was only superficially a tribute to the older Pakistan of wandering holy men. Ten years ago, the courtyard of this tomb was the meeting-place for all the diverse groups which Navaid calls Dervish. There was Datta Ganj Baksh, the medieval Sufi himself in his grave, and around him were pilgrims, beggars, mystics, sellers of pious artifacts, drummers, tattooists, dancers, snake charmers, fortune-tellers, men in trances. But most of these figures were now hidden in the narrow streets below the marble balustrade. The politician's gift both asserted the significance of the saint's tomb and obliterated the cultural environment which surrounded it. Their new architecture seemed to be echoing Navaid's vision of a single simple global Islam—a plain white empty courtyard and a marble and glass mosque, bland, clean, expensive—the 'Islamic' architecture of a Middle Eastern airport.

But I still could not understand why Navaid wanted to link these modern dervishes, one of whom was now shouting drunkenly at us from the street, to the medieval saints. 'Navaid, what do you mean by a Dervish? Are you complaining only about mystics, who belong to a monastic order?'

'Of course not.' Navaid gestured at the man who was now cursing our descendants. 'You think he is a mystic in a monastic order?'

'Then what's he got in common with a Sufi poet or a medieval saint?' I was confused by the way he put medieval intellectuals, mystics and poets in the same group as magicians on the fringes of modern society.

'They're all Dervish—you know where that word comes from— from the Old Persian word *derew*, to beg? What they have in common is that they are all rich idle beggars.'

I presumed that explained why he didn't call them 'Fakir', which means 'poor', or 'Sufi' which refers to their clothes.

'But why have you got such a problem with them?' I asked.

'What do you think? Those people down there,' he said pointing at the varied activities in the street, 'wear jewellery, take drugs, believe in miracles, con pilgrims, worship tombs—they are illiterate blasphemers.'

'Alright. But why do you reduce the Sufi saints to the same level?'

'Partly because people like you like them so much. Western

hippies love Sufis. You think they are beautiful little bits of a medieval culture. You're much happier with them than with modern Islam. And you like the kind of things they say. What is it the Delhi Dervish Amir Khosrow says?' Navaid recites:

I am a pagan worshipper of love,
Islam I do not need,
My every vein is taut as a wire
And I reject the pagan's girdle.

That's why I don't like them. Medieval Islamic mystics have no relevance to Islam in Pakistan.'

'Then why do you keep attacking them? Or comparing them to these men in the street?'

Navaid just smiled and wandered off down the courtyard.

Medieval mystics were, I was convinced, not irrelevant. It was they (not Arab invaders) who had converted the bulk of the Hindus to Islam in the first place, while their clothes, practices, poetry and prayers showed strong Indian influences. They were thus both the cause of Pakistani Islam and a reminder of its Hindu past. Furthermore, by drawing the link to the present, Navaid was conceding that the medieval 'Dervish' remained a live tradition in rural Pakistan.

Umar, by contrast, had not felt the need to recognize this. His modern Islam flourished among migrants into Pakistan's cities. He could thus ignore the half a million people who still danced at the tomb of Shahbaz Qalander, and the fact that his friends the politicians were credited with inheriting miraculous spiritual powers from men six centuries dead. His Islam, he felt, was the future. He could safely leave the Dervish behind in a marginalized, illiterate, impoverished world—leave them, in other words, in the rural communities where seventy per cent of Pakistanis still lived.

At last Navaid turned back towards me. 'When I said that Dervish were irrelevant, I meant that Islam is simple, anyone can understand it, it is public, it helps in politics, it does practical things for people. But for a Dervish, religion is all about some direct mystical experience of God—very personal, difficult to explain. Islam is not like that at all—it's there to be found easily in the Qur'an—we don't need some special path, some spiritual master, complicated fasting, dancing, whirling and meditating to see God.'

I could not imagine Navaid dancing. He was a reserved man, basically a puritan by temperament. When he admitted to being anything other than 'a Muslim pure and simple' he said he was a Wahhibi. His Islam, like Umar's, was in a modern Saudi tradition, the tradition of the plain white mosque. It rested on a close attention to the words of the Qur'an, it refused to be tied to any particular place or historical period, it was concerned with 'family life', the creation of Islamic states—an approach that was underwritten by extensive global funding networks. I could guess, therefore, why Navaid was troubled by an other-worldly medieval tradition with strong local roots, personal and apolitical, celebrating poverty, mystical joy, tolerance and a direct experience of God. I could also guess why he wanted to reduce this tradition to a roadside magic trick.

But I might have been wrong. Although Navaid was fifty he was, unusually for a Pakistani man, not married. He claimed never to have had a girlfriend. He was very poor but he did not get a job. Instead he spent his days discussing religion in the courtyards of the ancient mosques in the old city. He could recite a great deal of Persian poetry as well as most of the Qur'an. He was a wanderer and had lived for eleven years in Iran, from just after the revolution. He was a very calm and peaceful man, he had few criticisms of the West and he rejected most of the religious leaders in Pakistan. Although he attacked Dervishes, he knew the name of every obscure Dervish grave in Lahore. I left him by the outdoor mosque of Shah Jehan. He had seated himself under a large peepul tree, to recite a *dhikr*, a repetitive mantra for meditation favoured by the Sufis. As I walked off, I heard him repeating, 'There is no God but God…' with a half-smile on his face, entirely absorbed in the words and I was no longer certain who was the Dervish. □

GRANTA

MAREK MAREK
Olga Tokarczuk

TRANSLATED FROM THE POLISH BY
ANTONIA LLOYD-JONES

Olga Tokarczuk

There was something beautiful about that child—that's what everyone said. Marek Marek had white-blonde hair and the face of an angel. His older sisters adored him. They used to push him along the mountain paths in an old German pram and play with him as if he were a doll. His mother didn't want to stop breastfeeding him; as he sucked at her, she dreamed of turning into pure milk for him and flowing out of herself through her own nipple—that would have been better than her entire future as Mrs Marek. But Marek Marek grew up and stopped seeking her breasts. Old Marek found them instead, though, and made her several more babies.

But despite being so lovely, little Marek Marek was a poor eater and cried at night. Maybe that was why his father didn't like him. Whenever he came home drunk he would start beating Marek Marek. If his mother came to his defence, his father would lay into her too, until they'd all escape upstairs, leaving old Marek the rest of the house to fill with his snoring. Marek's sisters felt sorry for their little brother, so they taught him to hide at an agreed signal and from the fifth year of his life Marek Marek sat out most of his evenings in the cellar. There he would cry silently, without any tears.

There he realized that his pain did not come from the outside, but from inside, and had nothing to do with his drunken father or his mother's breast. It hurt for no particular reason, just as the sun rises each morning and the stars come out each night. It just hurt. He didn't know what it was yet, but sometimes he had a vague memory of a sort of warm, hot light drowning and dissolving the entire world. Where it came from, he didn't know. All he could remember of his childhood was eternal twilight, a darkened sky, the world plunged into gloom, the chill and misery of evenings without beginning or end. He also remembered the day electricity was brought to the village. He thought the pylons that came marching over the hills from the neighbouring village were like the pillars of a vast church.

Marek Marek was the first and only person from his village to subscribe to the district library in Nowa Ruda. Then he took to hiding from his father with a book, which gave him a lot of time for reading.

The library in Nowa Ruda was housed in the old brewery building and it still smelled of hops and beer; the walls, floors and ceilings all gave off the same pungent odour—even the pages of the books reeked as if beer had been poured over them. Marek Marek liked this smell. At fifteen he got drunk for the first time. It felt good. He completely forgot about the gloom, he could no longer see the difference between dark and light. His body went slack and wouldn't obey him. He liked that, too. It was as if he could come out of his body and live alongside himself, without thinking or feeling anything.

His older sisters got married and left home. One younger brother was killed by an unexploded bomb. The other was in a special school in Klodzko, so old Marek just had Marek Marek left to beat—for not shutting in the hens, for not mowing the grass short enough, for breaking the pivot off the threshing machine. But when Marek Marek was about twenty he hit his father back for the first time and from then on they beat each other up on a regular basis. Meanwhile, whenever Marek Marek had a little time and no money for drink, he read Stachura, the beat poet. The library ladies bought the collected works especially for him, covered in blue fabric that looked like jeans.

Marek Marek was still as handsome as ever. He had fair, shoulder-length hair and a smooth, girlish face. And he had very pale eyes, faded even, as if they had lost their colour through straining for light in dark cellars, as if they were worn out from reading all those blue-covered volumes. But women were afraid of him. Once, during a disco, he went outside with one, dragged her into an elder bush and ripped off her blouse. It's a good thing she yelled, because some other boys ran out and punched him. But she liked him; maybe he just didn't know how to talk to women. Another time he got drunk and knifed a guy who was friendly with a girl he knew, as if he had exclusive rights over her. Afterwards, at home, he cried.

He continued to drink, and he liked the way it felt when his legs made their own way across the hills while everything inside—and thus all the pain—was turned off, as if a switch had been snapped off and darkness had suddenly fallen. He liked to sit in the Lido pub amid the din and smoke and then suddenly to find himself, God knows how, in a field of flowering flax and to lie there until morning. To die. Or to drink at the Jubilatka and then suddenly to be snaking his way along the highway towards the village with a bloody face and a broken tooth. To be only partly alive, only partly conscious, slowly and gently ceasing to be. To get up in the morning and feel his head aching—at least he knew what hurt. To feel a thirst, and to be able to quench it.

Finally Marek Marek caught up with his father. He gave the old man such a battering against a stone bench that he broke his ribs and lost consciousness. When the police came they took Marek Marek away to sober up, then kept him in custody, where there was nothing to drink.

Between the waves of pain in his head, in his drowsy, hung-over state Marek Marek remembered that once, at the very beginning, he had fallen; that once he had been high up, and now he was low down. He remembered the downward motion and the terror—worse than terror, there was no word for it. Marek Marek's stupid body mindlessly accepted his fear and began to tremble; his heart thumped fit to burst. But his body didn't know what it was taking upon itself—only an immortal soul could bear such fear. His body was choked by it, shrank into itself and struck against the walls of his tiny cell, foaming at the mouth. 'Damn you, Marek!' shouted the warders. They pinned him to the ground, tied him up and gave him an injection.

He ended up in the detox ward, where with other figures in faded pyjamas he shuffled along the wide hospital corridors and winding staircases. He stood obediently in line for his medicine and swallowed it down as if taking communion. As he stared out of the window it occurred to him for the first time that his aim was to die as soon as possible, to free himself from this rotten country, from this red-grey earth, from this overheated hospital, from these washed-out pyjamas, from this drugged-up body. From then on he devoted every single thought to contriving a way to die.

One night he slashed his veins in the shower. The white skin on his forearm split open and Marek Marek's inside appeared. It was red and meaty like fresh beef. Before losing consciousness he felt surprised because, God knows why, he thought he saw a light in there.

Naturally he was locked up in isolation, a fuss was made and his stay in hospital was extended. He spent the whole winter there, and when he got back home he discovered that his parents had moved to their daughter's place in town and now he was alone. They had left him the horse, and he used it to bring down wood from the forest, which he chopped up and sold. He had money, so he could drink again.

Marek Marek

Marek Marek had a bird inside him—that's how he felt. But this wretched bird of his was strange, immaterial, unnameable and no more bird-like than he was himself. He felt drawn to things he didn't understand and was afraid of: to questions with no answer; to people in whose presence he always felt uncomfortable. He felt the urge to kneel down and suddenly start praying in desperation, not to ask for anything in his prayers, but just to talk and talk and talk in the hope that someone might be listening.

He hated this creature inside himself because it did nothing but increase his pain. If it weren't there, he would have drunk away quietly, sitting in front of the house and gazing at the mountain that rose before it. Then he would have sobered up and cured his hangover with the hair of the dog, then got drunk again without thinking, without guilt or decisions. The hideous great bird must have had wings. Sometimes it beat them blindly inside his body, flapping at its leash, but he knew its legs were fettered, maybe even tied to something heavy, because it could never fly away. My God, he thought, though he didn't believe in God at all, why am I being tortured by this thing inside me? The creature was immune to alcohol; it always remained painfully conscious; it remembered everything Marek Marek had done and everything he had lost, squandered or neglected; everything that had passed him by. 'Fuck it,' he mumbled drunkenly to his neighbour, 'why does it torment me like this, what's it doing inside me?' But his neighbour was deaf and didn't understand a thing. 'You've stolen my new socks,' he said. 'They were drying on the line.'

So the bird inside Marek Marek had restless wings, fettered legs and eyes filled with terror. Marek Marek assumed it was imprisoned inside him. Someone had incarcerated it in him, though he hadn't the faintest idea how that was possible. Sometimes, if he let his thoughts wander, he ran into those terrible eyes deep inside himself and heard a mournful, bestial lament. Then he would jump up and run blindly up the mountain, into the birch copses, along the forest paths. As he ran he looked up at the branches—which one would hold his weight? The bird went on screaming inside him, let me out, set me free, I don't belong to you, I'm from somewhere else.

At first Marek Marek thought it was a pigeon, the kind his father used to breed. He hated pigeons with their round, empty little eyes, their relentless mincing steps, their skittish flight, always changing direction. Whenever there was nothing left in the house to eat his father would make him crawl into the pigeon loft and extract the silly, docile birds. He passed them to his father one by one, holding them in both hands as his father deftly wrung their necks. He hated their way of dying, too. They died like things, like objects. He hated his father just as much.

But once, by the Frosts' pond, he had seen another kind of bird: it had hopped out at his feet and taken off heavily, rising above the bushes, soaring over the trees and the valley. It was large and black, with a red beak and long legs. It gave a piercing scream, and for a while the air went on rippling in the wake of its wings.

So the bird inside him was a black stork, except that it had fettered red legs and lacerated wings. It screamed and fluttered. He would wake up at night hearing this scream inside himself, a horrible, hellish scream. He sat up in bed terrified. Clearly he wouldn't fall asleep again until morning. His pillow stank of damp and vomit. He got up to look for something to drink. Sometimes there were a few drops left at the bottom of yesterday's bottle, sometimes not. It was too early to go to the shop. It was too early to be alive, so he just walked from wall to wall, dying.

When he was sober he could feel the bird in every part of his body, just beneath the skin. Sometimes he even thought he was the bird, and then they suffered together. Every thought that touched on the past or the doubtful future was painful. This pain made it impossible for Marek Marek to think anything through; he had to blur and dispel his thoughts to stop them from having any meaning. If he thought about himself, and what he used to be like, it hurt. If he thought about what he was like now, it hurt even more. If he thought about what he would be like in the future, and what would become of him, the pain was unbearable. If he thought about his house, at once he saw the rotting beams that would come crashing down any day now. If he thought about the field, he remembered that he hadn't sown it. If he thought about his father, he remembered that he had beaten him up. If he thought about his sister, he remembered that he had stolen money from her. If he thought of his beloved mare, he remembered how after sobering up he had found her dead with her newborn foal.

But when he drank, it was better. Not because the bird drank with him. No, the bird never got drunk, it never slept. But Marek Marek's drunken body and drunken thoughts took no notice of the bird's struggles. So he had to drink.

Once he tried to make himself some wine. Angrily he stripped the blackcurrant bushes—the garden was full of them—and with trembling hands threw them into a demijohn. He sacrificed some of his cash and bought sugar, then set up his concoction in the warmth of the attic. He was glad he would have his own wine, and that whenever he started to feel thirsty, he'd be able to go up there, stick in a tube and drink straight from the demijohn. But without even knowing, he'd drunk it all up before it had fermented properly. He even chewed over the must. He had long since sold the television and the radio and the tape recorder. In any case he couldn't listen to anything—he always had the flutter of wings in his ears. He sold the wardrobe with the mirror, the rug, the harrows, his bicycle, his suit, the refrigerator, the icons of Christ wearing his crown of thorns and the Virgin Mary with the heart on the outside, the watering can, the wheelbarrow, the sheaf-binder, the hay-tedder, the cart with rubber wheels, the plates, the pots and the hay—he even found a buyer for the manure. Then he went wandering about the ruins of the houses which had been abandoned by the Germans and discovered some stone troughs hidden in the grass. He sold them to a man who transported them to Germany. He would gladly have sold his tumbledown house to the devil, but he couldn't— it still belonged to his father.

His best days were when by some miracle he had managed to save a little alcohol until morning, so that as soon as he woke up he could take a slug without even getting out of bed. It made him feel blissful, and he would try not to fall asleep and lose that state of mind. He would get up dizzily and sit on a bench in front of the house. Sooner or later his neighbour always came by on his way to Nowa Ruda, pushing his bike. 'You stupid old tramp,' Marek Marek would say, raising a shaky hand in greeting. His neighbour would bestow a toothless grin on him. The socks had been found. The wind had caught them and blown them into the grass.

In November his neighbour brought him a black puppy. 'There you go,' he said, 'no need for you to go on grieving for your mare, though she was a fine horse.' At first Marek Marek took the dog into the house, but it drove him mad by pissing on the floor. So he set up an old bathtub outside the house, turned it upside down and propped it up on two stones. He hammered a hook into the ground and tied the puppy to it by a chain. This was his ingenious makeshift kennel. To begin with the dog kept whining and howling, but eventually it got used to it. It wagged its tail at Marek Marek whenever he brought it some food. With the dog around he felt better somehow, and the bird inside him calmed down a bit. But then in December the snow fell and one night there was such a bad frost that the dog froze to death. He found it in the morning buried in snow. It looked like a bundle of rags. Marek Marek shoved it with his foot—it was completely stiff.

His sister invited him for Christmas Eve, but he quarrelled with her immediately because she refused to serve vodka with the dinner. 'What sort of a Christmas Eve is it, for fuck's sake, without vodka?' he said to his brother-in-law. He put his coat back on and went out. People were already on their way to midnight mass to make sure they got good seats. He hung about near the church, staring at the familiar faces in the darkness. He bumped into his neighbour—even he was stumbling his way across the snow to the village. 'What a winter, eh?' the neighbour said, smiling broadly and clapping Marek Marek on the shoulder. 'Get lost, you silly old fool,' replied Marek Marek. 'Yes, yes, quite,' said the neighbour, nodding, and went into the church. People kept walking past Marek Marek, bowing to him coldly. In the vestibule they shook the snow off their shoes and went on inside. He lit a cigarette and heard the fluttering of tattered wings. Finally the bells began to ring, the congregation fell silent and the priest's voice rang out, distorted by a microphone. In the vestibule Marek Marek let the tips of his fingers skim the cold surface of the holy water, but he didn't cross himself. After a while the smell of steaming furs and festive overcoats dragged out from God knows where made him feel sick. Then he had an idea. He pushed his way back through the vestibule and went outside. The snow was falling hard, as if it was trying to cover up all the tracks. Marek Marek headed for the shop. On the way he stopped off at his sister's shed and took a pickaxe. He used it to break down the shop door, then stuffed his pockets with bottles of vodka, shoving them under his arms and down his trousers. He felt like laughing. 'They'll never bloody well catch me,' he said to himself and spent the whole night pouring vodka into the water tank by the stove. He threw the bottles into the well.

It was the best holiday of his life. As soon as he felt the slightest bit sober he knelt down by the tank, turned the tap, opened his mouth and vodka poured down his throat straight from heaven.

Just after the holiday the thaw began; the snow turned into nasty rain and the world looked like a sodden grey mushroom. The vodka was finished, too. Marek Marek didn't get out of bed. He felt cold and ached all over. He kept trying to think where he might find something to drink. He got it into his head that old Marta might have some wine. Her house was empty because she always went away for the winter. In his mind's eye he could see her kitchen with bottles of home-made wine standing under the table, although in fact he knew that old Marta never made any wine. But maybe this year she had, maybe she'd made some blackcurrant or plum wine and hidden it under the table. To hell with her, he thought, and tumbled out of bed. He walked shakily, because he hadn't eaten for several days and his head hurt, as if it was going to explode.

The door was locked. He kicked it open. The hinges gave a nasty creak. Marek Marek felt sick. The kitchen looked as if old Marta had only left the day before. The table was covered with a checked oilcloth that reached to the floor. On it lay a large bread knife. Marek Marek quickly peered under the table and saw to his surprise that there was nothing there. He began rummaging in the cupboards. He looked in the stove, in the wood basket, and in the chest of drawers where the bedlinen lay neatly piled. Everything smelled of winter damp—of snow, wet wood and metal. He looked everywhere, feeling the mattress and eiderdown, even thrusting his hand into some old gumboots. He had a clear vision of Marta in the autumn, before she left, packing away bottles of home-made wine. But he didn't know where. 'Stupid old bitch,' he said and burst into tears. He sat at the table with his head in his hands, and his tears fell on the oilcloth washing away some mouse droppings. He stared at the knife.

When he left he propped the door shut with a wooden stake because he liked old Marta and didn't want the snow to get into her kitchen. That same day the police called on him. 'We know it was you, anyway,' they said, adding that they'd be back.

Marek Marek lay down again. He felt cold, but he knew he wouldn't be able to keep hold of a hatchet for long enough to chop firewood. The bird was fluttering inside him, and the fluttering was making his body shiver.

Dusk fell suddenly, as if someone had put out the light outside. Freezing rain struck against the windowpanes in steady waves. If only I had a television, thought Marek Marek, as he lay on his back, unable to sleep. Several times in the night he got up and drank water from a bucket; it was cold and horrible. His body kept turning it into tears, which had started flowing that evening and went on till morning, filling his ears and tickling his neck. At daybreak he fell asleep for a while, but his first thought on waking was that there was no more vodka in the water tank.

He got up and peed into a pot. He started looking in the drawers for some string. When he couldn't find any he tore down an old faded curtain and pulled out the cable it had been hanging from. Through the window he saw his neighbour pushing his bike to Nowa Ruda. Suddenly Marek Marek felt blissful; the rain had finally stopped and grey winter light was pouring in through all the windows. The bird had gone quiet, too; maybe it was already dead. Marek Marek made a noose out of the cable and tied it to a hook by the door on which his mother used to hang frying pans. He felt like a smoke and started looking for a cigarette. He could hear the rustle of every scrap of paper, the creaking of the floor, and the pitter-pat on the floorboards when he spilled some pills. He couldn't find a cigarette, so he went straight up to the hook, placed the noose around his neck and slumped to the floor. He felt a massive pain in the back of his neck. Briefly the cable grew tighter, then it slackened and slipped off the hook. Marek Marek fell to the ground, not realizing what had happened. Pain radiated throughout his body and the bird began to scream again. 'I've lived like a pig and I'll die like a pig,' said Marek Marek out loud, and in the empty house it sounded like a challenge. His hands were shaking as he tied the cable to the hook again. He knotted it, tangled and twisted it. The noose was now much higher than before, not so high that he needed a chair, but not so low that he could sit down. He placed the noose over his head, swayed backwards and forwards on his heels for a moment, and then suddenly threw himself to the ground. This time the pain was so great it made his head spin. His mouth gasped for air, and his legs scrabbled helplessly for support, though that wasn't what he wanted. He struggled, amazed at what was happening, until all of a sudden he was seized with such great terror that he wet himself. He looked down at his feet in their threadbare socks, kicking out and slithering in pools of urine. I'll do it tomorrow, he thought hopefully, but he could no longer find any support for his body. He threw himself forward again and tried to prop himself up on his hands, but just then he heard a crash in his head; a bang, a shot, an explosion. He tried to clutch at the wall, but his hand just left a wet, dirty mark. Then he stopped moving, because he still hoped that everything bad would pass by without noticing him. He glued his eyes to the window and a vague, fading thought occurred to him: that his neighbour would come back. Then the bright rectangle of the window disappeared. ☐

GRANTA

THE WAY YOU DO IT

DO IT

Rachel Cusk

The apartment was small. It lay in the basement of one of the new giant chalets that were going up around the edge of the village, six-storey structures fancifully clad in varnished yellow pine that stood at angles to one another in the dirty snow like oversized doll's-houses. Their apartment was supposed to sleep five people. They could hardly fit into it with their rucksacks. They stood around waiting for the tour guide to come and sort it out but when she arrived, a tanned German girl in tight white clothes, she opened her eyes very wide and said no, there has been no mistake, this is for five people. She opened a cupboard and a bed fell out of it. They had to crowd into the kitchenette so that she could demonstrate how the sofa also unfolded. When she had gone, Thomas and Jane moved in unison to the only bedroom, where there was a double bed. Christian and Lucy placed their coats on the sofa. Christian and Lucy had been together longer, but Thomas and Jane were married and talked about having a baby. Martin was married with a child but he had come alone. He took the bed in the cupboard, which necessitated that he sleep with his head directly below the boot rack.

Later they walked up and down the main street looking for a bar. The centre of the little town was lined with boutique windows showing well-lit tableaux of leather and gold. One or two couples, stout and richly dressed, their heads wreathed in steam, stood on the frozen pavements looking in. Now that it was dark the cold was almost airless. Great black walls of night stood just beyond the small illuminations of shops and street lights, thick and impenetrable, so that although they were outside they seemed to be contained within an annex of their claustrophobic apartment. Usually when he came here Martin stayed at a small hotel where men with mournful eyes and drooping moustaches breakfasted silently in the windowless dining room. Twice they passed this hotel: he walked past its modest entrance without saying anything to the others. Looking up he saw the window of the room on the top floor that he and Serena had stayed in last year. The lights were on; there were people in there, and in some strange way it seemed to Martin that it was himself, that he and Serena were in there, eternally living moments of their past. They found a bar that was cladded with pine from floor to ceiling. It was crowded with people speaking German and French. Thomas overheard someone saying that more snow was forecast.

'That's great,' said Jane. She set her mouth in a line and folded her arms on the table, as though she had arranged the snow previously and was glad, but not surprised, to hear that it had arrived.

'Can you ski when it's snowing?' said Lucy.

'Of course you can,' said Christian.

'I've only been skiing once,' said Lucy to Martin. 'Years ago.'

'It comes back,' said Martin.

'I fell over,' said Lucy, 'and skidded all the way down the hill into one of those tow lifts. Somebody's ski went right into my head. I've still got the scar.'

She lifted back her heavy brown hair and searched among the roots with her fingers. Martin saw the dead whiteness of her scalp, speared with swarming dark wires of hair. Thomas was arranging matchsticks on the table top around his bottle of beer.

'Two moves,' he said, 'to get the bottle inside the box without touching the bottle.'

'Without touching the bottle,' said Christian.

'I'm terrible at these,' said Lucy.

'It's pretty difficult actually,' said Jane. She surveyed the bar with a benevolent gaze. Presently she got up and went to look at some framed black-and-white photographs hanging on the wall.

'Come on,' said Thomas.

'Wait,' said Christian. He was leaning forward with his face close to the matchsticks. A vein stood out on his forehead. 'Hang on, I'm going to get it.'

'The way you do it,' said Thomas, 'is like this.'

He moved the matchsticks.

'You didn't say we could do that,' said Christian.

'Okay, okay, I've got one for you,' said Lucy. 'A man is driving along one night with his son and they have a crash. The father dies but the son is still alive and they take him to hospital.'

'What's this?' said Jane, coming back to the table.

'It's a riddle,' said Lucy. 'So the father's dead and they take the son to hospital. They rush him into the operating theatre for surgery. The surgeon takes one look at the boy and says, stop, I can't do the operation, that's my son lying there.' She looked around the table. 'So what's happened?'

'Are you not allowed to operate on your own child?' said Jane. 'Tom, are you not allowed to operate on your own child?'

'So the man in the car thinks the child is his son,' said Thomas. 'And the surgeon also thinks he's his son.'

Christian and Lucy nodded together.

'Are they a gay couple?' said Jane.

Lucy shook her head, her lips pursed.

'The surgeon's a woman,' said Martin. 'She's his mother.'

'Right!' Lucy pointed a finger at him exultantly.

'But you said "he",' said Jane.

'No I didn't,' said Lucy.

'No she didn't,' said Christian.

Thomas got up to get more beers.

'Have you spoken to Serena yet?' asked Lucy.

'No,' said Martin. 'She's probably in bed by now. I'll phone her in the morning.'

'She must have wanted to come,' said Lucy, her faced screwed up in sympathy as though watching someone in pain.

'Yeah.' Martin nodded.

'Did she mind you coming?'

'I don't think so. She's got her mother staying for the week.'

'I think it's really good the way you two are so independent,' said Lucy.

The bar was too hot. Its sealed pine interior seemed to erase the memory of proportion. Suddenly Martin could no longer remember the size of anything, the mountain on which they were perched, the infinity of space and darkness above and below them, nor how far he was from his city, his house and the rooms in which he lived.

'It's snowing,' announced Jane.

They walked back to the apartment. Snow fell on their hair and coats like the soft touches of a thousand ghostly fingers. They walked with muffled footsteps. Thomas ran ahead and lobbed a snowball back at them and the women shrieked. In the apartment Martin waited in the cramped bathroom while Christian and Lucy got undressed. When he came out the room was in darkness. He could see the mound of their bodies in the bed.

'Goodnight,' he said. He got into the narrow camp bed and eased his head back into the cupboard. He woke later to an angled, unfamiliar darkness. His mind inhabited it with its rudimentary life. When he thought of his wife and child he felt like something that had been discarded from his own existence, a component, like a wheel, that had come loose and spun away. He wondered whether Serena had the baby in bed with her. He felt amputated and yet strangely continuing to exist, to grow into the new grooves of minutes and hours like some kind of botanical experiment involving the plotted torture of sunlight.

In the morning he got up and dressed before the others were awake. He manoeuvred himself through the cramped maze of furniture. As he opened the apartment door Lucy's arm flailed up from beneath the bedclothes. He surfaced into the freezing, sunless glare of the street. The sky was white. The air was thin and coldly drenching. It seemed to form crystals in his mouth as he breathed. He bought a croissant from a bakery and ate it as he walked to the lifts. The streets were already full of skiers, streaming in from the tributaries of side streets. Their heavy boots thundered on the pavements. He fed himself into the crowd and was borne through the barriers and into a lift. As they ascended he looked around. The sight of the mountain in daylight was like waking from the futility of a dream. It began to show its peaks and crevices, its colossal flanks, as the lift rose higher. Blue-green waterfalls hung in frozen cascades down rock faces. Trees smoky with frost stood in clouds above the snow. There were children on the lifts ahead of him. Their parents sat to either side of them, as erect as sentries. His own daughter was three weeks old. He imagined them skiing together, when she was older. He had the feeling that this was the correct thing to imagine under the circumstances. These were privileged people. They were rich and safe; they were together. They didn't mean anything to him—they were merely a part of the retraction he must make to get back to where he had been. The thought of his daughter filled him with spurts of nervous warmth, and with the alarm of someone who has dropped a plate and is watching it in the last seconds of its wholeness, before it hits the floor.

The snow was good. Martin knew it through the first contact of his skis. The cloud had cleared and the sky was visibly deepening with blue. He could see the massive, sculpted peaks of other mountains. Their forms seemed to recall the world in a primitive state, in the swirl of creation. Other skiers shot by him, their bodies straight and graceful, swaying from side to side with the precision of metronomes and then vanishing in a spray of powder. He skied at first cautiously and then fast as the rhythm returned to him. By the end of the first run he felt his head cleared of thought. It was like the gauze of illness lifting from the body. He took the lift back up to the top. Suspended above the piste in the sun he was vacantly happy. Other people hung around him in the air, huddled, anonymous, like machines in a state of pause. He skied down again and came back up on the lift. The third time, halfway down, he forked off to the left where the piste divided. The slope faced a different way here. Large, bald blisters of ice shone through the snow. He went down a gully and skidded out the other end to find himself at the top of a broad, icy wall. People were going down it in big curves, slipping metres at a time. He stopped to consider what route he would take through them. Just below him a woman had stalled with her skis facing the wrong way, towards the edge. She was bent over, as though she were looking for something. Her legs were far apart and she clawed the air with her hands. While Martin watched, one of her skis slipped and she shrieked, frantically trying to flatten herself against the slope. A man was peering up at her from a few metres below, shielding his eyes from the sun. Martin recognized Christian.

'Come on!' Christian shouted. 'You've just got to turn.'

'I can't!' Lucy shouted.

'Just turn! Just put your skis down the slope and turn!'

Lucy started to cry. She made a whooping noise that travelled in echoing chimes down the valley.

'Come on!' shouted Christian. He lifted his poles and drove them straight down again into the snow. Then he shook his head and looked up into the air. Lucy roared. A moment later she went sliding and shrieking down another few metres. Christian didn't watch her. He turned and faced out towards the valley in a posture of contemplation.

Martin skied down to Lucy. She was still crying loudly. Close up her face was a wreck of emotion. Deep grooves of anger striated the skin. Tears and mucus were smeared over her red cheeks. Threads of saliva hung from her mouth.

'Follow me down,' he said. 'Just look at my skis and don't look at anything else. Turn where I turn.'

He had no idea whether this would work. He merely desired to unpick her from the snag of what seemed vaguely to him to be her femininity. He wanted to comb it out, the whole tangle of women, until it was straight and clear. He set off slowly. When he looked back he expected not to see her there, but her dark form was looming just behind him. They passed Christian, who seconds later passed them and skied on down to the bottom without stopping. He was waiting for them at the cafe near the lifts. Lucy behaved towards Martin as though some intimacy had passed between them. She was flushed and excited and kept gripping his arm. They had coffee at an outside table. Christian was directly in the sun and his face was screwed up into a piggish mask. Martin felt burdened by their company. He wished he hadn't chosen to come to this part of the resort; he wished he had stayed where he was happy. Thinking this made him realize that happiness was for him an act of subterfuge. The whole flow of his life was towards becoming embroiled. In the hospital, after the baby was born and Serena had fallen asleep, he had sat holding his daughter in a chair beside the bed and she had looked at him with unfocused, empty eyes; and he had felt in that moment oppressed by her need and by his sense that an onerous job had fallen to him by virtue of his being there awake while her mother slept. His daughter was corresponding with him, assuming that he was the first thing in the world; she was already building herself on his foundations and it was too late to stop her. After that it was he who rose, who walked the silty floor of the night with her while her limitless cries unspooled. Serena, always tired or in pain or somehow unhappy, always in the end victimized by the things she had created, seemed to exist more and more in a state of unconstrained emotion. The world of doing lay beneath it all like a settlement beneath the waters of a flood, tragic, unavailing. The baby got on her nerves. She said things like that much as Lucy had stalled on the slope, because it felt true. That was why Martin was here, to see if it really was.

In the evening they went to a different bar, that rocked like the hull of a ship with the loud voices and ruddy faces of skiers. Martin and Lucy and Christian ate dense, oleaginous plates of potatoes and sausage and cheese. Jane and Thomas had cooked for themselves earlier in the tiny kitchen. Jane talked of their day, in which the two of them had travelled by bus to a different part of the resort to ski.

Thomas was Martin's oldest friend, but these days he never saw him alone. Jane kept Thomas away from his old life, as though he were an addict and it a source of temptation. Jane annoyed Martin. Chewing his food, he felt as though his mouth were full of her. She looked at him sharply, head cocked, sensing his distaste.

'How's Serena coping?' she asked.

'I haven't spoken to her yet.'

'How's the breastfeeding going?'

'Fine,' said Martin untruthfully. 'Great.'

Jane didn't believe that you could just do it, have a baby. Her manner towards Martin was that of a person delegated to visit a criminal suburb, offering rehabilitation. Jane and Thomas were ironing out their lives in preparation for parenthood, starching and folding and putting away their youth, their excitement, their spontaneity.

'Has she started expressing her milk?'

Martin was seized by the desire to slap her, to exhort her violently to think about something else. Get out of here, he wanted to shout, go and get drunk, go dancing, make love in a cable car!

'No,' he said. 'Not yet.'

He stopped at a hotel on the way home to telephone. Serena's mother answered. Serena was asleep. The baby was fine, she was right there on her lap. Martin asked her if she was getting any sleep and she said not much. I've got the rest of my life to sleep, she said. She's a party animal, your daughter. He guessed from that that Serena wasn't getting up at night. A stone of worry lodged itself in his chest. She had become distraught almost straight away about being woken. She would lie on her back in the dark and cry while the baby cried in her cot next to their bed. Martin always got up quickly now and got the baby out of the room before she could wake Serena up. Sometimes they fell asleep together on the sofa downstairs. He gave her bottles of formula milk that he mixed and stood in a row before he went to bed. The midwife had said Serena would never establish breastfeeding that way, but he didn't see what else he could do. When he got back to the apartment the others were asleep.

They had two more days of good weather and then clouds closed in around the mountain, swaddling the pistes and lifts in fog. Martin hung around the village alone while the others went ice skating. He had become, somehow, detached from the group. His heroics with Lucy seemed to have created a rift between himself and Christian. They had joined forces with Jane and Thomas, travelling about on buses together to distant pistes and even spending one afternoon when the weather was good sightseeing in the local town. Thomas was a good skier; Martin didn't know how he could stand it, the confinement, the wasted time. Martin's presence on the holiday began to seem more and more brutal. All around him people were giving in to each other, denying themselves. Staring through gift-shop windows with his wife and baby hundreds of miles away, he felt ridiculous. He had finally spoken to Serena. She had an infection in her breasts, so breastfeeding had been abandoned. He was silently aggrieved by this, by the fact she had just stopped without asking him. He felt conspired against in his absence. He felt too that he had failed to protect his daughter. It had been gestating in him, this feeling, and now his hours of inactivity had brought it to life. The baby was his. As a child, he had been for a period fixated by the realization that he was bound to existence by a series of tethers. His shadow, his heartbeat, the ceaseless work of breathing had all, for a while, fascinated and oppressed him. Sometimes he tried not to breathe. Sometimes he would climb a wall or a tree to see if his shadow followed him. He had in his mind a narrow, high place where he would be sufficient to himself.

By afternoon the lifts were open and he went up. People had given up on the day and the mountain was more or less empty. He skied under the ropes at the edge of the piste and headed off into wilderness. This was what he liked best, skiing in the trees. Today he skied dangerously, wildly dodging rocks, hurtling down unmarked valleys. It was still cloudy and he could only see a few feet in front of him. He felt a vicious carelessness of himself. He revelled in his skill and in his right to expend himself. He wound down a long tree-studded slope and came out fast the other end, going over the next incline without stopping. It was bare and very steep; at the bottom he could see the village lights. He turned his skis straight down the hill, wondering if he could make the village in one run. He was going so fast that he nearly closed his eyes, like someone falling asleep at the wheel of a car. Just then his skis abruptly levelled out, and by the time he realized he had hit a path he had nearly crossed it. He skidded sideways but the momentum of the hill threw him over the path and into empty space on the other side. He didn't know what had happened. There was a thick crust of snow overhanging the sheer drop below the path and somehow he was splayed on it, clinging, with nothing beneath him. Someone was speaking to him in French. A ski pole nosed against his face and he grabbed it and felt himself dragged back on to the path. He had lost his skis. When he stood up he fell over straight away. The man helped him up. It was a ski monitor. He was shaking his head and shouting. Martin couldn't speak. The man began to speak in English. You are very lucky, he said. I follow you, you are very lucky. Martin said that he was sorry. Mad, said the man, fou. He offered to walk with Martin back to the village but Martin waved him on. The mountain was turning blue with dusk. His legs twitched violently as he walked slowly down the path towards the village. It was dark by the time he got back to the apartment. The others were out. He got into bed and lay curled on his side.

The next day was the last day. Martin rented new skis and went up with Lucy and Christian. Christian had spent most of the week waiting for Lucy as she crawled and skidded and cried her way down the mountain. Martin offered to ski with her somewhere easy so that Christian could have some time off. He said he didn't feel up to much else, after yesterday. Christian was visibly grateful. He was all right, Martin thought. He took Lucy down to the nursery slopes, where blindingly white expanses of snow rolled out mildly to all sides. It was a pillowy, sensationless landscape that seemed to have been manufactured by his own consciousness. Lucy ploughed sturdily through it, crouched over.

'You see, I can do it when it's like this,' she said at the bottom.

He was filled with the desire to be tender. The top of the mountain, its steep faces, its spikes, stood embedded in his heart like a claw. By lunch time he felt bored and detached. They met up with Christian and he handed Lucy over. The fact of his return was with him now. It was like a wall in front of him. He skied some difficult runs and found that his accident hadn't changed anything. The reality of Serena and the baby was beginning to show through the veil of his absence, coming in glaring flashes as if through rents in his dreams. He tried to set the afternoon afloat, but the thought of what awaited him brought him down from the mountain early. He packed his things back at the apartment and lay on the bed reading a book. He fell into a grey sleep and was woken by Thomas throwing a towel at his head.

'Coming up?' he said. His face was sardonic and excited, conversational, as though two people lived in it.

The others had gone to see a film. The resort was floodlighting one of the pistes. Thomas and Martin went up on the lifts in the dark. Martin told him a bit about Serena, their conversation, the problems with the baby, and to his surprise Thomas was unstoppered and his essence, what he used to be and what Martin realized he must be still, flowed out. Martin wondered how he could keep the secret of himself all through his days and nights with Jane. Or maybe it wasn't like that, maybe Thomas had already accepted what he, Martin, could not seem to. Martin talked on, and Thomas began to seem more and more to him like a point of contact both earthly and divine, a hieratic being, a robed father to whom Martin, the vagrant, the unquiet soul, had returned to seek counsel. They got off the lifts. Hardly anyone else was there. Floodlights had been placed in the snow, forming a yellow river that meandered out of sight. The mountain looked ethereal with the prohibition of its darkness lifted. Martin felt himself connected to a series of moments in his life, which seemed to disclose themselves deeper and deeper in himself one after the other, like a chain of lights. Thomas set off ahead of him, hooting and waving his arm as he snaked down the ghostly piste. Martin watched him until he disappeared. The sky was a dome of stars. He would never, he thought, be here again. He hesitated like a diver over the still surface of water, and launched himself.　　□

Keep good company with this
FREE ISSUE OFFER!

A one year (four-issue) subscription is $37.
You save $14, more than 27%. That's better
than getting a whole issue of Granta, FREE!

There are over 65,000 readers to Granta,
in every corner of the world.

Why not join them?
Or give a subscription as a gift?

You can save up to $60 on the bookshop
price ($12.95 an issue), and get a
regular supply of outstanding
new writing, delivered to your home.

GRANTA
www.granta.com

FREE ISSUE OFFER

Every issue of Granta features outstanding new fiction, memoir, reportage, and photography. Every issue is a handsome, illustrated paperback—because the writing itself endures. Every issue is special. That's why Granta is published only four times a year: to keep it that way. Subscribe and you'll get Granta at a big discount, delivered to your home. (Granta makes a great gift, too: thoughtful, personal, and lasting.)

- A one year (four-issue) subscription is $37. You save $14, more than 27%. That's better than getting a whole issue of Granta, FREE!

- A two year (eight-issue) subscription is $65. You save $38.

- A three year (twelve-issue) subscription is $95. You save $60.

"*Granta* is a wonderful thing. Only the *New Yorker* has an equivalent power to snare you unawares, and you can't fit that into your coat pocket." —*Time Out*

NO POSTAGE
NECESSARY
IF MAILED
IN THE
UNITED STATES

BUSINESS REPLY MAIL
FIRST-CLASS MAIL   PERMIT NO. 115   JACKSON, MS

POSTAGE WILL BE PAID BY ADDRESSEE

GRANTA
P O BOX 23152
JACKSON MS 39225-9814

GRANTA

HIDE THE CAN
Deirdre O'Callaghan

Arlington House, a large red-brick Victorian building in Camden Town, north London, is the largest hostel of its kind in Europe. It houses nearly four hundred men of whom more than half are Irish. The hostel—which reached bursting point in the 1970s, with a thousand occupants—was built in 1905 to provide basic accommodation for single working men. Many of its later residents have been men who came over from Ireland in the 1950s, 1960s and 1970s looking for casual work on building sites in London. Though a lot of them eventually went back to Ireland, some of them did not, and now Arlington House is the nearest thing they have to a permanent home. Beds and rooms are let on a weekly basis and the staff are trained to provide support for the sick, the mentally ill and the alchohol-dependent.

The photographer Deirdre O'Callaghan, who moved to London from Cork in the early 1990s, has been visiting Arlington House over the past four years, taking pictures inside the hostel, joining the men on day trips to the coast, getting to know some of the regulars. 'They emigrated not through choice, stayed though reluctant, and never returned out of pride,' she says. But recently, some of the men from the hostel have been able to go back home for a week or two each year, under the Aisling Project, a charitable scheme which arranges trips back to Ireland. For some of the men this is the first time they have been back to their native country and reunited with their families for twenty or thirty years.

Some of Arlington House's residents including, overleaf, 'Forty Pints'

Tim Healey in the kitchen: I'm still waiting for my golden handshake, I should get it in another two years.
Overleaf: inside one of the community rooms. Some areas of the hostel are designated wet and others dry.

Michael Farrell: When I first came here, there were so many nationalities, I felt like a lost sheep, straying from land to land. There's a lot of sheep here—white, black, yellow, and kangaroo sheep all the way from Australia.

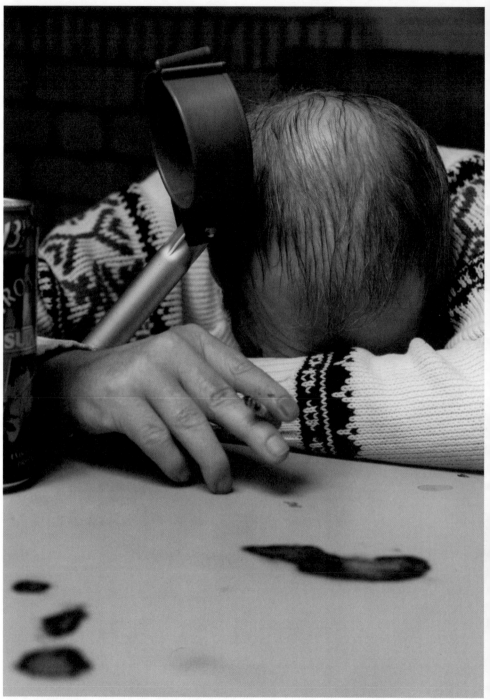

Val: This morning I was watching that Kilroy programme on TV and they had all these kids on talking about growing up without a father and I identified with them. Then they had the fathers on, and all I could think was: 'Why the hell did you leave them?'

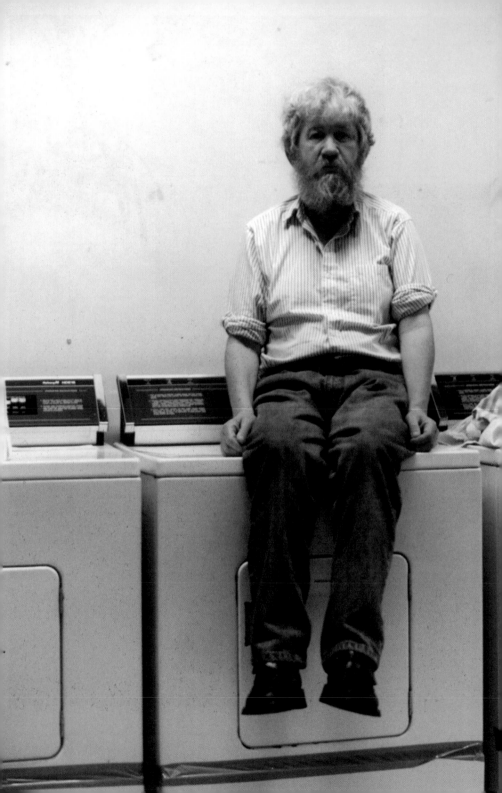

In the laundry: Gerry from Kerry who thinks he's from Derry

Watching television: BBC1

BBC2

Patrick, in his room in Arlington House

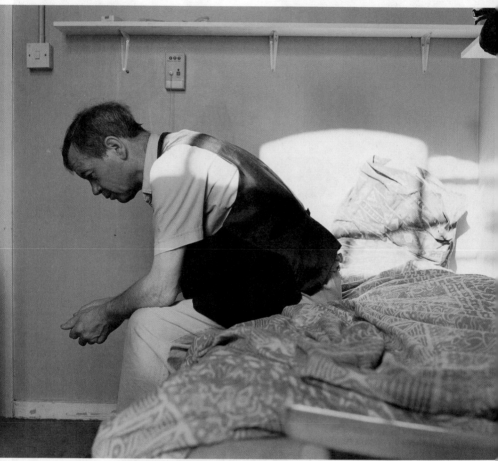

Pat: I come from Roscommon. I used to be in the pub trade—well, the catering side of it—I was a pastry chef. I was doing it all my life, but I drank my way out of it. I lost my daughter through drink, I lost my dear girl through drink, I lost my flat in Wood Green through drink. Drink has ruined my life. I'm in here through drink instead of having my own place. I have an enlarged liver through drink, my legs are weak through drink, I can't sleep at night unless I have a drink.

Deirdre O'Callaghan: Are those real pearls John?
John McCann: Well I wouldn't be feckin' wearing them if they weren't.

Back to
Ireland:
the ferry
crossing
from
Fishguard
to
Rosslare.

On the beach at Rosslare

Michael: God I'd love
to be able to bite into
an apple. I've only got
two pegs in the front.
My false teeth are in
a drawer at home.
They've have been
there since I got them.
It would be great to
have your own
choppers.

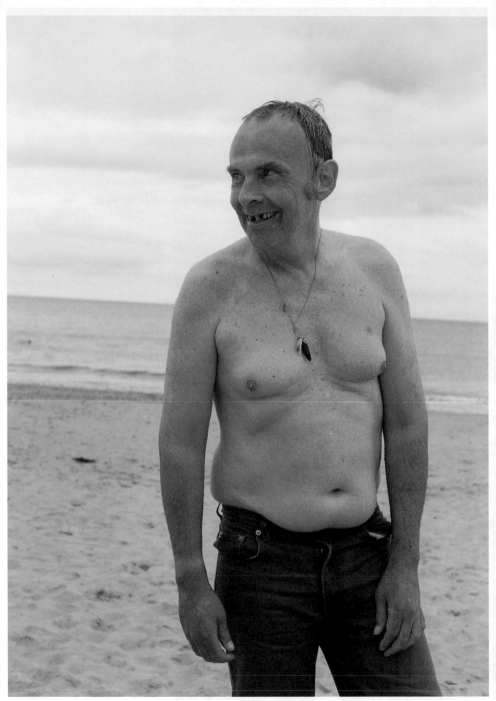
Jim Rowan, on the beach at Rosslare

A day trip
to Brighton

GRANTA

THE GREAT RETURN
Milan Kundera

TRANSLATED FROM THE FRENCH BY
LINDA ASHER

Prague, 1968

The hotel dated from the last years of Communism: a sleek modern building of the sort built all over the world, on the main square, very tall, towering by many storeys over the city's roof tops. Josef settled into his seventh-floor room and went to the window. It was seven in the evening, dusk was falling, the street lights went on, and the square was amazingly quiet.

Before leaving Denmark he had considered the coming encounter with places he had known, with his past life, and had wondered: would he be moved? left cold? delighted? depressed? Nothing of the sort. During his absence an invisible broom had swept across the landscape of his childhood wiping away everything familiar; the encounter he had expected never took place.

Near the hotel, a tall building exposed its bare side, a blind wall decorated with a gigantic picture. In the twilight the caption was unreadable and all Josef could make out was two hands clasping, enormous hands, between sky and earth. Had they always been there? He couldn't recall.

He was dining alone at the hotel restaurant and all about him he heard the sound of conversations. It was the music of some unknown language. What had happened to Czech during these two sorry decades? Was it the stresses that had changed? Apparently. Hitherto set firmly on the first syllable, they had grown weaker; the intonation seemed boneless. The melody sounded more monotonous than before, drawling. And the timbre! It had turned nasal, which gave the speech an unpleasantly blasé quality. Over the centuries, the music of any language probably does change imperceptibly, but to a person returning after an absence it can be disconcerting: bent over his plate, Josef was listening to an unknown language whose every word he understood.

Back in his room, he picked up the telephone and dialled his brother's number. He heard a joyful voice inviting him to come over right away.

'I just wanted to tell you I'm here,' said Josef. 'Do excuse me for today, though. I'm knocked out. Are you free tomorrow?'

He wasn't even sure his brother still worked at the hospital. 'I'll get free,' was the answer.

He rings and his brother, five years older than him, opens the door. They grip hands and gaze at each other. These are gazes of enormous intensity, and both men know very well what is going on: they are registering—swiftly, discreetly, brother about brother—the hair, the creases, the teeth. Each knows what he is looking for in the face before him and each knows that the other is looking for the same thing in his. They are ashamed of doing so, because what they're looking for is the probable distance between the other man and death—or, to say it more bluntly, they are looking in the other man's face for signs of death. To put a quick end to that morbid scrutiny they cast about for some phrase to make them forget those few grievous seconds—some exclamation, or question, or if possible (it would be a gift from heaven) a joke (but nothing comes to their rescue).

'Come,' the brother finally says and, taking Josef by the shoulders, leads him into the living room.

'We've been expecting you ever since the thing collapsed,' the brother said when they sat down. 'All the émigrés have already come home, or at least put in an appearance. No, no, that's not a reproach. You know best what's right for you.'

'There you're wrong,' said Josef with a laugh. 'I don't know that.'

'Did you come alone?' the brother asked.

'Yes.'

'Are you thinking of moving back for good?'

'I don't know.'

'Of course, you'd have to take your wife's feelings into consideration. You got married over there, I believe.'

'Yes.'

'To a Danish woman,' said his brother, hesitantly.

'Yes,' Josef said, and did not go on. The silence made the brother uncomfortable, and just to say something, Josef asked, 'The house belongs to you now?'

In the old days the flat was part of a three-storey income property belonging to their father; the family (father, mother, two sons) lived on the top floor and the other two floors were rented out. After the Communist revolution of 1948 the house was expropriated and the family stayed on as tenants.

'Yes,' answered the brother, visibly embarrassed. 'We tried to get in touch with you, but we couldn't.'

'Why was that? You do know my address!'

After 1989, all properties nationalized by the revolution (factories, hotels, flats, land, forests) were returned to their former owners (or, more precisely, to their children or grandchildren). The procedure was called restitution: it required only that a person declare himself owner to the legal authorities and, after a year during which his claim might be contested, the restitution became irrevocable. That judicial simplification allowed for a good deal of fraud, but it did avoid inheritance disputes, lawsuits, appeals, and thus brought about, in an astonishingly short time, the rebirth of a class society with a bourgeoisie that was rich, entrepreneurial, and positioned to set the national economy going.

'There was a lawyer handling it,' answered the brother, still embarrassed. 'Now it's already too late. The proceedings are closed. But don't worry, we'll work things out between us and with no lawyers involved.'

Just then the sister-in-law came in. This time that collision of gazes never even occurred: she had aged so much that the whole story was clear from the moment she appeared in the doorway. Josef wanted to drop his eyes and only look at her later, secretly, so as not to upset her. Stricken with pity, he stood up, went to her, and embraced her.

They sat down again. Unable to shake free of his emotion, Josef looked at her; if he had met her in the street, he would not have recognized her. These are the people who are closest to me in the world, he told himself, my family, all the family I have, my brother, my only brother. He repeated these words to himself as if to make the most of his emotion before it should dissipate.

That wave of tenderness caused him to say: 'Forget the house business completely. Listen, really, let's be pragmatic—owning something here—that's not my problem. My problems aren't here.'

Relieved, the brother repeated: 'No, no. I like equity in everything. Besides, your wife should have her say on the subject.'

'Let's talk about something else,' Josef said as he laid his hand on his brother's and squeezed it.

They took him through the flat to show him the changes since he left. In one room he saw a painting that had belonged to him. When he'd decided to leave the country, he had to act quickly. He was living in another town at the time and since he needed to keep secret his intention to emigrate, he could not give himself away by doling out his possessions to friends. The night before he left, he had put his keys in an envelope and posted them to his brother. Then he'd phoned him from abroad and asked him to take anything he liked from the flat before the state confiscated it. Later on, living in Denmark and happy to be starting a new life, he hadn't the slightest desire to find out what his brother had managed to salvage and what he had done with it.

He gazed for a long while at the picture: a working-class suburb, poor, rendered with that bold welter of colours that recalled the Fauve artists from the turn of the century—Derain, for example. And yet the painting was no pastiche; if it had been shown in 1905 at the Salon d'Automne together with the Fauves' paintings, viewers would have been struck by its strangeness, intrigued by the enigmatic perfume of an alluring visitor come from some faraway place. In fact, the picture was done in 1955, a period when doctrine on Socialist art was strict in its demand for realism. This artist, who was a passionate modernist, would have preferred to paint the way people were painting all over the world at the time, which is to say in the abstract manner, but he also wanted his work to be exhibited, therefore he had to locate the magic point where the ideologues' imperatives intersected with his own desires as an artist; the shacks evoking workers' lives were a nod to the ideologues and the violently unrealistic colours were his gift to himself.

Josef had visited the man's studio in the 1960s when the official doctrine was losing some of its force and the painter was already free to do pretty much whatever he wanted. In his naive sincerity, Josef had liked this early picture better than the recent ones and the painter, who looked on his own proletarian Fauvism with a slightly condescending affection, had cheerfully made him a gift of it. He'd even picked up his brush and, alongside his signature, written a dedication with Josef's name.

'You knew this painter well,' remarked his brother.

'Yes. I saved his poodle's life for him,' Josef said.

'Are you planning to go see him?'

'No.'

Shortly after 1989 a package had arrived at Josef's house in Denmark: photographs of the painter's latest canvases. Created now in complete freedom, they were indistinguishable from the millions of other pictures being painted around the planet at the time. The painter could boast of a double victory: he was utterly free and utterly like everybody else.

'You still like this picture?' asked the brother.

'Yes, it's still very fine.'

The brother tilted his head toward his wife: 'Katy loves it. She stops to look at it every day.' Then he added: 'After you left, you told me to give it to Papa. He hung it over the table in his office at the hospital. He knew how much Katy loved it and before he died he bequeathed it to her.' After a little pause: 'You can't imagine. We lived through some dreadful years.'

Looking at the sister-in-law, Josef remembered that he had never liked her. His old antipathy (she'd returned it in spades) now seemed to him stupid and regrettable. She stood there staring at the picture with an expression of sad impotence on her face, and in pity Josef said to his brother: 'I know.'

The brother began an account of the family's story: the father's lingering death, Katy's illness, their daughter's failed marriage, then on to the cabals against him at the hospital, where his position had been gravely compromised by the fact of Josef's emigrating. There was no tone of reproach to that last remark, but Josef had no doubt of the animosity with which the brother and sister-in-law must have discussed him at the time, indignant at the paltry reasons Josef might have alleged to justify his emigration, which they certainly considered irresponsible: the regime did not make life easy for the relatives of émigrés.

In the dining room, the table was laid for lunch. The conversation turned lively, with the brother and sister-in-law eager to inform him of everything that had happened during his absence. The decades hovered above the dishes, and his sister-in-law suddenly attacked him: 'You had some fanatical years yourself. The way you used to talk about the Church! We were all scared of you.'

The remark startled him. 'Scared of me?' His sister-in-law held her ground. He looked at her: on her face, which only minutes earlier had seemed unrecognizable, her old features were coming out.

To say that they'd been scared of him was nonsense, actually, since the sister-in-law's recollection could only concern his school years, when he was between sixteen and nineteen years old. It is entirely possible that he used to make fun of believers back then, but his taunts couldn't have been anything like the government's militant atheism and were just aimed at his family, who never missed Sunday Mass and thereby incited Josef to be provocative. He had graduated in 1951, three years after the revolution, and when he decided to study veterinary medicine it was that same taste for provocation that inspired him: healing sick people, serving humanity, was his family's great pride (already, two generations back, his grandfather was a doctor) and he enjoyed telling them all that he liked cows better than humans. But nobody had either praised or deplored his rebellion. Because veterinary medicine carried less social prestige, his choice was just interpreted as a lack of ambition, an acceptance of second rank within the family, below his brother.

Now at the table he made a garbled effort to explain (to them and to himself both) his psychology as an adolescent, but the words had trouble getting out of his mouth because the sister-in-law's set smile, fastened on him, expressed an immutable disagreement with everything he was saying. He understood that there was nothing he could do about it, it was practically a law: people who see their lives as a shipwreck need to hunt down the guilty parties. And Josef was doubly guilty, both as an adolescent who had spoken ill of God and as an adult who had emigrated. He lost the desire to explain anything at all and his brother, subtle diplomat that he was, changed the subject.

His brother: as a second-year medical student he had been barred from the university in 1948 because of his bourgeois background. So as not to lose hope of resuming his studies later on and becoming a surgeon like his father, he had done all he could to demonstrate his support for Communism, to the point where one day, sore at heart, he wound up joining the Party, in which he stayed until 1989. The paths of the two brothers diverged: first ejected from university and then forced to deny his convictions, the elder felt himself a victim (he would feel that way forever). At the veterinary school, which was less coveted and less tightly monitored, the younger brother had no need to display any particular loyalty to the regime: to his brother's eyes he seemed (and forever would seem) a lucky little bastard who knew how to get away with things; a deserter.

In August 1968, the Russian army had invaded the country. For a week, the streets in all the cities howled with rage. The country had never been so thoroughly a homeland, or the Czechs so Czech. Drunk with hatred, Josef was ready to hurl himself against the tanks. Then the country's statesmen were arrested, shipped under guard to Moscow and forced to conclude a slapdash compromise, and the Czechs, still enraged, went back indoors. Some fourteen months later, on the fifty-second anniversary of Russia's October Revolution—now imposed on the country as a national holiday—Josef had climbed into his car in the market town where he had his animal clinic and set off to see his family at the other end of the country. Arriving in their city, he slowed up; he was curious to see how many windows would be draped with red flags which, in that year of defeat, were nothing else but signals of submission. There were more of them than he expected: perhaps the people displaying them were doing so against their actual convictions, out of prudence, with some vague fear. Still, they were acting voluntarily, no one was forcing them, no one was threatening them. He had pulled up in front of his family home. On the top floor, where his brother lived, there blazed a large flag, hideously red. For a very long moment Josef contemplated it from inside his car; then he turned on the ignition. On the trip home he decided to leave the country. Not that he couldn't have lived here. He could have gone on peacefully treating cows here. But he was alone, divorced, childless, free. He reflected that he had only one life and that he wanted to live it somewhere else.

At the end of lunch, sitting over his coffee, Josef thought about his painting. He considered how to take it away with him, and whether it would be too unwieldy in the plane. Wouldn't it be easier to take the canvas out of the frame and roll it up?

He was about to discuss it when the sister-in-law said: 'You must be going to see N.'

'I don't know yet.'

'He was an awfully good friend of yours.'

'He still is my friend.'

'In 'forty-eight everyone was terrified of him. The Red Commissar! But he did a lot for you, didn't he? You owe him!'

The brother hastily interrupted his wife, and he handed Josef a small bundle: 'This is what Papa kept as a souvenir of you. We found it after he died.'

The brother apparently had to leave soon for the hospital; their meeting was drawing to a close, and Josef noted that his painting had vanished from the conversation. What? His sister-in-law remembers his friend N., but she forgets his painting? Still, although he was prepared to give up his whole inheritance and his share of the house, the picture was his, his alone, with his name inscribed alongside the painter's! How could they, she and his brother, act as if it didn't belong to him?

The atmosphere suddenly grew heavy and the brother started to tell a funny story. Josef was not listening. He was determined to reclaim his picture and, intent on what he wanted to say, his distracted glance fell on the brother's wrist and the watch on it. He recognized it: big and black, a little out of style; he had left it behind in his apartment and the brother had appropriated it for himself. No, Josef had no reason to be incensed at that. It had all been done according to his own instructions; still, seeing his watch on someone else's wrist threw him into a strange unease. He had the sense he was coming back into the world as might a dead man emerging from his tomb after twenty years: touching at the ground with a timid foot that's lost the habit of walking; barely recognizing the world he had lived in but continually stumbling over the leavings from his life; seeing his trousers, his tie on the bodies of the survivors, who had quite naturally divided them up among themselves; seeing everything and laying claim to nothing. The dead are timid. Overcome by that timidity of the dead, Josef could not muster the force to say a single word about his painting. He stood up.

'Come back tonight. We'll have dinner together,' said the brother.

Josef suddenly saw his own wife's face; he felt a sharp need to address her, talk with her. But he could not do that. His brother was looking at him, waiting for his answer.

'Please excuse me, I have so little time. Next visit,' and he gave them each a warm handshake.

On the way back to the hotel, his wife's face appeared to him again and he blew up: 'It's your fault. You're the one who told me I had to go. I didn't want to. I had no desire for this return. But you disagreed. You said that not going was unnatural, unjustifiable—it was even foul. Do you still think you were right?'

Back in his hotel room he opens the bundle his brother gave him:

an album of photographs from his childhood, of his mother, his
father, his brother, and, many times over, little Josef. He sets it aside
to keep. A couple of children's picture books; he tosses them into
the wastepaper basket. A child's drawing in coloured pencil, with the
inscription 'For Mama on her birthday', and his clumsy signature;
he tosses that away. Then a notebook. He opens it: his school diary.
How did he ever leave that at his parents' house?

The entries here date from the early years of Communism but,
his curiosity somewhat foiled, all he finds is accounts of his dates
with girls from school. A precocious libertine? No indeed; a virgin
boy. He leafs through the pages absently, then stops at these rebukes
addressed to one girl: 'You told me love was only about bodies. Dear
girl, you would run off in a minute if a man told you he was only
interested in your body. And you would come to understand the
dreadful sensation of loneliness.'

Loneliness. The word keeps turning up in these pages. He would
try to scare them by describing the fearsome prospect of loneliness.
To make them love him, he would preach at them like a parson: that
unless there's emotion, sex stretches away like a desert where a
person can die of sadness.

He goes on reading, and remembers nothing. So what has this
stranger come to tell him? To remind him that he used to live here
under Josef's name? Josef gets up and goes to the window. The
square is lit by the late afternoon sun, and the image of the two hands
on the big wall is sharply visible now: one is white, the other black.
Above them, a three-letter acronym promises 'security' and
'solidarity'. No doubt about it, the mural was painted after 1989,
when the country took up the slogans of the new age: brotherhood
of all races; mingling of all cultures; unity of everything, of everybody.

Hands clasping on billboards—Josef's seen that before! The
Czech worker clasping the hand of the Russian soldier! It may have
been detested, but that propaganda image was indisputably part of
the History of the Czechs, who had a thousand reasons to clasp or
to refuse the hands of Russians or Germans! But a black hand? In
this country, people hardly knew that black people even existed. In
her whole life his mother had never run into a single one.

He considers those hands suspended there between heaven and
earth, enormous, taller than the church belfry, hands that shifted the

place into a harshly different setting. He scrutinizes the square below him as if he were searching for traces he left on the pavement as a young man when he used to stroll it with his schoolmates.

'Schoolmates.' He articulates the word slowly, in an undertone, so as to breathe in the aroma (faint! barely discernible!) of his early youth, that bygone, remote period, a period forsaken and mournful as an orphanage. He feels no affection for that dimly visible, feeble past; no desire to return; nothing but a slight reserve, detachment.

If I were a doctor, I would diagnose his condition thus: 'The patient is suffering from nostalgic insufficiency.'

But Josef does not feel sick. He feels clear-headed. To his mind, the nostalgic insufficiency proves the paltry value of his former life. So I revise my diagnosis: 'The patient is suffering from masochistic distortion of his memory.' Indeed, all he remembers is situations that make him displeased with himself. He is not fond of his childhood. But as a child, didn't he have everything he wanted? Wasn't his father worshipped by all his patients? Why was that a source of pride for his brother and not for him? He often fought with his little friends and he fought bravely. Now he's forgotten all his victories, but he will always remember the time a fellow he considered weaker than himself knocked him down and pinned him to the ground for a loud count of ten. Even now he can feel on his skin that humiliating pressure of the turf. When he was still living in Bohemia and would run into people who had known him earlier, he was always surprised to find that they considered him a rather courageous person (he thought himself faint-hearted), with a caustic wit (he considered himself a bore), and good-hearted (he remembered only his stinginess).

He knew very well that his memory detested him, that it did nothing but slander him, therefore he tried not to believe it, and to be more lenient towards his own life. But it didn't help: he took no pleasure in looking back, and he did it as seldom as possible.

What he would have other people, and himself, believe is that he left his country because he could not bear to see it enslaved and humiliated. That's true; still, most Czechs felt the same way— enslaved and humiliated—and yet they did not run off abroad. They stayed in their country because they liked themselves and because they liked themselves together with their lives, which were inseparable from the place where the lives had been lived. Because Josef's memory was malevolent and provided him nothing to make him cherish his life in his country, he crossed the border with a brisk step and with no regrets.

And once he was abroad, did his memory lose its noxious influence? Yes. Because there, Josef had neither reason nor occasion to concern himself with recollections bound to the country he no longer lived in. Such is the law of masochistic memory: as segments of his life melt into oblivion, man sloughs off whatever he dislikes, and feels lighter, freer.

And above all, abroad, Josef fell in love, and love is the glorification of the present. His attachment to that present drove off his recollections, shielded him against their intrusion; his memory did not become less malevolent, but—disregarded, kept at a distance—it lost its power over him.

The life we've left behind us has a bad habit of stepping out of the shadows, of bringing complaints against us, of taking us to court. Living far from Bohemia, Josef had lost the habit of keeping his past in mind. But the past was there, waiting for him, watching him. Uneasy, Josef tried to think about other things. But when a man has come to look at the land of his past, what can he think about if not his past? In the two days left to him, what should he do? Pay a visit to the town where he'd had his veterinary practice? Go and stand, moist-eyed, before the house he used to live in? He hadn't the slightest desire to do that. Was there anyone at all among the people he used to know whom he would—sincerely—like to see? N.'s face emerged. Way back, when the rabble-rousers of the revolution accused the very young Josef of God knows what (in those years everyone, at some time or another, stood accused of God knows what), N., who was an influential Communist at the university, had stood up for him, without worrying about Josef's opinions and family background. That was how they'd become friends, and if Josef could reproach himself for anything, it would be for having largely forgotten about the man during the twenty years since his emigration.

'The Red Commissar! Everyone was terrified of him!' his sister-in-law had said, implying that, out of self-interest, Josef had attached himself to a friend of the regime. Oh, those poor countries shaken by great historical dates! When the battle is over, everybody stampedes off on punitive expeditions into the past to hunt down the guilty parties. But who were the guilty parties? The Communists who won in 1948? Or their ineffective adversaries who lost? Everybody was hunting down guilty parties and everybody was being hunted down. When Josef's brother joined the Party so as to go on with his studies, his friends condemned him as an opportunist. That had made him detest Communism all the more, blaming it for his craven behaviour, and his wife had focused her own hatred on people like N. who, as a convinced Marxist before the revolution, had of his own free will (and thus unpardonably) helped to bring about a system she held to be the greatest of all evils.

When his brother said, 'You got married over there, I believe,' he answered, 'Yes,' with no further remark. His brother might merely have used some other turn of phrase, and rather than saying, 'You got married,' asked, 'Are you married?' In that case Josef would have answered, 'No, widowed.' He hadn't meant to mislead his brother, but the way the query was phrased allowed him, without lying, to keep silent on his wife's death.

During the conversation that followed, his brother and sister-in-law had avoided any mention of her. That must have been out of embarrassment: for security reasons (to avoid being questioned by the police) they had denied themselves the slightest contact with their émigré relative and never even realized that their forced caution had soon turned into authentic lack of interest. They knew nothing about his wife, not her age or her given name or her profession, and by keeping their silence now they hoped to disguise that ignorance, which showed up the terrible poverty of their relations with him.

But Josef took no offence. Their ignorance suited him fine. Since the day he buried her, he had always felt uncomfortable when he had to inform someone of her death, as if by doing so he were betraying her in her most private privacy. By not speaking of her death, he always felt he was protecting her. For the woman who is dead is a woman with no defences: she has no more power, she has no more influence, people no longer respect either her wishes or her tastes, the dead woman cannot will anything, cannot aspire to any respect or refute any slander. Never had he felt such sorrowful, such agonizing compassion for her as when she was dead.

Jonas Hallgrímsson was a great romantic poet and also a great fighter for Iceland's independence. In the nineteenth century all of small-nation Europe had these romantic patriot poets: Petöfi in Hungary, Mickiewicz in Poland, Preseren in Slovenia, Macha in Bohemia, Shevtchenko in Ukraine, Wergeland in Norway, Lönnrot in Finland, and the like. Iceland was a colony of Denmark at the time and Hallgrímsson lived out his last years in the Danish capital. All the great romantic poets, besides being great patriots, were great drinkers. One day, dead drunk, Hallgrímsson fell down a staircase, broke a leg, got an infection, died, and was buried in the Copenhagen cemetery. That was in 1845. Ninety-nine years later, in 1944, the Icelandic Republic declared its independence. From then on, events hastened their course. In 1946, the poet's soul visited a rich Icelandic industrialist in his sleep and confided: 'For a hundred years now my skeleton has lain in a foreign land, in the enemy country. Is it not time it came home to its own free Ithaca?'

Flattered and elated by this nocturnal visit, the patriotic industrialist had the poet's skeleton dug out of the enemy soil and carried back to Iceland, intending to bury it in the lovely valley where the poet was born. But no one can stop the mad course of events: in the ineffably exquisite landscape of Thingvellir (the sacred place where, a thousand years ago, the first Icelandic parliament gathered beneath the open sky), the ministers of the brand-new Republic had created a cemetery for the great men of the homeland. They ripped the poet away from the industrialist and buried him in the pantheon that at the time contained only the grave of another great poet (small nations abound in great poets), Einar Benediktsson.

But again events rushed on, and soon everyone learned what the patriotic industrialist had never dared admit: standing at the opened tomb back in Copenhagen, he had felt extremely disconcerted. The poet had been buried in a paupers' field with no name marking his grave, only a number, and the patriotic industrialist—confronted by a bunch of skeletons tangled together—had not known which one to pick. In the presence of the stern, impatient cemetery bureaucrats, he did not dare show his uncertainty. And so he had transported to

Iceland not the Icelandic poet but a Danish butcher.

In Iceland, people had initially tried to hush up this lugubriously comical mistake, but events continued to run their course and in 1948 the indiscreet writer Halldór Laxness spilled the beans in a novel.

What to do? Keep quiet. Therefore Hallgrímsson's bones still lie 2,000 miles away from his Ithaca, in enemy soil, while the body of the Danish butcher—who although no poet was a patriot as well—still lies banished to a glacial island that never stirred him to anything but fear and repugnance.

Even hushed up, the consequence of the truth was that no one else was ever buried in the exquisite cemetery at Thingvellir, which harbours only two coffins and which, thereby, of all the world's pantheons—those grotesque museums of pride—is the only one capable of touching our hearts.

A very long time ago, Josef's wife had told him that story. They thought it was funny, and a moral lesson seemed easily drawn from it: nobody much cares where a dead person's bones wind up.

And yet Josef changed his mind when his wife's death became imminent and inevitable. Suddenly the story of the Danish butcher abducted to Iceland seemed not funny but terrifying.

The idea of dying when she did had been with him for a long time. It was due not to a romantic tendency but rather to a rational consideration: if ever his wife should be struck by a fatal illness, he had determined he would cut short her suffering. To avoid being indicted for murder, he planned to die as well. Then she actually did fall gravely ill, and suffered terribly, and Josef no longer had a mind for suicide, not out of fear for his own life, but because he found intolerable the idea of leaving that very beloved body to the mercy of alien hands. With him dead, who would protect the dead woman? How could one corpse keep another one safe?

Long ago, in Bohemia, he had watched over his mother's dying agony. He loved her very much, but once she was no longer alive, her body ceased to interest him. To his mind, her corpse was no longer she. Besides, two doctors—his father and his brother—took care of the dying woman, and in the order of importance he was just the third family member. This time, everything was different. The woman he saw dying belonged to him alone. He was jealous for her body and wanted to watch over its posthumous fate. He even had to admonish himself: she was still alive, lying in front of him, she was speaking to him, and he was already thinking of her as dead. She was gazing up at him, her eyes larger than ever, and his mind was busy with her casket and her grave. He scolded himself for that as if it were a shocking betrayal, an impatience, a secret wish to hasten her death. But he couldn't help it. He knew that after the death, her family would come to claim her for their family vault, and the idea horrified him.

Contemptuous of funeral concerns, in writing their wills some time earlier, he and she had been too offhand; their instructions on disposing of their possessions were very rudimentary and they hadn't even mentioned burial. The omission obsessed him while she was dying, but since he was trying to convince her that she would beat death, he had to hold his tongue. How could he confess to the poor woman who still believed she would recover? How could he confess what he was thinking about? How could he talk about the will? Especially since she was already slipping into spells of delirium and her thinking was muddled.

His wife's family, a big influential family, had never liked Josef. It seemed to him that the struggle ahead for his wife's body would be the toughest and most important he would ever fight. The idea that this body would be locked into an obscene promiscuity with other bodies—unknown and meaningless—was unbearable to him, as was the idea that he himself, when he died, would end up who knew where and certainly far away from her. To let that happen seemed a defeat as huge as eternity, a defeat never to be forgiven.

What he feared came about. He could not avoid the shock. His mother-in-law railed against him: 'It's my daughter! It's my daughter!' He had to hire a lawyer, hand over a bundle of money to pacify the family, hastily buy a cemetery plot, act more quickly than the others to win this final combat.

The feverish activity of a sleepless week fended off his suffering, but something even stranger occurred: when she was in the grave that belonged to them (a grave for two, like a two-seater buggy), in the darkness of his sorrow he glimpsed a ray—a feeble, trembling, barely visible ray—of happiness. Happiness at not having let down his beloved; at having provided for their future, his and hers both.

After his wife's death, Josef noticed that without daily conversations, the murmur of their past life grew faint. To intensify it, he tried to revive his wife's image, but the lacklustre result distressed him. She'd had a dozen different smiles. He strained his imagination to recreate them. He failed. She'd had a gift for fast funny lines that would delight him. He couldn't call forth a single one. He finally wondered: if he were to add up the few recollections he still had from their life together, how much time would they take? A minute? Two minutes?

That's another enigma about memory, more basic than all the rest: do recollections have some measurable temporal volume? Do they unfold over a span of time? He tries to picture their first encounter: he sees a staircase leading down from the pavement into the cellar of a brasserie; he sees couples here and there in a yellow half-light; and he sees her, his future wife, sitting across from him, a brandy glass in her hand, her gaze fixed on him, with a shy smile. For a long while he watches her holding her glass and smiling. He scrutinizes this face, this hand, and through all this time she remains motionless, does not lift the glass to her mouth or change her smile in the slightest. And there lies the horror: the past we remember is devoid of time. Impossible to re-experience a love the way we reread a book or re-see a film. Dead, Josef's wife has no dimension at all, either material or temporal.

Therefore all efforts to revive her in his mind soon became torture. Instead of rejoicing at having retrieved this or that forgotten moment, he was driven to despair by the immensity of the void around that moment. Then, one day, he forbade himself that painful ramble through the corridors of the past and stopped his vain efforts to bring her back as she had been. He even thought that by his fixation on her past existence he was betraying her, relegating her to a museum of vanished objects and excluding her from his present life.

Besides, they had never made a cult of reminiscence. Not that they'd destroyed their private correspondence, of course, or their diaries with notes on errands and appointments. But it never occurred to them to reread them. He therefore determined to live with the dead woman the way he had with the living one. He now went to her grave not to reminisce but to spend time with her; to see her eyes looking at him, and looking not from the past but from the present moment.

And now a new life began for him: living with the dead woman. There is a new clock organizing his time. A stickler for tidiness, she used to be irritated by the mess he left everywhere. Now he does the housework himself, meticulously, for he loves their home even more than he had when she was alive: the low wooden fence with its little gate, the garden, the fir tree in front of the dark-red brick house, the two facing easy chairs they'd sit in at the end of the working day, the window ledge where she always kept a bowl of flowers on one end, a lamp on the other; they would leave that lamp on while they were out so they could see it from afar as they came down the street back to the house. He respects all those customs, and he takes care to see that every chair, every vase is where she liked to have it.

He revisits the places they loved: the seaside restaurant where the owner invariably reminds him of his wife's favourite fish dishes; in a small town nearby, the rectangle of the town square with red, blue, yellow painted houses—a modest beauty they found enthralling. Or, on a visit to Copenhagen, the wharf from where every evening at six a great white steam ship set out to sea. There they could stand motionless for a long time watching it. Before it sailed, music would ring out—old-time jazz, the invitation to the voyage. Since her death he often goes there, he imagines her beside him and feels again their mutual yearning to climb aboard that white nocturnal ship, to dance on it and sleep on it and wake up somewhere far, very far, to the north.

She liked him to dress well, and she saw to his wardrobe herself. He hasn't forgotten which of his shirts she liked and which she did not. For this visit to Bohemia, he purposely packed a suit she'd had no feeling for either way. He did not want to grant this journey too much attention. It is not a journey for her, or with her.

When Communism departed from Europe, Josef's wife kept pressing him to go see his country again. She intended to go with him. But she died, and from then on all he could think about was his new life with the absent woman. He tried hard to persuade himself that it was a happy life. But is 'happiness' the right word? Yes, happiness like a frail, tremulous ray gleaming through his grief—a resigned, calm, unremitting grief. A month earlier, unable to shake the sadness, he recalled the words of his deceased wife: 'Not going would be unnatural of you, unjustifiable—even foul.' Actually, he thought, this trip she had so urged on him might possibly be some help to him now, might divert him, for a few days at least, from his own life that was giving him such pain.

As he prepared for the trip, an idea tentatively crossed his mind: what if he were to stay over there for good? After all, he could be a vet as easily in Bohemia as in Denmark. Till then, the idea had seemed unacceptable, almost like a betrayal of the woman he loved. But he wondered: would it really be a betrayal? If his wife's presence is non-material, why should she be bound to the materiality of one particular place? Couldn't she be with him in Bohemia just as well as in Denmark?

He has left the hotel and is driving around in the car. He has lunch in a country inn, then he takes a walk through the fields: narrow lanes, wild roses, trees, trees. Oddly moved, he gazes at the wooded hills on the horizon and it occurs to him that twice in his own lifetime the Czechs were willing to die to keep that landscape their own. In 1938, they wanted to fight Hitler; when their allies, French and English, kept them from doing so, they were in despair. In 1968, the Russians invaded the country and again they wanted to fight; condemned to the same capitulation, they fell back into that same despair again.

To be willing to die for one's country: every nation has known that temptation to sacrifice. Indeed, the Czechs' adversaries also knew it: the Germans, the Russians. But those are large nations. Their patriotism is different: they are buoyed by their glory, their importance, their universal mission. The Czechs loved their country not because it was glorious but because it was unknown; not because it was big but because it was small and in constant danger. Their patriotism was an enormous compassion for their country. The Danes are like that, too. Not by chance did Josef choose a small country for his emigration.

Much moved, he gazes out over the landscape and reflects that the history of his Bohemia during this past half-century is fascinating, unique, unprecedented, and that failing to take an interest in it would be narrow-minded. Tomorrow morning, he'll be seeing N. What kind of life did the man have during all the time they were out of touch? What had he thought about the Russian occupation of the country? And what was it like for him to see the end of the

Communism he used to believe in, sincerely and honourably? How is his Marxist background faring with the return of this capitalism that's being cheered along by the entire planet? Is he rebelling against it? Or has he abandoned his convictions? And if he's abandoned them, is that a crisis for him? And how are other people behaving towards him? Josef can hear the voice of his sister-in-law who—as huntress of the guilty—would certainly like to see N. handcuffed in court. Doesn't N. need Josef to tell him that friendship does exist despite all of History's contortions?

Josef's thoughts return to his sister-in-law: she hated the Communists because they disputed the sacred right of property. And then, when it came to me, he thought, she disputed my sacred right to my painting. He imagines the painting on a wall in his brick house in Copenhagen and suddenly, with surprise, he realizes that the working-class suburb in the picture, that Czech Derain, that oddity of History, would be a disruption, an intrusive presence on the wall of that place. How could he ever have thought of taking it back with him? That painting doesn't belong there where he lives with his dear deceased. He'd never even mentioned it to her. That painting has nothing to do with her, with the two of them, with their life.

Then, he thinks: if one little painting could disrupt his life with the dead woman, how much more disruptive would be the constant, unrelenting presence of a whole country, a country she never saw!

The sun dips towards the horizon. He is in the car on the road to Prague. The landscape slips away around him, the landscape of his small country whose people were willing to die for it, and he knows that there exists something even smaller, with an even stronger appeal to his compassionate love: he sees two easy chairs turned to face each other, the lamp and the flower bowl on the window ledge, and the slender fir tree his wife planted in front of the house, a fir tree that looks like an arm she'd raised from afar to show him the way back home.

B uilt on a slope, the house showed just one storey at street level. When the door opened Josef was assailed by the amorous onslaught of a huge German shepherd. Only after a while did he catch sight of N. laughing as he quieted the dog and led Josef along a hallway and down a long stairway to a two-room garden flat where he lived with his wife; she was there, friendly, and she offered her hand.

'Upstairs,' N. said, pointing to the ceiling, 'the flats are much roomier. My daughter and son live there with their families. The villa belongs to my son. He's a lawyer. Too bad he's not home. Listen,' he said, dropping his voice, 'if you want to come back here to live, he'll help you—he'll take care of things for you.'

These words reminded Josef of the day forty years earlier when, in that same voice lowered to indicate secrecy, N. had offered his friendship and his help.

'I told them about you...' N. went on, and he shouted towards the stairwell several names which must have belonged to his progeny. When Josef saw all those grandchildren and great-grandchildren coming down the stairs, he had no idea whose they were. Anyhow, they were all beautiful, stylish (Josef couldn't tear his eyes off a blonde, the girlfriend of one of the grandsons, a German girl who spoke not a word of Czech), and all of them, even the girls, looked taller than N.; among them he was like a rabbit caught in a tangle of weeds visibly springing up around and above him.

Like fashion models strutting a runway, they smiled wordlessly until N. asked them to leave him alone with his friend. His wife stayed indoors and the two men went out into the garden.

The dog followed them, and N. remarked: 'I've never seen him so worked up by a visitor. It's as if he knows what you do for a living.' Then he showed Josef some fruit trees and described his labours laying out the grassy plots set off by narrow pathways, so that for some time the conversation stayed distant from the subjects Josef had vowed to raise. Finally he managed to interrupt his friend's botanical lecture and ask him about his life during the twenty years they had not seen each other.

'Let's not talk about it,' said N., and in answer to Josef's enquiring look he laid an index finger on his heart. Josef did not understand the meaning of the gesture: was it that the political events had affected him so profoundly, 'to the heart'? Or had he gone through a serious love affair? Or had a heart attack?

'Some day I'll tell you about it,' he added, turning aside any discussion.

The conversation was not easy: whenever Josef stopped walking to shape a question better, the dog took it as permission to jump up and set his paws on Josef's belly.

'I remember what you always used to say,' N. remarked. 'That a person becomes a doctor because he's interested in diseases; he becomes a vet out of love for animals.'

'Did I really say that?' Josef asked, amazed. He remembered that two days earlier he had told his sister-in-law that he'd chosen his profession as a rebellion against his family. So had he acted out of love, and not rebellion? In a single vague cloud he saw filing past him all the sick animals he had known; then he saw his veterinary clinic at the back of his brick house where, tomorrow (yes, in exactly twenty-four hours!), he would open the door to greet the day's first patient. A slow smile spread across his face.

He had to force himself back to the conversation barely begun. He asked whether N. had been attacked for his political past. N. said no, according to him people knew he had always helped those the regime was giving trouble. 'I don't doubt it,' Josef said (he really didn't), but he pressed on. How did N. himself see his whole past life? As a mistake? As a defeat? N. shook his head, saying that it was neither the one nor the other. And finally Josef asked what N. thought of the very swift, harsh re-establishment of capitalism. Shrugging, N. replied that under the circumstances there was no other solution.

No, the conversation never managed to get going. Josef thought at first that N. found his questions indiscreet. Then he corrected himself: not so much indiscreet as outdated. If his sister-in-law's vindictive dream should come true and N. were indicted and tried in court, maybe he would reassess his Communist past to explain and defend it. But in the absence of any such trial, that past was remote from him these days. He didn't live there any more.

Josef recalled a very old idea of his, which at the time he had considered to be blasphemous: that being a Communist has nothing to do with Marx and his theories. It was simply that the period gave people a way to fulfil the most diverse psychological needs: the need to look nonconformist; or the need to obey; or the need to punish the wicked; or the need to be useful; or the need to march forward into the future with youth; or the need to have a big family around you.

In good spirits, the dog barked and Josef said to himself: the reason people are quitting Communism today is not that their thinking has changed, or undergone a shock, but that Communism no longer provides a way to look nonconformist, or obey or punish the wicked, or be useful, or march forward with youth, or have a big family around you. The Communist belief no longer answers any need. It has become so unusable that everyone drops it easily, never even noticing.

But the primary purpose of his visit was still unfulfilled in him: to make it clear to N. that in some imaginary courtroom he, Josef, would defend him. To achieve this he would first show N. that he was not blindly enthusiastic about the world that had sprung up here since Communism, and he described the big advertisement on the square back in his home town, in which an incomprehensible-acronym-agency proposes its services to the Czechs by showing them a white hand and a black hand clasped together. 'Tell me,' he said, 'is this still our country?'

He expected to hear a sarcastic response about worldwide capitalism homogenizing the planet, but N. was silent. Josef went on: 'The Soviet empire collapsed because it could no longer hold down the nations that wanted their independence. But those nations—they're less independent than ever now. They can't choose their own economy or their own foreign policy or even their own advertising slogans.'

'National independence has been an illusion for a long time now,' said N.

'But if a country is not independent and doesn't even want to be, will anyone still be willing to die for it?'

'Being willing to die isn't what I want for my children.'

'I'll put it another way: does anyone still love this country?'

N. slowed his steps: 'Josef,' he said, touched. 'How could you ever have emigrated? You're a patriot!' Then, very seriously: 'Dying for your country—that's all finished. Maybe for you time stopped during your emigration. But they—they don't think like you any more.'

'Who?'

N. tipped his head towards the upper floors of the house, as if to indicate his brood. 'They're somewhere else.'

During these remarks, the two friends came to a halt. The dog took advantage of it: he reared up and set his paws on Josef, who petted him. N. contemplated this man-dog couple for a time, increasingly touched, as if he were only just now taking full account of the twenty years they hadn't seen each other: 'Ah, I'm so happy you came!' He tapped Josef on the shoulder and drew him over to sit beneath an apple tree. And at once Josef knew: the serious, important conversation he had come for would not take place. And to his surprise, that was a comfort, it was a liberation! After all, he hadn't come here to put his friend through an interrogation!

As if a lock had clicked open, their conversation took off, freely and agreeably, a chat between two old mates: a few scattered memories, news of mutual friends, funny comments and paradoxes and jokes. It was as if a gentle, warm, powerful breeze had taken him up in its arms. Josef felt an irrepressible joy in talking. Ah, such an unexpected joy! For twenty years he had barely spoken Czech. Conversation with his wife was easy, Danish having turned into a private jargon for themselves. But with other people he was always conscious of choosing his words, constructing a sentence, watching his accent. It seemed to him that when Danes talked they were running nimbly, while he was trudging along behind, lugging a twenty-kilo load. Now, though, the words leaped from his mouth on their own, without his having to hunt for them, monitor them. Czech was no longer that unknown language with the nasal timbre that had startled him at the hotel in his hometown. He recognized it now, and he savoured it. Using it, he felt light, as if after a weight-loss treatment. Talking was like flying, and for the first time in his visit he was happy in his homeland and felt that it was his.

Stimulated by the pleasure beaming from his friend, N. grew more and more relaxed. With a complicitous grin he mentioned his long-ago secret mistress and thanked Josef for having once served as an alibi for him with his wife. Josef did not recall the episode and was sure N. was confusing him with someone else. But the alibi story, which took N. a long time to tell, was so fine, so funny, that Josef ended up conceding to his supposed role as protagonist. He sat with his head tilted back, and through the leaves the sun lit a beatific smile on his face.

In that state of well-being N.'s wife surprised them: 'You'll have lunch with us?'

He looked at his watch and stood up. 'I've got an appointment in half an hour!'

'Then come back tonight! We'll have dinner together,' N. urged warmly.

'Tonight I'll already be back home!'

'By "back home" you mean...'

'In Denmark.'

'It's so strange to hear you say that. So then this isn't home to you any more?' asked N.'s wife.

'No. It's there.'

There was a long silence and Josef expected questions: if Denmark really is your home, what's your life like there? And your wife? Are you happy? Tell us! Tell us!

But neither N. nor his wife asked any such question. For a moment, a low wooden fence and a fir tree flickered across Josef's mind.

'I must go,' he said, and they all moved towards the stairs. As they climbed, they were quiet, and in that silence Josef was suddenly struck by his wife's absence; there was not a trace of her here. In the three days he'd spent in this country, no one had said a word about her. He understood: if he stayed here, he would lose her. If he stayed here, she would vanish.

They stopped on the pavement outside, shook hands once again and the dog leaned his paws on Josef's belly. Then the three of them watched Josef move away until he vanished from their sight. □

GRANTA

ZAGHROUDA
Jonathan Tel

If a dove flew from Jerusalem to Ramallah, about halfway along its journey it would pass a low hill around the eastern slope of which a village straggles; as it left the village it would flap over the roof of a cafe, and seated at one of the rickety tables outside the cafe as likely as not there would be two old men, in black-and-white checked keffiyah and shin-length abayeh, who would be sharing a narghile, inhaling puffs of honey-scented smoke and exhaling it into the good fresh air. The men are the same age, give or take a few hours. They are wrinkled and (underneath their keffiyah) bald as babies. Their voices are hoarse from age and tobacco. The topic of their conversation, of course, is how much better everything used to be in the old days.

Because of the coincidence of their shared birthday, soon after they were born they were laid side by side on a quilt, and compared critically by their respective fathers. The Turkish qadi, who was in charge of the region at the time, gave permission for an entourage of male relatives to fire Lee-Enfield rifles in the air as a salute for the newborns. However it took a week for this tribute to be organized, and by then the British had conquered Palestine and the fathers were arrested as suspected spies. The sons learned an important lesson from this. Throughout their long lives they have done nothing brave or glorious. But on the other hand they have survived.

The names the men commonly go by are Abu Radwan and Sinatra. They are both great-grandfathers, and have many relatives who should by rights be caring for them. But in practice they only trust each other. They have been allied throughout this life. They have every expectation of continuing to be allied in the afterlife.

Their conversation drifts to a matter of absorbing interest to them, though to nobody else in the village—the Pan-Arabist Movement of the 1950s and 60s. Were Egypt and Syria right to have joined their countries as the United Arab Republic in February 1958? So fiercely had the men disputed this question they had refused to speak to each other until September 1961, when Syria had pulled out, the UAR had dissolved, and Abu Radwan and Sinatra's disagreement had become moot. With time, their views have mellowed, and the gap between their positions has narrowed, but they still debate the matter with warmth.

'Ah, if only King Hussein had accepted Shukri al-Kuwatly's plea to bring Jordan into the coalition—that was the golden opportunity we all missed,' Abu Radwan laments. He is older than his friend by three hours: he feels he may speak with authority.

'No, you've got it wrong,' says Sinatra. 'It was Syria's fault for not bringing Iraq into the fold.' He barks names and dates, listing broken promises and failed opportunities. He takes a puff of the narghile, and rather loses his train of thought. 'From that point on, everything went downhill.' He rests a hand on Abu Radwan's arm to demonstrate that his refutation of his friend's position is not intended to dishonour him.

The owner of the cafe, commercially considerate, has unrolled a green awning which, in the spring breeze, billows above the old men like a flag. They shift their chairs back a few centimetres, to remain within the shade.

The cafe looks out over a patch of dusty earth, where nothing much is happening.

In theory the cafe commands a view—but to see it one would have to gaze over the top of a head-high cement wall on the far side of the waste ground. Abu Radwan and Sinatra have better things to do at their time of life than to stand on tiptoe and admire the vista. All they can observe of it, then, is blue sky, and a portion of the bluish hill on the far side of the valley. On top of that hill there is a row of apartment buildings, the colour of the earth, which pertains to a Jewish settlement there.

Among the things they cannot see (though occasionally they can hear it) is the busy bypass road that stretches through the valley, used mostly by cars and trucks with Israeli licence plates, driving to and from Jerusalem.

For several minutes Abu Radwan has been delivering his standard disquisition on the rise of Nasserism during the early- to mid-1950s, and Sinatra has been nodding his support. On this subject they are in hearty agreement.

'...Not only did Gamal Abdel Nasser nationalize the Suez Canal, but he had all the best tunes,' says Abu Radwan, by way of conclusion.

'Yes, songs you can sing along to,' says Sinatra.

Whereupon the two old men take the opportunity to tilt their heads back and launch into a chorus of 'Ya ya ya Gamal, leader of millions'.

Having repeated the entire song several times, they sip a refreshing glass of sweetened mint tea.

Then, ritually, they each ask how many children the other has. Of course they know the answers, but this is a polite conversation to have with friends, or indeed with strangers, and will serve to fill several minutes, this as every morning. They are proud of being old men, relishing the power the role brings with it, and one of the privileges of old age is the right to pose the same questions over and over.

'I have seven children,' Abu Radwan answers, 'three boys and four girls.'

'My cock is stronger than yours,' Sinatra says triumphantly, 'for I have five children, all boys.'

There are things that are not said. Of Abu Radwan's seven, one boy and one girl died in childbirth; one boy lives in Kuwait and the other in Detroit, so he has no son to care for him; ten years ago a daughter died when her kitchen caught fire; another daughter was divorced under shameful circumstances thirty-four years ago and he has not spoken to her since. As for Sinatra's five sons, the youngest has been jailed by Arafat's Force 17 for alleged drug-dealing, while the eldest dresses in women's clothing and calls himself Fatma.

'Another smoke?'

'Certainly,' says Sinatra.

Without turning his head, he calls to the cafe owner, who brings out a fresh wad of tobacco (the rose-scented kind, this time), and who revives the charcoal in the narghile by blowing on it. Sinatra assists, by inflating his cheeks then puffing hard, like a child trying to put out the candles on a birthday cake.

As if invoked by the recent talk of children, children are now playing on the waste ground. Boys, perhaps six or eight of them (it is impossible to make an exact count) are in constant motion, like bees over clover. None of the boys is older than twelve. They are playing some game which involves running to and fro. When a boy touches the wall, he is 'safe'.

The oldest boy wanders a little away from the others. He takes off his New York Knicks T-shirt. He creeps sideways in a stealthy crouch...suddenly he smashes the T-shirt down on the ground. Trapped within the T-shirt—paradoxically evident only when it is screened from view, for who would pay attention to it normally?—is

a pigeon. A kind of conjuring trick, in reverse. The boy grins. The
dazed pigeon attempts to bat its wings; it is warm between his hands.
He knots the T-shirt, and hugs the trapped bird, uninjured but
puzzled, to his chest. A good boy, he will take the pigeon home to his
mother for lunch.

Meanwhile the other boys have begun playing a game, 'Traffic'.
One boy stands with his back to the others, facing the wall. He calls
out, 'Green light!' His friends sneak up behind him. Suddenly he
looks over his shoulder. 'Red light!' The boys freeze. If anyone is still
in motion, his name is called and he has to go all the way back to
the starting line (which is defined as the limit of the shadow of the
cafe awning—directly in front, therefore, of the two old men). If
however the catcher does not glance around sharply enough, then
his pursuers will close in on him. Inevitably, sooner or later, he will
be poked between the shoulderblades. He will have lost the game—
and the victor will take on the role of the hunted one.

The shadows shift. The day heats up. The old men spread their
legs wider, under the lap of the abayeh.

Sinatra raps his fingers rhythmically on the brass tray on the table,
on which their now drunk glasses of mint tea sit. The mint leaves
and stalks themselves survive, damp and greenish, as if recently
hauled up from the bottom of the sea.

Abu Radwan idly stirs the mint with his teaspoon, perhaps
dreaming of searching for sunken treasures, pieces of eight,
doubloons...

Sinatra too examines the residue of liquid at the bottom of his
glass. By an association of ideas, he recalls another Nasserite anthem.
'We said we would and we have built the hi-igh dam!' he warbles.

Abdel is reluctant to join in on this one, so tricky to sing, but he
cannot resist vying with his friend when it comes to the 'hi-igh'.

Meanwhile the oldest boy has stored his pigeon for safe-keeping
beside the cafe. Nearby he finds a heavy lump of limestone, which
had been in use as a makeshift doorstop. The stone is as large as his
own head; he picks it up and lets it fall, with the aim of breaking it
up into smaller, more manageable pieces.

One of the other boys (spurred on to compete with the old-timers'
singing, perhaps) has taken his Walkman out of his pocket. He
removes the headphones. Several boys gather around to listen. The

cassette is a pirated version of a pop star belting out his latest hit, fresh from Cairo. It is the McFalafel jingle. The boys nod solemnly, in tempo. But the batteries are weak. The voice slows and deepens, like that of a jinn trapped in a bottle, and then fades out entirely.

By dint of determined pecking, the pigeon manages to free its head from its bonds. It peers out from its T-shirt wrapping.

The old men thump their fists on the table, and together they take the Dam Building Song from the top.

By now all the boys have chosen a stone—of varying dimensions and weight—in proportion to their own size.

They stand close together, not far from the wall (or parapet, as it might be called, if one thinks of it that way) and more or less in unison they lob their stones over it. The younger boys simply throw their stone upward in whatever way they can. But the older ones copy the stylish techniques of basketball players they have seen on TV—one-handedly launching the ball so that it flies through the hoop, in their imagination.

As to where the stones are landing, they can only guess. The taller boys spring repeatedly into the air, to snatch a succession of quick peeks over the wall. The smallest boy (he can't be more than five) begs one of the older boys (his brother, it seems, if we are to take his request literally; though perhaps he is saying 'brother' in an honorific sense) to aid him. The older one places both hands around the younger one's waist, and hoists him, as if hauling a sack of cement. It is doubtful that the little boy can see anything significant, even so.

In all probability, the stones would have done nothing more drastic than trickle down the hillside. Conceivably but implausibly, some stone might have skipped down to the bypass road, where it might have fallen on a Zionist windshield which, should it be non-reinforced, might have shattered...

At any rate the boys are eager to continue this activity. With devotion and thoroughness, they pick up stones and throw them, time and again.

Meanwhile Abu Radwan rings his spoon against the tray. He calls for more boiling water and sugar, to recompose his and his friend's tea.

Politely—but not as politely as all that (for the cafe owner, naturally, would prefer it if these customers would order fresh glasses), their wants are supplied.

There are five cubes of sugar in the bowl. Abu Radwan and Sinatra each take two. Both men have a sweet tooth. Who should get the last cube? They are drawn by the contradictory impulses of greed and generosity. They look into each other's eyes. They smile, each knowing what the other is thinking.

At last Abu Radwan seizes the prize, puts it in his glass, and stirs the tea vigorously.

'What is mine is mine by right!' he sings out, in his cracked voice. And Sinatra laughs—for Abu Radwan is quoting the song that the groom chants on his wedding day, while the male relatives dance the Sword Dance.

The stone throwing continues.

The sun shifts higher in the sky. Abu Radwan and Sinatra move their chairs all the way back now, against the side of the cafe.

Once again they discuss politics—the absorbing question of what should have happened during 1958–61. They re-state their positions with scarcely less vigour than before.

They sip their tea. As was bound to happen sooner or later, the old men begin to cry. Not passionate tears, not the tears of youth, but steady, unstoppable, necessary.

Their tears roll down their cheeks and salt their sweet tea. Their tears fall on their clothing and on the brass tray and on the table top and on the dry earth.

The cafe owner, crying himself, comes out bringing them two halves of a cut onion. 'Squeeze these close to your eyes,' he says through his tears. 'The more you cry, the better it is for you.'

And then the children, who naturally are also crying, retreat from their positions by the parapet, and withdraw to near the cafe, farther from the wafting cloud of tear gas.

Several of the children have masked their faces with their own T-shirts, as a minimal protection against the gas.

One of the boys has a genuine gas mask (a relic from the Gulf War). He wears it with panache. Though the thing looks formidable, it is unlikely the filter is still activated, and in any case it is too large for him so the fit cannot be airtight. Surely in secret he also is crying.

The oldest boy is torn between two desires. On the one hand he would like to mask himself with his T-shirt. On the other hand, to do so would mean letting the pigeon go.

Bold, not to say impudent, notwithstanding his flowing tears, he asks to borrow Sinatra's keffiyah.

'Certainly not,' says Sinatra.

The expression on Abu Radwan's face is such that the boy does not even attempt to make the same request of him.

The boy runs inside the cafe—and soon comes out with a dishrag he has borrowed from the owner, tied over his mouth and nose.

Fortunately quite a strong breeze is blowing. The awning pumps up and down. The gas disperses, and general weeping ceases.

The children do not remove their improvised masks though. Masked, they feel empowered. They look at one another—their old friends become semi-anonymous—with respect and wonder.

The smallest boy is crying still—tears of frustration. He has been trying to tie his Donald Duck T-shirt around his head, but since the ratio of skull-size to chest-size is greater in his case, it will not stay put. He has asked his elder brother to do something, but in this matter even his brother, his own flesh and blood, cannot help. His brother merely pulls the T-shirt over the little boy's neck, and tugs his arms through the armholes, and tells him to grow up. Among all these transformed children, the little boy's round face, gleaming with tears, alone is pristine.

Thrilled by their adventure, the remaining boys chat among themselves and also to the two old men.

'You have to be careful, sir, not to eat Zionist chocolate,' the gas-masked boy advises Abu Radwan, forward and deferential at the same time.

'What nonsense!' says Abu Radwan. 'What do I need chocolate for, at my age?'

'No, it is true,' the same boy insists. 'I heard it from my cousin. He told me they are putting radioactive chocolate in Snicker bars.'

'True? False?' enquires Abu Radwan, open-minded.

'What is "radioactive"?' Sinatra asks.

A different boy explains, 'Radioactive means it's hot.'

'When it is hot it is no good,' Sinatra confirms sagely, exhaling horns of smoke. 'It melts in your hand.'

This inspires Abu Radwan to tell everybody a long involved story about how he went to a funeral of some young fellow who had been shot with a rubber bullet in Ramallah, a martyr. He didn't know the family well, but he felt he ought to go. '…Well, the man's wife was weeping, which was very bad of her, everybody kept telling her not to disgrace the family. And the relatives were giving out sweetmeats. Trays of delicious knaafe and halwa, and, yes, miniature Snicker bars. You can get a family-size packet in the souk, that has twenty tiny bars inside; it's economical. Anyway, the sisters and sisters-in-law were throwing them down from a window. And the mother was very good, she kept trilling her zaghrouda, just as if it was her dead son's wedding!'

'It would not have happened in the good old days,' says Sinatra.

'But that is my point,' says Abu Radwan. 'We are not in the good old days.

'And then what?' says Sinatra.

'Then we all drank sweetened coffee and went home,' says Abu Radwan.

At this point Sinatra tries to sing a zaghrouda himself—simultaneously voicing a fixed note while flapping his tongue—but he cannot achieve it. It sounds rather as if he is mimicking a car alarm. He bursts out coughing.

Abu Radwan is too wise even to attempt so foolish a feat.

But the boys are young enough and excited enough to strive to make this sound. They have to adjust their masks first, to free up their mouths and noses. Consecutively, and then concurrently, they each produce a zaghrouda, with varying degrees of success. The oldest boy's voice is breaking—his is a horrible screech. But the youngest boy has a pure sweet tone.

Abu Radwan pats the little boy's head. 'You are a canary,' he tells him.

'You are an angel,' Sinatra says.

The cafe owner has come out, clapping his hands over his ears. 'You are a bunch of tomcats!' he shouts.

'And what about his wife?' Sinatra asks.

'Whose wife?' says Abu Radwan.

'Whose do you think?' says Sinatra. 'Did she repent her sinful weeping, and sing a zaghrouda instead?'

'How should I know?' Abu Radwan says. 'You think I look at other men's wives? This was a funeral, not a dance hall!'

Since by now the day is hot, the old men retreat inside the cafe. They sit down beneath the electric ceiling fan.

The owner carries in on their behalf their tray of tea, and their narghile.

Once more, they receive flavoured tobacco. Once more, hot water is added to their soggy mint leaves.

As for the boys, since they have nothing better to do, they set about throwing stones again. Naturally they are determined to do it even better this time, more like the images of boys throwing stones that you see on TV.

It really would look more professional if they could borrow a keffiyah or two, but if the old men won't lend theirs, then there's no help for it.

From time to time the boys adjust their own, and one another's, T-shirt masks. The boy in the gas mask has found it too uncomfortable, and has instead knotted his T-shirt around his head in the manner of his friends. Somebody notices a plastic bag blowing across the ground, and blocks it with his foot, the way you stop a soccer ball.

Abu Maneh Fine Tailoring is printed on it in elegant Kufic lettering. This is put over the head of the youngest boy, so he too will be properly masked (albeit unable to see out) and will not shame the others. His brother tucks it well in, inside the neck of his T-shirt.

Now the boys form a rough line, side by side, facing the parapet. A stone is in every hand. Dramatically, as if posing for an imagined TV camera, they lift their arms, levering them well back.

The cafe owner is nowhere in sight. Presumably he is in his shack behind the cafe, sleeping with his wife, as he usually does at this hour, when business is reliably slack.

Inside the cafe, Abu Radwan, though he is seated upright on a hard wooden chair, has his head tilted to one side; he is snoring.

As for the other old man, he is crooning to himself quietly, in Arabic, 'I Did it My Way'.

Meanwhile the pigeon, a Houdini of a bird, escapes from the T-shirt. It struggles into the air, circles the village, and disappears.

For all their spirit and poise, then, nobody is observing the seven boys who are crouched close by the parapet, throwing stone after stone at the unseen enemy beyond—nor the eighth boy, the littlest, who, with the plastic bag over his head, is kneeling on the waste ground. He leans forward as if praying, then rolls to one side, still.

□

GRANTA

THE LITTLE PLATE OF CHILDHOOD

Todd McEwen

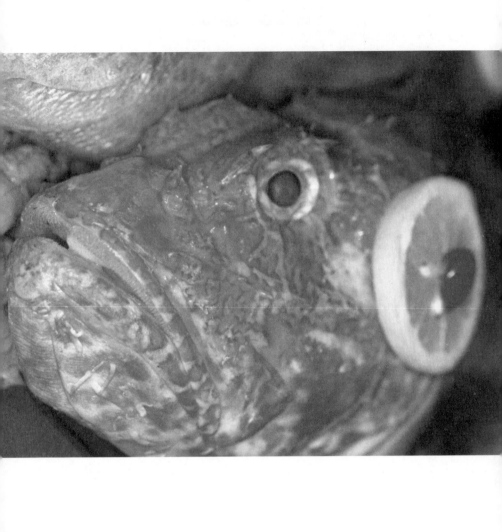

Why I hate food

—at the mention of food a fight always gradually breaks out. Something has happened to the way people eat; there are too many TRIBES about it. There is the tribe of those who eat only at home, their tiny kitchens stuffed with cookbooks. If they have space they have built kitchen *islands*, under spotlights, grand opera kitchens where the dinner guest drowses drunkly and slowly starves while watching his fat, obsessed host prepare the meal—there is a man on Thompson Street who has an APPLAUSE sign over his island. Its burners in the night. You see it from the imagined safety of your ship. The drums, the drums.

Some will only eat in restaurants—they can't, *won't* make you coffee or a drink, even in *anticipation* of the restaurant. But the largest tribe are those who cannot eat the GOOD FOOD WHICH IS FREELY AVAILABLE ON EVERY CORNER IN THIS OUR TOWN. It's right in front of them—but if *sustenance* is mentioned, so is a *taxi*. You could be walking past the GRAND CENTRAL OYSTER BAR even, but no, *NO*, being *proximate* to a place *rules it out*; complicated negotiations must be entered into between everyone in the party and you are then forced into a taxi—*the forcemeat stuffing of a taxi*—and hurtled somewhere far uptown, far downtown, and preferably across town from where you realized you were hungry. So hungry. Or *thought* you were hungry! Hasn't your appetite disappeared after one of these *contretemps* asserted of course in the friendliest possible way?

As we go about town, we encounter a number of altercations, hold-ups, muggings, which *look like crimes*—we step around them in the street, on the subway steps, people locked in combat, yes— we observe little tussles out the window of our office or the bus. Person A has Person B by the lapels; C uses her stilettos unfairly. But most of these contests aren't crimes—they are people arguing about where to eat. *It really has come to this.* Our town is so disconnected from its sources of supply that where to dine has become a life-and-death struggle—it seems nothing has changed since the Neolithic (excepting perhaps napery). Arguing about where to eat is just as exhausting as chipping your arrow-head and going out to try and kill a capybara; eventually in surprise succeeding, and then hauling it home, chopping it up and heating it in some unimaginable way.

And supermarkets are all run by JACK ASSES. They take even more time than capybara.

I truly hate food, I said to Isidor. I just can't take it any more. F*** food! Of course, *f***food*, I thought immediately, food for sex—not Bob Guccione spilling chocolate syrup on the rattan, you idiot, but the bachelor picking up little snacks to salt the appetite of his intended—carbohydrates and *rounded* things that might be popped between red lips—things that are slimy—f***food, I called it. Isidor became very uneasy when I used this term as it sounded like a put-down of food, and he could not bear for *food* to be denigrated—F*** FRUIT especially, I loudly said in a bad mood one day in Union Square. It's really just sugar and water in a suspiciously plasticky wrapping. Really bad for you. My teeth always ached at the thought of biting apples.

—*I hate food!*

Isidor became wide-eyed, his eyes morose blue at this.—Keep your voice down, he said under his breath.

—It's all the preparation, I said, the horrible amount of time, even as a child it drove me MAD to watch people making food, my poor mother, the gas, my father raging at his brazier, trying to make it fun, trying to make it...MANLY? Every moment I've spent shopping, cooking, eating and washing dishes I've wished I were smoking, reading, drinking or screwing. Don't you see how important it is to recognize the restaurant, the delicatessen, the pretzel-and-chestnut man as THE ONLY SOURCES OF FOOD? Otherwise you'll end up crying in the street. *Sanctify* the delicatessen, said I, the restaurant and their waiters which are closest to your front door, no matter how bad. What better example of the American spirit, of cooperation? Of the primal transaction? I give you something of value, shells or cigarettes, and you feed me.

—But why are you fetishizing it? said Izzy. That holy transaction takes place at McDonald's 2,000 times per hour.

—Ach, that doesn't count.

—Your argument is a good one, said Isidor, except I happen to know it places you at the mercy of Mary Jo's Deli.

I know I know and all the feebleness of upper Broadway, I thought, and yes I am made sick with fear standing in Mary Jo's watching flies buzzing in the fittings, how never a single one finds its way even by accident to its blue electric Zing Zing; and yes I EAT CARDBOARD and greeny baloneys because I'm sticking to my theory and it's a good one. Mine is the only theory that helps the ecology of the city and saves me time. Provides jobs.

And what is the point of living in a city unless you want to save time? If you want to *waste* time go to Larchmont or Vermont or Montana or Montevideo—where you may pay handsomely to waste your time, waiting in line to buy gasoline or having children—or better, *you can pay people to waste your time FOR you.* Out there. Isn't this the essence of the city? You live in town because you want someone to make your morning coffee for you. Don't you think it's CHEATING to prepare food in your own home?

—It is only drink that nourishes and ennobles, I said. Admit it! If everyone would *just admit* that then we could send all our wheat overseas to those hungry people—they're not allowed to drink, anyway. We get what we need, they get what they need. —I don't know, said Isidor.

Look what happens to the idea of food when, years ago, you are allowed to run your fingers over the prominent contours of the vulva—nothing more—of this girl from Hunter College for three or four hours on a rainy afternoon. In the shower afterwards you could still see the dull mark on your wrist, the elastic of her underwear incised there. Your poor hand in the exact same position for three hours. You withdrew it from her jeans, blood-gorged numb and purple—if only it had been another extremity—and suggested dinner, which she took as calmly as she had the mauly diddling since three o'clock.

—I'm a vegetarian, she breathed, doing up the many buttons.

In the old neighbourhood, *vegetarian* meant either a Muenster cheese sandwich or that Chinese food which having been most boiled in the world was losing its molecular integrity. In a state ricocheting between guilt and largesse you took this two-bump beauty (thinking all evening of the pronounced quality of her labia, bump-bump, bump-bump under your fingers) to THE FARMYARD—'New York's Old-Established Vegetarian Restaurant', here, in the West Forties.

Bump bump, the taxi on sleeping policemen outside a garage—rain had come on while you lay on your bed, she staring at the ceiling and you wondering what the hell was happening with your life—nothing. The driver pointed out a modest door and a dingy lighted stair—the taxi went off in a series of puddles and bangs and you took the bored woman's arm out of rocketing chivalry. Thunder, suddenly, musically, insistently; lightning across the front of the building, which took on a sinister look thanks to the crenellations of a hamburger joint on the corner. At the same moment the restaurant's venerable sign faltered and—bzzzt—THE FARMYARD—went out.

Bump-Bump went up the stairs, you following, observing with vexation nautical lacing at the back of her jeans—your recent prison; the scene which greeted you in the dining room robbed you of air and drew you together—at last she grabbed you, in horror-movie uncertainty. The low brow of the shabby peanut-oiled *maître d'* indicated a SEA beyond of the truly distressed and decrepit, the lame, the halt dining as best they could. Here a man with a growth on his cheek *twice* the size of the growth on the ham-and-salad tub man at Mary Jo's Deli—hell, twice the size of what he was having for dinner; there a family of hunchbacks in their seventies or eighties *having their food cut up for them* by a waiter with a glass eye. No one a recognizable morphic type, shape, or colour, and—you know—that's saying something in this our town. But Bump-Bump rushed to sit down—you lost interest in her body entirely at this point except for beginning to SCOUR HER COUNTENANCE for incipient pallor, growths, twistings, to affirm your moral insertion of her into this menagerie.

The food was classical Vegetarian (stultifyingly capital V)—everything vegetal fungal and udderal chopped up and moulded at ferocious industrial temperature and pressure to *resemble meat*—only despite these extreme processes the semblance was but slim; each dish with a sickly dairy taste—cold *moussaka* run over by the dog-catcher. Bump-Bump ordered diffidently and seemed determined to notice nothing. When the limping waiter snatched the cover from the platter you stared in fury at your cool parsnipwursts—a shocking reiteration of the late afternoon and its rain—the girl's vulva like that on a Greek statue—and you could barely resist fingering the depression between the two.

Lump lump, going down. Nothing to be said, apparently, the stuff did require a lot of chewing—it was dawning on you that far from coming to THE FARMYARD to improve their lot, these wretches, whom you were more likely to have encountered in a fun-house—had in this place, from this food—GOT that way.

No proper ending—New York never lets anything die off completely between two people—but a sequel. Several months later in Mary Jo's, Bump-Bump, with bigger eyes and smile, faced you off near the potato chips. *Accosted* you just as you were staggering and feeling ill at the sight of the growth on the ham-and-salad tub man's face, wondering if he dined at THE FARMYARD. And she incredulously says, *You're buying baloney!?*, and above his ranged fluorescent furrows of browning caking salads, the ham-and-salad tub man salivates at her.

Let us take a trip down Alimentary Lane—before our food moved to New York and became perverted, as mother would say. Here, on a winter evening, is your plate—a jolly Georgian coaching scene—the plate is *brown and white*—and here is just *enough* juice from your little chop pleasantly to obscure the scene ('Catching the Mail'). Your little chop is just half an inch thick—an animal has been sacrificed in your honour, but there is no suggestion of pride or plumpness or luxury in your little chop. There is something insistent about its quality as *fuel*—it is a piece of coal for your engine and since this is a WEEK NIGHT, a SCHOOL NIGHT, it's to be regarded as nothing more—there is a sterility, a NURSE-LIKE quality about mother's kitchen, is there not? Is the little chop itself your nurse? You think about it on the corner of 53rd and Madison, it is a smell you can conjure anywhere (and have done, even to put yourself to sleep in a lonely room), your little chop, the broiler, the hood, the kitchen, the hot handles of the pots and pans, the clock, the light, the beans, the rice. Down with potatoes, the role of carbohydrate will this evening ladies and gentlemen be played by White Rice, not sticky together like school rice from a scoop but not the featheriest and most separate either. Difficult to photograph, a circumspect mound, a tussock of rice with a pat of butter upon it—the butter photographs distinctly and the rice is as always a white shape with disturbing shadows. For all New York's claims to cover the waterfront of gastronomy, this is a smell you will never find here, not even in the most ordinary corner luncheonette or the plainest Sixth Avenue hotel serving the biggest dumbest hicks:

—the little plate of childhood.

This is all *in* you now, these poorly rotogravured and pastel molecules, inside you and perhaps nourishing something still, some idea of what dinner might be like for someone of RECTITUDE, someone with *character*, god damn it. I still don't know what half the stuff was that I ate.

Sure all you eat or all you tell everyone at the bar you eat is brown rice and vegetables delicately sautéed or oven roasted—how you stay in good trim for a city boy or girl, the balance, god's own roughage slicing all the gin and nicotine out of you. But as Isidor points out, that's all a pathetic throwback to the little plate of childhood—except for the boring little piece of meat jumping up and down, *begging* to be carried away by the postilions of the mail.

One day recently in Isidor's bookshop I discovered the source of this iniquity. I unearthed, under the many overlays and corruptions of our need for food and drink in this our town, the colour, texture, temperature, the proteins ('building blocks'—sheesh!), the nourishment, the MEANING of our youth. He stocks tons of ephemera which can make you very uncomfortable about your country and your birthright. In the dark cookery aisle I beheld a thing from the antique land we all came from, where, woe, mother would get hold of the recipe page in the local paper.

Down East Clam Dunk	*The verbe-comme-nom school of cuisine.*
Blue Cheese Bologna Wedges	*The FUN staple meat*
Cream of Baked Bean Soup	*Are you kidding?*
Frank 'n Vegetable Soup	*What they did to the letter N! Formerly a kind and useful letter.*
Luau Barbecued Ribs	*Ah, Hawaii! Shangri-La of the mid-Fifties imagination; now merely the headquarters of minor drug dealers and gas guzzlers.*

The Little Plate of Childhood

Waikiki Kabobs	*Spelling just wasn't a problem to our parents. Also try our Waikiki Nog.*
Fiesta Corn Pudding	*Can you imagine real Mexicans sitting around with bowls of this? They'd hang it from a string and beat the shit out of it.*
Company Cauliflower	*They arrive, you take their coats, all is early Kennedy jollity, and then their eyes light on...!*
Party Dream Salad	*Which sums up the entire catalogue of aspiration 1950–65.*
Baked Salad of the Sea	*Aside from the phrase 'of the sea', which enriched many lives, there was the idea that BAKING made something ready for the table, that it was physically possible to BAKE ANYTHING, as per—*
Baked Cheese Sandwiches, Baked Cheese 'n Ham Sandwiches, Ham 'n Blue Cheese Old Tyme Baked Sandwiches	*How many lives? The ups, the downs, the doomed marriages?*

I could bear it no longer. —Say, I called out to Isidor, *Cheesy Ponytail Franks. Place frankfurters in roll. Place sandwiches on rectangles of aluminum foil. Seal carefully and twist ends to give ponytail look!* Izzy rushed over. There in the dark cookery aisle we cackled and wept together. As he paged through this warped book, Isidor acquired a distant, bilious expression. He teetered. —Are you surprised that you hate casseroles? he said to me suddenly. Don't you hate the word and its associated house-filling smell, that of a big earthenware half-glazed dish with a frightening, hollow handle? Doesn't the word *casserole* itself SMELL, of unimaginatively used onions? —You're so right, I said. It's terribly creepy, serving dollops of stuff *straight from the cooking vessel*. It strikes at the heart of sensibility. It *deprives waiters of work*.

I pointed out *Baked Tuna Ring*. —Oh, said Iz, anything that could be formed into a ring was good. You reel from all that post-war sloth. People *will* paint it, said Izzy, as an energetic American time, but really they wanted everything piping hot. They wanted it all mixed up with cheese. And look: by the time you got to dessert, you'd no energy left to keep cooking: *Refrigerator Cake, No-Bake Confetti Brownies.*

—Yes, I said, even though preparing the entrées merely involved stirring onion soup mix into...something. I feel sick.

Serving Butter Attractively.

Chipped Beef.

Canned Pears.

Cottage Cheese—What Is It?

No wonder that Isidor and I, reared on this kind of thing, are conflicted in our attitudes to food—and everything else for that matter. But while I can hardly bear to think about food, was *driven away from it at an early age*, our atomic cuisine had determined Isidor on loving food. Trauma ensued. If someone visits me, whether uptown or out of town, the first thing Isidor asks them is *Did he feed you?*

The Discovery of Fish

—and its waiters—took place on a damp day long ago, Isidor and I standing half-relaxed on the prosaic rain-corner of Seventh Avenue and 34th Street. A Monday afternoon, perhaps a public holiday, though you couldn't tell due to the absence of people who *stroll.*

We had just come out of Penn Station, —*that low-ceilinged Hell*, said Isidor, of course you won't remember the old Penn Station. —No, I said, I won't, and I'd rather not remember this one either. —I'm telling you, said Isidor, in Hell all the ceilings will be very low, with hot spotlights which singe the acoustical tile surrounding them so it looks like someone has been cooking French toast on the ceiling. Architects have got to go.

I cast about for something to contrast with the present moment on the dull rain-corner, though contrast is hard-won in the West Thirties. We had just visited Isidor's parents by train. Isidor's mother believed I was a 'Negro' and gave me special, though off-balance, treatment. Isidor's father was fairly sure I was not, though he took it up with her in the kitchen. —He is more or less like us, what is the matter with you? he said, picking his noonday fight. —Hoo hah! said Mrs Katz, 'more or less'!

There was very little contrast between the Katzes' house and the Erie-Lackawanna Railroad. Sitting on the wicker seats was just as stultifying as sitting on the couch of any parent.

There are days, aren't there? Rare ones, when you feel like doing, and can actually do, what normal, relaxed people do. —Radio City, I said, thinking of the huge comforting dark to be found there on days such as this; as you take your wallet out of your coat while passing under the illuminated name LEON LEONIDOFF. —It's dwindling but it's still there, said Isidor, and I respect that. You hear me? I *respect* that. Let's go.

Yet we remained there on the corner, cold and bleary from the Erie-Lackawanna, two boys of nineteen without their mommas. I was reminiscing over Mrs Katz's food, if truth be told. Isidor was put out with me for appreciating it. —What the hell do you mean by thanking her for her flanken? he had said. How dare you thank my murderer? —Oh well, I said, I don't know. Iz spat on what turned out to be a mouse in the gutter. On my mind was the silver and red marquee at the Music Hall, the warm dark, long purple lights, the smell of a thousand damp coats tidily attended to. I looked up and down 34th Street—halfway toward Eighth I saw a mirroring of the neon in my thoughts, a warm old sign in the middle of the block. Isidor and I were susceptible to commercial overgrowths, barnacles of this kind. PADDY'S CLAM HOUSE. As if one, without speaking, we turned in the rain and walked toward it, the orange-white-green neon promising comfort of an old and inexpensive sort. Paused at the door. —Do you eat fish? said I. —Well, no, said Iz. And pushed on the door and we were enveloped in the steam and scream of a Fish Restaurant; where we always should have been.

There was a bar. Right as you went in—not original, but there, a little apology for those who came during times of great uproar and had to wait for a table. The charm of small glasses of 'Piel's' for 25¢; part of the spell was looking at the ¢. —One of the last ¢ signs, said Isidor, it must be. We felt like birdwatchers; one could keep a log. I looked at my printed napkin, PADDY'S CLAM HOUSE, and felt finally a part of the history of my family, all the fish they'd swallowed. —My grandfather in his derby in the clam-houses of San Francisco, I said to Iz. He gave me a rare tongue-lashing once, outside Alioto's, he said Chowder, surely you will eat *chowder*, everybody eats CHOWDER?! I said I would have one of the awful hamburgers they grudgingly fry you on a corner of the grill in fish restaurants, but he wouldn't let me be seen with him in Alioto's if I wasn't going to eat fish. He was always going on about eggs, eggs will *kill* you, every egg a *bullet*, yet his favourite thing was to rush into Alioto's in his raincoat and eat six dozens of fried clams. —Hypocrisy is on the rise, said Isidor.

I thought of my grandfather going over to a bar while waiting for the cable car to be turned at the foot of Powell Street: he liked the way the sun shone through the little clerestories at him. The bar smelled of brass and hat and glass-smear. It wasn't called a bar at all; oddly, the sign outside said LAUREL DRINKS, and the wiseguy boys of the neighbourhood perpetually and freshly wrote SHE DOES? underneath it with pencils and charcoal and dog poo. Boys like the one he once was, when he felt the height of the city dizzying, and the freedom which came with dizziness: the freedom to pull the plait of the Chinaman who sold his mother vitriol, the freedom to tie a dog to the California Street cable by its tail, the freedom to hop on and hop off any moving conveyance for any reason. No conductor or Confucian or mother had ever caught him.

The bartender gave us big menus. —I don't, uh, said Isidor, what do you—. You should have seen us, side by side, in the mirror behind the bar, perusing our first Fish Restaurant menu, two small worried fellas, perusing it like it'd never been perused. The bartender thought we might be FOREIGNERS who COULDN'T READ.

—I gotta table for you guys, said a waiter, this way. We followed him into the din, into the SEA of white cloths, chairs, coats, people and their fingers, people talking about their ties, their sisters, businesses, some spoke of cars, f*** cars. Being at 34th and Seventh, there was a bit of talk of drapery. —My parents are afraid of fish, said Isidor. —Yeah well that's very tough, said the waiter; —It's the sensuality, I offered, as we sat. —No, it isn't, said the waiter. —They're from Poland, said Isidor. —What do you want from me, I said, I'm afraid too. My dad used to take me to a trout farm; we floated on a lot of slimy water and caught fish who were drugged and hypnotized to OBEY. The whole thing made me very apprehensive, especially the fact that these fish tongued up their own silt all day which was scraped off the bottom of the pond and made into pellets which became their suppers. —They ate their own *defaeces*? said Isidor. —How'd they avoid scraping up mud too from the bottom? —It was lined with cement, I said, blushing with awareness that I was unworthy of sitting here. What truck had I with fish—save the truck which came and emptied the brainwashed trout into that hideous basin in the semidesert? I leaned toward Iz. —I used to throw up at the end, I said, it was the quality of the water we were floating on and this orange pop out of this cooler-which-didn't-cool-it. I'd had no contact with a fish and no expectation of eating one, but *blugggh*! —Pretty funny, said Isidor, looking around, nervous. He felt the conversation was inappropriate for other tables.

It is odd of myself always to have despised the very idea of fish, considering that when young my favourite place was a tidal pool; that at night after perusing *The Illustrated Book of the Sea* I always dreamed of a life under the waves, swimming effortlessly with my special friends the giant sunfish and the nautilus... That is until things got complicated and *they all turned into dreams of suffocation.* — My mother would boil a king crab all day, I said to Iz. The smell filled the house, even the *sofa cushions*. We had to brain her with the pot lid to get her to quit.

—It's extensive, I almost said universal, said Isidor, the child's hatred of fish; it's sex of course—salty, raw, pungent, inflamed, raving, pervading and like it a mystery to which they are not admitted. They are excluded from fish and from the rites of the parental bedroom and so they hate and fear both. —Thank you, I said, after a pause during which we both thought we *had* been a wee bit audible. Where anyway is all this *salty pervading* sex you've been having? You're skating, you know, awful close to the old fishpussy thing. We are not men like that, men who think that pussy is fish and fish pussy! Men who work for a living! —Would you *stop* talking about this? said a man at the next table. —See, I have problems with, continued Isidor, red, low—I could never get past the affinity cats have for fish and couldn't sort the metaphor. —What metaphor, I said, it isn't a—

—Ha ha ha! What do *you* guys know about *pussy*? said the waiter, standing there; rocking on the balls of his feet. Big smile, greying hair combed back, short white jacket, beneath it a short white apron, black trousers and shoes. White shirt and black bow tie; towel and pad in hand: I could have given his description to any policeman.

Smiling, engaged, affably hostile—he had taken in our conversation at the salient word and was including himself in; had already put Isidor and me in his 'little world'. But expressions like this are very irritating—there is only *one* world, after all, and those who would make other worlds usually have the purposes of capitalism in mind—'*Welcome to the World of Golf*'—or belittlement—'He's in his own world'—(twirl finger by temple).

—**What'll ya have today**—

The menu was large and daily set in tiny Fournier type. Bluefish, clams, snapper, crackers, sauces—these things raced in arcs of ice water around our heads. Isidor was stunned by the menu and its choice, all the words he was unused to conjuring—

—**Okay fellas what can I get yiz**—

I too clammed up as I stared at the verification of everything I had ever encountered, in a way—the fingers of an old weirdo in my palm, the glistening of girls, the manners of the staff of the IRT—. Isidor, subsumed in the menu, saw the city's past, and in the new words found poetry, found his calling: an invisible, partly Gershwin stair was built right beside him which led in several years to the door of his bookshop. You could almost hear the hammers and saws. The waiter's pad was thick; orders now being sweated in the kitchen curved round it to the back; a stripe of royal blue carbon paper; it seemed properly a quality of the waiter's plump hand, spoke richesse just like the menu—

—**...fellas!**

Of a sudden we plunged and ordered, I a dish of steamed clams, since that was a thing Grandfather had belittled me about, and a finnan haddie, which I conceived looked like himself in his derby. And salad—that is, iceberg lettuce and one seventh of a small tomato under thick putty-coloured goo. *Please*. And Isidor *chowder*, New England to be sure—if he was going to eat this it ought to have the Brahmin's sting, the surroundings of PADDY's notwithstanding. He had long coveted the hexagonal cracker. And bluefish, as it sounded clean, proper, big game. Maybe. No one is too sure of their Hemingway any more.

—*No bluefish*, said the waiter, looking off to the side and turning over a page of his pad—as if there were *never* bluefish—isn't this the kind of thing that drives you nuts—you go into a place where the menu is printed in Fournier *every day* and immediately the guy tells you *no bluefish*. That is New York, pal. —*Then snapper*, said Isidor; he hoped by doing this not to have his stock lowered in the kitchen or with the waiter. Snapped his menu shut like he came there always. —You wanna stay with your beers there? said the waiter, one eyebrow moving one centimetre. Oh there must be drink with fish as surely as there must be l'astringent après le rasage. —White wine, Isidor fairly shouted; then he looked up at the waiter through his appealing brows—what kinds do you have, he said. —All kinds, fellas, said the waiter, moving quickly away from us and making a violent sign to the little bartender, yelling *TWO WINES!*

I goggled at the place, the black-and-white waiters moving with many difficulties through the autumn exhalations of the coats and the energetic, ordinary talk in the air. A whole realm to share with Isidor! —When I was a child, on the motherf***ing television, I said, there were vast restaurants under the sea—the waiters were penguins and lobsters played castanets in the floor show. —Yeah, I know, said Izzy, the orchestra was all traif. As usual after visiting New Jersey, Isidor was feeling tinges of guilt. —But there's nothing wrong with this! I think we have *got* to have more and more restaurants and waiters and glassware and fish and white wine for everyone, said Isidor looking around excitedly, or everything is going to EXPLODE. Civilization *really will be lost* in slips between pizza box, computer keyboard and drooly lips.

—Yes! A Fish Restaurant, clamorous yet efficient, is the obvious model for government! I said to Isidor. For how is anything going to get *sorted out*, out there in that god damn country, unless everyone can get together? That's how the country was *founded*, god damn it, people *got together*, in a room, a Fish Restaurant...

I felt I understood the city for the first time—how it actually works, how it is the engine of civilization and liberation—saw the place of delicatessens, waiters and restaurants in a great scheme, and of the FISHES themselves. It really couldn't have been planned better by Moses (Robert) himself. I give you something of value and you feed me. What could be...greater? More historic? PADDY'S was so like life...everyone was being mistreated. O God they loved it. It generates an energy which runs the city along ineluctable lines. It

Todd McEwen

explains *everything* that our town is a Fish Restaurant, that it raves and pervades, that there is noise and rudeness, rudeness which is salt spray, the pungent flesh of things which get done. The source of all rudeness, or bracing American character, may be the flesh of fish, which TANGS, and keeps us in mind of the old city, the old mental capital, keeps us on the old cold streets of sunsets and harsh ideas, keeps us going back and forth across New York Bay on the *Mary Murray* and the *Cornelius G. Kolff*, over the fishes, our fuel. Would that it kept us fighting the Revolutionary War, which everybody out there in that god damn country has ceased to do.

It suddenly struck me that waiter panache and aplomb, a *real* waiter's, are needed to survive in town today; to preserve the forms of civilization. —Isn't the waiter's attire the ideal town wear? I said to Isidor.

The Apron—none of the city's dribblings, especially in spring, would get on you, the rusty water from awnings, melony sludge from disappearing ice at the fruit stand. Nor do your own spillages, unbalances of beer, pose any threat to your true costume, nor do the cigarette-ash coffee and milk covered tables of the Village—pffft!— the INDUSTRIAL LAUNDRY takes care of your apron overnight at agonizingly high temperature and pressure.

The Clean White Shirt—a religion in itself, gentlemen, your credo to the world: you maintain; you endure. You can be as ordered, as eternal a *tabula rasa* as the white tiles, on which, granted, you may have lain, of the giant Men's Room of any great hotel. What we put on *over* the clean white shirt, an apron, a shopkeeper's coat, a suit sharp-cornered enough to prick people turning the corner of Pine Street, doesn't matter—just for the moment.

The Towel—why you don't see everyone carrying a towel in New York I don't know, unless that's what they have in those plump briefcases and bags, lots of nice white towels. Never *known* such a place for getting stuff on you, never *seen* so many people who need a bit of wiping before they get to the office. If each had his waiter's towel, there would never again come that moment when you must stutter obvious things to the groomed, embalmed, refrigerated receptional beauty, having just blown in off 100° Fahrenheit Street to drip and flake and *breathe* all over the frighteningly clean formica of her station. (Confidential to Mr L. Bean of Freeport: *'These robust*

182

100% Egyptian cotton Belgian waiter's fore-arm towels are the best we've seen…' Missing a trick there.)

What *is* that stuff on the banister of the IRT, south stairs, 14th Street station (downtown side)? It's there every day. Again—towel—rectified. A fresh start. By the low dread rumblings of the great Laundry of the Night.

And the Black Trousers, thanks to their buddy the apron, don't show cigar ash, soot, fish blood, that stuff on the IRT banister (south stairs). Sober companions of the clean white shirt, ready for *anything* after work, the quiet assertion of faith in people if they would *just get serious*; if they would be Scottish or Portuguese just for a little while?

It would be an admirable goal to be the rudest fish waiter in New York; it would make you the kind of king of all this. I propounded a theory of waiter attire for myself and over the coming months adopted this costume for years, black trousers and clean white shirt. Dressed this way, I thought, I will quietly show people where to sit, just anywhere, or even what to do. I'll get money and tips. Pick up valuable Pine Street information from people I encounter every day. I could become

THE CAPTAIN OF THE NEIGHBOURHOOD.

—New York is the last place where the graces of waiting table are real, said Isidor. An honourable profession in decline, like those of signwriter, street-sweeper, tobacconist, whore. Do you think anyone is paid a living wage to bring you a biscuit in *Seattle*, or even a piece of meat? Even though they nourish and sustain all those uptight people of the Northwest? —Pffft! I said. —*It used to be a living*, Izzy said. Waiters raised happily disorganized families in the shadow of the hotel, their collars open on Sundays.

Imagine who comes to call when you offer a job waiting table *these* days. By the Sixties college students had all but replaced waiters from the union hall; then in the Seventies it was high-school students, then in the Eighties it was Reagan and so the most unbelievable collection of retard-Os, junior high girls on drugs, pathetic PhDs, out-and-out nutcases—no one would stay more than a month or two, unionize *that* if you will. Where were all the guys with little moustaches? Imagine Reagan destroying everyone's livelihood and sense of well-being just like that! Imagine Reagan *your waiter*. He destroys practically every job that he can't do himself, then falls victim to his own obliteration of the economy and he's serving you your meal:

—*Waiter? Waiter. We also ordered some new potatoes.*

—*Well, you know...on new potatoes...a lot of people in this country...I've spoken with them...and...well, they think that old potatoes are...well...*

—*Shut up!*

—The waiter is the backbone of civilization, I said to Izzy, and ultimately its saviour. —I agree, waiters are at the heart of everything, said Isidor. Let's judge everyone we know by how they treat the waiters. Before we finally and officially all become waiters in the city of tomorrow, the last way we will have of relating to one another. *Waiters all!* yelled Isidor. Although, he said with menace, some of us would like to think we are waited UPON. —But we all *serve something*, said I. There is no real neutrality, aloofness, no escape of one's streetly responsibilities in New York. There is no doing nothing. Always there is duty!

PADDY'S CLAM HOUSE braced, scarified, excoriated and cajoled us. The fish we ate went down in a trance. It was a little under- and overcooked—the food at PADDY'S was never very good—it tasted of not much except New York and ice water. What mattered were the textures and the texts of that hour. Isidor's meal was deep, mine horizontal.

The waiter put the check in front of Isidor the same way he had put down our plates, as if serving was not so much an intimate transaction as it was a reminder that we were merely part of the Great Chain of Being. No familiarities or banter now.

—Do you realize we will never again discuss genitals with that guy? said Isidor, as we moved toward the hanging coats blocking the door like a mob that might turn ugly. —We could hang around, I said, see when he gets off.

As usual after visiting New Jersey, Isidor was feeling the horn and wanted intoxicating. In the fine spray of indifference, brine and sarcasm of the Fish Restaurant he imagined bright legs in the Radio City Music Hall; legs like sardines. For the first time Isidor and I experienced that lust for the glistening streets given by the flesh of the sea. □

GRANTA

GIVE IT UP
FOR BILLY
Edmund White

Harold's lover Tom didn't come with him to Key West that winter. Tom thought the heterosexual snowbirds (those who winter in the south) were too old in Key West and the younger gays who worked there year round were too stupid. Since South Beach had become the destination for A-list gays (celebrated decorators, real-estate speculators, media moguls and their satellites, muscle builders and models), Key West had turned into a backwater for balding gay couples from Toledo, the sort who owned and operated their own neighbourhood dry-cleaners and whose foreheads burned easily in the semi-tropical sun. These guys, the Toledo dry-cleaners, immediately took up with a similar couple from Lubbock they'd just met. The foursome were happy to go on a glass-bottomed boat out to the reef or to play bridge at night back at their all-male compound where the only men under thirty worked behind the desk.

Harold didn't mind how dowdy Key West had become with its main street lined with Israeli-owned T-shirt shops, its commercialization of Papa Hemingway's bearded face on the coasters at Sloppy Joe's bar on Duval, or its conch train that puttered down shaded streets and informed the tourists in shorts and sun hats about the Hemingway House and his cats with six toes or about Truman's Little White House or the Audubon House. Harold accepted that the world was becoming a product to be consumed by the world's leading industry, mass tourism. He looked at Japanese tourists as models for us all. They didn't seek out private, authentic experiences while travelling, or so at least he imagined. They didn't claim to be the exception, to be solitary and romantic. They weren't a headache for their group leader. No, they were content to buy the best known, most easily recognized luxury brand names at airport shops and to take their photos of the Whaling Museum or the Eiffel Tower or the Oldest House from the exact spot the guide indicated. Harold had been coming here for a few weeks every winter over the last twenty years and he'd seen Key West go from a rough town of drifters and trailer trash to an elegant stronghold with artistic pretensions, including an annual literary conference on themes such as 'Nature Writing' or 'Journaling' or 'Fact or Fiction?'. Property prices had gone up tenfold.

And he was no longer young and wouldn't figure on anybody's A or B list. He was sixty-three, in a few days to be sixty-four, and about to retire from the New World History department of Princeton with a handsome teacher's pension portfolio. He had an arthritic neck and cataracts he wanted to have removed as soon as they were a bit riper. Tom, his forty-five-year-old lover, worked for Johnson & Johnson in public relations. Tom ran several miles a day and had no wrinkles, possibly because he used Retin-A.

They had an extremely open, easy-going relationship. Their heterosexual friends—and almost all of their friends were heterosexual in Princeton—said they envied them their relaxed attitude toward each other's extramarital adventures. Actually the adventures were embarrassingly rare and the friends found their non-possessiveness confusing since it seemed to mark yet another spot where there wasn't a perfect fit between homosexual and heterosexual couples. People liked homosexuals if they were a sort of fun-house reflection of their own image. They didn't want them to be completely different.

What no one knew was that Harold and Tom had long since given up having sex with each other. It was as if their original friendship had flared up into sexuality and jealousy for a few years before subsiding back into mutual esteem. Harold wanted Tom to have fun, even sexual fun, so long as he didn't fall in love with someone else and leave him. He couldn't bear to live alone in Princeton. Or anywhere, for that matter. Though Princeton, with its acres of mansions and lawns and its lonely winter nights and its absence of all gay presence, seemed particularly daunting for a single gay man. Recently Tom had begun to date a woman from his office, someone who did community relations, and she represented a more serious threat to their life together. Women played for keeps, Harold believed. He thought female seriousness was biological and had something to do with sperm being cheap and eggs dear, or was it to do with spreading a favourable mutation quickly through the species, but such theories always struck him as kitsch. He knew that straights took their lives more seriously than gays did, and straight women most of all. He also knew that Tom had begun to despise the Chelsea-style gay men they saw when they went into New York City for dinner or a concert. Tom couldn't resist making a nasty comment every time they passed a muscle boy. Anyone who looks like that must be putting in four hours a day at the gym, he'd snarl. For Harold it was not an issue. Neither Chelsea Boys nor skinny East Village bohemians looked at him. Nobody did.

Tom would say, I'm glad we don't live in the gay world. It embarrasses me, it's so mindless and narcissistic. Give me the eternal verities any day—children, the future, self-discipline, altruism.

Harold relaxed back into his old Key West routines. He rented a bike and went everywhere on it, even on cold nights and rainy days. Literary friends his age thought it absurd that he didn't rent a car and drive around in dignity as they did. They thought it ridiculous that he insisted on teetering around with his big po-po hanging out over the saddle, but Harold loved the boyhood associations of riding a bike, especially at night down the cat-busy lanes and under giant palms churning in the wind. Most of the time he was tired and a bit dazed, as if coming out from under a sedative, but when he was alert, as he was at midnight on his bike, he felt as he always had.

He'd looked forward to going back to Scooter's, the go-go bar, which in the past had been on the edge of town where Truman Avenue shaded into Highway 1. It had been a rowdy but innocent place where skinny, Florida blonds and small compact brunettes from Montreal came out on the tacky runway, one by one, in jeans and layered shirts. Each did two numbers, the first one clothed and the second stripped down to a G-string. The unseen announcer at the end would say, 'Okay, fellas. Give it up for Ronnie,' a locution Harold had never heard before; apparently it meant 'Applaud Ronnie'.

He found that there were more and more things he didn't know about. Almost all the guests on late-night talk shows he'd never heard of—pop singers or actors in TV series, which he didn't watch. He didn't follow sports and never knew the names of tennis players and football stars. He could identify most of the current and past names in New World studies, of course, as well as many of the principal figures in American history. He was convinced he knew more about his period, Woodrow Wilson's America, than about George W. Bush's.

Scooter's had moved into town. The bar was now smaller and cleaner and better lit. Instead of putting on stage any kid blowing through town, it now had a small permanent cast of dancers, mostly non-English speakers: a big blond Estonian, an intensely black Senegalese with biceps as round as cannonballs, a wispy Czech, a sulky Spaniard, a smiling Macedonian. They would dance for twenty minutes on one of the two podiums at the far end of the room, then jump up on to the bar and coax tips out of customers before working the room.

They'd dance standing up on the bar and customers would stick dollar bills in their gym socks, but after a while they'd crouch down, their legs spread wide, and let the older men touch their thighs and crotches. The tips were rarely more than a dollar or two, whereas at Teacher's, the heterosexual strip bar, the men handed out tens and twenties. Were gay men poorer or less competitive or did they think it a waste to pay out a lot of money to a member of their own sex? The seedy festive air of the old Scooter's was gone, with its tables and chairs gathered around the stage and the lights red or white, strong or soft, which the boys had kicked on with their toes, like Marilyn Monroe in *Bus Stop*. They no longer had an overhead pipe to do pull-ups on. And gone was the cubbyhole separated from the room by glass beads where customers could have extra feels in the dark for twenty bucks: lap dancing, it was called.

Now the proximity of the heavy foot traffic up and down Duval, those herds of tourists grazing along, released from the big cruise ships, acted as an inhibiting presence on the men in the new Scooter's. The whole place was just too visible and few locals dared to drop in.

But it was better than nothing. In Princeton there were no go-go boys and in New York there were too many drag queens for Harold's taste and not much lap dancing. He admired transvestites—their courage, their art, their antic sense of fun—but they didn't turn him on. In Princeton, of course, for so many years the boys had been his students: superb, untouchable. Now that at last he was about to retire, he was the age of their grandfathers and unlikely to attract anyone. He sometimes fancied an older man, but they seldom looked his way. Almost no one looked his way.

Night after night Harold, after a dinner with elderly literary or scholarly friends, would bicycle down the nearly empty streets to Duval, which was always busy, and to Scooter's. Gay bars, straight bars, closing restaurants, a big disco, the Ripley's Believe-It-or-Not, the handsome spotlit facade of the Cuban Cultural Center, the slow passage of cruising cars and pickup trucks up and down the main drag, the clang-clang of bells rung by professional bicyclists conveying one or two passengers in open rickshaws—it was all exciting, an animated little world. Harold chained his bike to a lamp post, visited the outdoor ATM and ambled into Scooter's. He liked the glow of naked young flesh under the spotlights, the smell of freshly poured beer, the pools of attention as men gathered around a dancer drifting like a big, showy camellia through the crowd. He liked to sit at the bar and look up at these kids with their powerful legs, sweat-drenched torsos, broad shoulders and unfocused smiles. Sometimes one of them would drip on him. They were nude and extravagant as hothouse flowers blooming above all these old men. In Italy he'd once seen rose bushes threaded through gnarled olive trees: that was the effect. The boys were more often than not bewitched by their own reflections, which they studied in the mirror with alternating smiles and frowns. As one would turn sideways and suck in his gut you could just hear him asking himself if he was really getting a beer belly as his pal Tommy claimed.

The men, of course, had once been boys, too, but not boys like these, not usually. These men were chemical engineers or hotel managers or accountants: nerds. Two of them whom Harold had met were English and ran a bed-and-breakfast in Brighton. A few, no doubt, had been good-looking, but not in the way these dancers were. Back then, very few men worked out and almost no gays. These dancers had gym-built bodies, legs bowed with muscle, tiny waists giving it up to flaring torsos and wide shoulders, thick necks, cropped heads. 'Give it up for Bobby'—that was the phrase that kept ringing in his head for no good reason. These dancers were shaved, tattooed, bronzed, tinted; even their pubic hair, when they revealed a glimpse of it, was just a shaped, trimmed patch, cut to the quick to make their genitals look still bigger. Everything—sneakers or combat boots, thong or towel, nipple ring or diamond ear-bob—had been thought out, but even so they had a reckless, raucous assertiveness that came through their primping like a trumpet through a thicket of quivering strings. Most of them were straight and spent the dollars they earned on local girls. He'd seen them stumbling out of the Hog's Breath Saloon with girls. Harold liked them all, all of the boys, and when one of them strolled around the room in a gold G-string and gathered a group of old men (hands liver-spotted, backs twisted, mouths radiant with new teeth),

Harold couldn't help but picture Susannah and the Elders by, was it Titian? That beautiful naked girl emerging from her bath, her flesh coveted by all the old men peeking through the bushes.

It took two or three days for Harold to decide he liked Billy the most. Billy was about five foot ten and he had a splash of peroxided hair, though in recent years peroxide no longer signified 'cheap' or 'effeminate'. Now it read 'punk' or just 'young'—nothing clear, in any case. Billy had a knowing smile and a faint scar that traversed his nose. Just a seam, really. A ghost of asymmetry. He had a solemn, level gaze, something serious and noncommittal but friendly about his manner. He had what personal ads on gay websites called a 'six-pack stomach'.

He also had an immense uncut penis which once or twice a night he worked up and gave quick glimpses of. Sometimes, when he danced on a dais, he pulled his shorts open and looked down at his penis, which he could see but the audience couldn't. He'd mime the sound, 'Wow', and bug his eyes, as if he'd never seen it before. But he went lightly on the comedy. He wasn't a camp. He was a serious, virile man but not forbidding, certainly not unapproachable. A man's man, who treated customers as if they were almost pals, though he definitely maintained a professional distance.

Harold gave him five-dollar tips and never groped him. Sometimes Harold said friendly, non-committal things, like, 'The air conditioner's on the blink tonight?' or, 'Where'd they get this music?'. After four or five days Billy would come over to Harold on his break. If Harold was seated at the bar, Billy would lean against him, throw a hot, heavy arm around his shoulders. 'That guy over there,' Harold would say, 'was sure pawing you.'

Billy said, 'These guys must think we're really naive. Man... That guy said he'd just bought a mansion quote-unquote in Key West and had decided he wanted to spend the rest of his life with me. He said he was a multimillionaire quote-unquote and would leave me well provided for. He'd take me away from all this.' Billy opened a hand, then let it fall to his side.

'Jesus...' Harold muttered with feigned disgust at the guy's chutzpah. But why not? If the guy were alone, not long for this world, rich enough to feather his last nest with a nice gigolo, why

not buy a young man who looked thirty and seemed unusually solid.
'I said to him, Why not tip me a few dollars right now if you're so
rich, but the cheap bastard never parted with a penny.'

'Hey, Billy,' Harold said, wrapping a hand around his tight little
waist, 'where are you from anyway, Australia?'

'Zimbabwe.'

'Oh.'

'Do you see?'

'Yes I see. Former Rhodesia.'

'You'd be amazed how many Americans think it's next to Tibet.'

'Hopeless…'

Harold groaned. Billy had a polite, deferential manner, an
impenetrable but friendly regard, a deep reserve. He might throw
his arm over Harold's shoulder but it all felt like a professional
engagement; Harold could almost hear the meter ticking.
A very tall blond man in his late thirties wearing a raspberry-
coloured polo shirt, pleated khakis and gold-bitted loafers signalled
Billy, who excused himself. Harold didn't want to stare but he saw
the seated man draw Billy down on to one leg and idly stroke his
hairless, oiled thigh. There was no lust in it, just intimacy, and the
man spoke rapidly, even in a businesslike way, while Billy nodded
agreement. They could have been two spies exchanging information
while pretending to be dancer and client. In five minutes the
conference was over and the man had elbowed his way out of the
bar, uninterested in the other dancers, though he did shake hands
with the bouncer at the door and even spared him a smile.

The next day Harold watched a porno film his landlord lent him;
the eventless sub-plot was about twins from Hungary, identical down
to the tiniest mole on the right forearm or the small, cantilevered
buttocks or the overlapping incisors. They seemed happiest when
stepping off each other's joined hands and doing a backflip into the
pool and the most embarrassed when they had to kiss, and fondle
each other's smallish identical erection with an identical hand. They
had identical ponytails. The main story was unrelated, all about a
superb, dark-haired boy with flawless skin who so enjoyed being
penetrated by a blond Dracula that he begged the monster to bite
his neck—a declaration so miraculously romantic that Dracula was
turned back into an ordinary human being. And saved. From what?

Harold wondered. Eternal life? Eternal youth? Harold worried about dying. He had de-dramatized every moment in his life, giggled at the over-the-top romantic scenes in movies, accepted his mother's death with equanimity, even indifference, though when he'd won a scholarly prize for his book on Wilson at Versailles, he'd wept, since his mother wasn't alive to enjoy his moment of glory. Egotism, he'd told himself. Egotistical foolishness. Life at Princeton, the university and the town, was so unchanging that he couldn't remember many key dates in his life there other than his five sabbatical years and the beginnings and ends of his three previous affairs.

He couldn't quite figure it out, but it was as if he'd worked out a strategy that if he didn't bear down too hard on his life it would leave such a faint impression it wouldn't what? Count? Be noticed? Go through the carbon on to a master copy? He'd almost never been alone. He'd always had a live-in companion, although in the Sixties he had still had to pretend that Jack, the man of the moment, was just rooming in his spare bedroom. By the mid-Seventies the mores had so changed that he and Jack had been invited everywhere as a couple.

There had been so few ripples in his life. He'd produced only three books, but two were significant and still in print. He'd inched his way up the ladder to tenure and a full professorship. He'd had three or four star students who were now distinguished Americanists. One was even contemplating early retirement.

He felt he'd somehow slipped through. He'd not had to serve in Vietnam, at first because he'd been in graduate school and then because his asthma had been so crippling. Later, the disease had just gone away, even though central New Jersey was both polluted and saturated with pollen, the industrial Garden State. He'd been just a few years too old to become a hippy, and he was never tempted to drop out. He'd supported the student rebels in 1968, but no more so than had most of the other junior faculty. He'd come out when he was in his fifties, back in the 1980s, when gender studies had become trendy and he was able to renew his scholarly image by arguing in an oft-cited essay that the First World War had been a forcing shed for modern gay identity. He'd exercised moderately, had never drunk to excess, he'd been afraid to try intravenous drugs, and he'd smoked marijuana just twice, both times with a Puerto Rican trick, and had felt nothing. Just when Aids had become a real danger he'd met Tom, who was then in his early twenties and virtually a virgin. They'd been faithful for nearly a decade and by then had mastered safe-sex techniques, which they used with all their other new tricks.

But he knew he wasn't going to slip past old age, sickness and death. No one did. He wasn't Dracula. He was considered practical and realistic and he'd take all the most rational steps toward the grave or rather the crematorium. The other day Tom had read out loud a passage from a new novel, 'He was accumulating as many experiences as possible so he'd feel less alone when he died,' but Harold suspected the author of irony. It didn't work that way. Harold thought most novelists were irresponsible and those he'd known weren't very perceptive or worldly. That's why he seldom read fiction.

Harold knew that at best he had just twenty or twenty-five more years to live, which didn't sound very long. The previous twenty years had gone by so fast. Time was speeding up just as it was running out, like the last of the water draining from a sink. Back in the early Eighties Key West had been a good time-thickener because he'd known so few people and had done nothing but lie around and read. But now the island was so busy with elderly activity—luncheons, readings, cocktail parties, art openings—that the days sped by. Key West made Princeton seem tranquil by contrast.

Harold didn't tell Tom every detail about Billy during their daily phone calls but Tom certainly got the highlights. Tom had enough on his plate. Roger, their old wire-haired fox terrier, had become so ill with leukaemia and was in such pain from arthritis that Dr Wilkins had put him to sleep.

Harold knew he was being irrational, but he thought they should have waited until he, Harold, could have said goodbye to the dog. 'Closure? Is that it?' Tom asked. 'Everybody in America suddenly wants closure. Well, I wasn't worrying about your peace of mind, Harold.'

A long silence set in. To change the subject Harold asked Tom about Liz.

'Her name is Beth. She's fine. We're seeing a lot of each other. How's Billy? When are you going to go to bed with him?'

'I'm not sure what my next move should be.' Harold was grateful for this fake conversation to replace the real, painful one.

'Ask him over in the afternoon. If that man in the Gucci shoes is keeping him, the late afternoon may be the only time he's free.'

'Don't you think it's odd he's from Zimbabwe?'

Tom laughed. 'You don't keep up with the news but Zimbabwe is going through hell. The black president, Mugabe, has encouraged roving bands of black ex-soldiers to kill the white settlers and expropriate their farms, and the soldiers know nothing about farming and the crop yields are diminishing and the World Bank or whatever won't extend them any more loans; it's a nightmare. As for gay life, the gay guide forbids readers to go there at all. People suspected of homosexuality are pushed off a cliff—or is that Yemen? Anyway, it's dire, darling. Your little Billy has come to Key West to come out.'

Harold said admiringly, 'You always can orient yourself to a new person or situation within seconds. Whereas I feel like some sort of moral Mr Magoo.'

'That's right. I'm perfect,' Tom said. He didn't take compliments well and was specially immune to Harold's, which were too flowery and heartfelt for someone like Tom, brought up on jokey, shrugging sitcom dialogue.

That night Harold invited Billy to drop by his place the following afternoon for a drink.

'I don't drink.'

'For a fruit juice.'

'But not orange or grapefruit,' Billy said. 'They're too acidic. Maybe a herbal tea would be best, or mineral water flat.'

'What?'

'Non-sparkling. It's better for the digestion.'

Although Harold found alimentary pedantry to be tiresome, he welcomed it as a diversion from the real question: Why should they get together at all?

'I can come by after my workout around four-forty-five or four-fifty,' Billy said.

Despite the precision, he didn't show up until five-fifteen. He came speeding up in a red convertible with the top down and the stereo blaring a Mariah Carey tape (something Tom would have sniffed at).

For Harold, who liked no music after early Stravinsky, it was all the same to him. The barbarians had broken through the gate, they were the rulers, there was nothing more to worry about.

They sat outside on a little veranda surrounded by shoulder-height bamboo walls. Harold had brought back from the expensive supermarket cooked shrimp, smoked mackerel bits, blue corn chips, and several kinds of water; as much as he could carry in his bicycle basket without losing control. Billy drank the water but didn't touch the food.

When Harold asked Billy what were his plans in life, the young man said, 'You know the tall guy who comes into the club to see me?'

'Yes. Who is he?'

'His name is Ed. He's an agent for models. He arranged for me to be in *Frisk*. Here, I brought you the February issue. It's in the car.'

Harold had always imagined most of the readers of the 'women's magazine' *Frisk* were gay men, closet cases who needed a heterosexual alibi in order to study other men's bodies. Maybe there were women readers, too. Certainly in this issue, he thought as he thumbed through it, there was a lean man in his fifties, a guy with a small penis and a beautiful face, and there was a photo essay titled 'A Romantic Evening by the Fire', which showed a woman being undressed by an entirely depilated man. A hardcore gay magazine wouldn't have had any of these variations—the older man or the woman, but the guys would have had shaved bodies.

Billy's pictures made up the lead story. He was shown in various stages of undress, though the last spread revealed just how immense his 'manhood' was, to use the language of the magazine. The text called him by a different name, Kevin, and said he was a corporate lawyer in Boston.

'So you want to be a model?'

'I'm already thirty and if I watch my diet and work out every day maybe I can stretch it out till I'm forty, but I'm saving every cent. Some day maybe I'll go into public relations. Right now I'm just making a quick buck. I can't work in America anyway, not at a legitimate job; I don't have a green card. Most of my money I'm sending back to my mum to install an electric fence around her house.'

'Shouldn't you get her out of Zimbabwe altogether?'

'The cities aren't dangerous, not yet. She has a very nice house and servants. You can't believe how far the US dollars I send her go. Anyway, she's running the family business.'

'What is your family business?'

Billy looked at Harold in a penetrating way—frank, level, unsmiling. 'Funeral parlour. My mum and dad emigrated from England to Rhodesia in the late Sixties. They had a thriving business. When I was eighteen my dad sent me back to London for a two-year course in embalming techniques, grief counselling, and funeral accountancy. Then he died and I took over the business. My mum is the business manager. She's the one who has all the contacts in the community.'

'Black as well?'

'About a third of our clients are black.'

From the very beginning Harold had picked up on something...formal about Billy. When they were just standing around Billy lowered his head, let a non-committal smile play over his lips. He hooked his hands behind his back and widened his stance like a soldier at ease. Now Harold could easily picture Billy in a white shirt, dark tie and dark suit, producing a white handkerchief for the sobbing widow.

Harold asked Billy whether he'd been gay in Zimbabwe. 'No, it's too dangerous. I had a girlfriend, though I spent a lot of time looking at her brother. She knew. We didn't talk about it, but she knew. I desired her, too. In fact, she's the most beautiful girl I've ever seen. She's going to move to London any day now.'

'Are you bisexual?'

Billy looked vaguely cornered and said, 'Let's just say I'm sexual.' Harold could tell it was a line he'd said many times before.

Billy took Harold for a ride in his car out to another island. His cell rang and he laughed and murmured into it, but he wasn't speaking English. When he hung up, Harold asked, 'Was that Afrikaans?'

'Zulu. Well, our kind of Zulu.'

'Were you speaking to someone in Zimbabwe?'

'Yes, it was my mate Bob. Great guy. We always have a bit of a chinwag once a week.'

'Is he black?'

'What? Oh. No. He's white.'

'You speak Zulu to another white guy?'

'We go back and forth.'

Harold thought no one could argue that a Zulu-speaking, African-born Zimbabwean was an outsider.

Whenever Harold asked something about politics in Zimbabwe, Billy maintained a low-key tone. *Sixty Minutes* had just done a frightening segment on the deterioration of the country. In one scene a group of armed black men in rags crossed a lush, well-tended field and approached a young white farmer. Their discussion seemed more a dispute over something like a parking ticket, heated but containable, yet in another scene the charred, bloated dead bodies of other white settlers were shown.

Someone taped the programme for Billy, who seemed shocked, silenced when he saw it. 'I knew that young farmer. I knew him.'

'The president was such an obvious hypocrite,' Harold said. But Billy appeared to be way beyond outrage or anger.

They had sex every afternoon. Harold paid him two hundred dollars a session. After a few days he suggested they lower the fee to a hundred-fifty dollars, but Billy was firm. 'I need all I can get, Harold,' he said.

Billy would appear around five in his red convertible outside Harold's gate. They'd sip some herbal tea and then move into the bedroom for a 'massage'. Harold would apply a thick cocoa butter with an oppressively sweet smell to Billy's back and shoulders, then to his muscular buttocks, finally to his calves and thighs. It smelled like a Mars Bar.

Harold didn't really like massaging Billy's body, which felt too hard and unyielding. There was no mystery to it. It was like armour, not responsive flesh. Billy would talk in fits and starts, giving the news of the day, and Harold felt like his trainer. The problem was that Harold didn't really dote on other men, never had. He wasn't an idolater, though Billy was cut out to be an idol.

Decades and decades ago, back in the 1950s, Harold had been famous for his smooth skin; even the three women who had touched and held him had envied him his skin. He'd been lithe, small-sexed, boyish, though he'd dressed in chunky tweeds and worn wire-rims and seldom smiled with his thin lips. But for the handful of men who'd bothered to lift his fragile glasses off and liberate him from his heavy, thickening clothes, he'd been a bijou. Once when he'd been in Paris as a tourist he'd been picked up by a couturier who lived in Sartre's old apartment. The man, all sprouting whiskers and smoker's cough, had stood back, slightly amazed at the boyish genie he'd summoned up out of the drab clothes: *'Mais tu es un bijou, un petit bijou,'* he'd said as he opened his hands, as if to bear witness. Harold still felt a bit like that, a jewel, and he half expected to amaze other men. On the phone his voice, apparently, sounded like a piping, eager, over-educated kid's, holding a laugh in, and young people who met him first on the phone warmed up to him, called him 'Hal' and said funny, sly things to him. Later, when they saw he was old, they were taken aback.

After Harold had massaged Billy's back he tapped his ass, as a trainer might, with an unsuggestive touch, and Billy turned over. There, suddenly, was the enormous uncircumcised penis, white and marbled and somehow assembled, like sausage meat. And Harold applied himself to it, performed fellatio as if this were just a customized kind of massage, given the shape of the body part. Billy kept his eyes closed and made not a sound until the actual moment of explosion, and even then Harold suspected it was less a sensual moan than a warning to back off in the interests of safe sex.

Harold invited Billy to his sixty-fourth birthday party on another island not far away. They all sprayed themselves against the clouds of mosquitoes and Harold's friends, a dozen of them, artists and writers and teachers in their fifties and sixties, were charmed by Billy, who stood about with his hands hooked behind him, his eyes lowered; the perfect mortician.

He was unassertive but friendly and open. He talked about Zimbabwe and his fears for his mother and sister. 'I'm trying to raise a bit of money so that my sister can emigrate to Australia.'

'We saw the *Sixty Minutes* show,' someone murmured sympathetically.

'I knew that farmer. My sister has a beautiful farm, but she can never sell it now. I've got to get her out of there as soon as I can afford it. Every day counts.'

Billy played with someone's four-year-old daughter and even laced an arm around the waist of a big-eyed, short-haired woman who'd divorced her husband recently, though the husband was present if subdued. A man who wrote a column on labour problems for *The Nation* kept asking Billy questions about his job as a dancer. Billy smiled mildly; he had no hesitation in responding. Surely, Harold thought, he must be enjoying this freedom. He was never free in Africa.

One of the guests, a sculptor, invited them to his studio to pose for him. 'I'm doing terracotta figurines of lap dancers at Teacher's, women dancers and male customers, so I might as well do some gay pairs, if you're up to it. I don't know what will come of it, if anything.'

They went to Sid's studio two days later, in the afternoon, at their usual hour. Sid paid Billy ten dollars for posing. By this time Harold's straight friends had all seen the issue of *Frisk* and they were all astonished by the size of Billy's penis. 'But is that trick photography?'

'No,' Harold said, lowering his eyes modestly.

Sid's wife said, 'And he's a hell of a nice guy, too. He played with Annabelle's daughter for hours. I asked him to dance next month for our guests on Captain Bob's boat; we're giving a big party. Too bad you won't be here.' It struck Harold as odd that straight people would want a go-go boy to dance for them, but Key West prided itself on being offbeat.

Harold enjoyed holding Billy's calves and staring up at him. Billy was wearing just a G-string, whereas Harold was in a shirt and slacks. Sid had rigged up a platform that simulated a bar. He kept pushing them closer together, not because he wanted intimacy. No, he just wanted to simplify their forms into a pyramid. Once again Harold thought of roses emerging out of a gnarled, twisted olive tree. Harold dreaded their sex sessions. The rancid, sweet smell of the cocoa butter, which Billy had brought with him that first time and had left behind, sickened him. The butter had almost been used up. He disliked the lengthy massage of this nearly inert and unfeeling body and the sausage-making, which ended with a single groan. He resented the ruinous expense, which Harold thought he couldn't reduce or eliminate, since it was going to save Billy's mother and sister. Harold couldn't even convince himself he was bringing any special pleasure to Billy, since Billy complained that Harold's teeth were too sharp and hurt him. Of course Harold had never faced such a big challenge before.

Suddenly it was over. The vacation had come to an end. Harold had given his straight friends in Key West something to deplore or admire, in any event to discuss. Did they suspect Harold was paying Billy and so handsomely? Or did they think all the usual rules didn't apply to gay life and that young Susannahs gave freely, copiously of their charms to their Elders? He suspected his friends thought he was exploiting Billy, but in fact Billy was exploiting him, with his full complicity. Harold sympathized with Billy's family's plight and respected Billy's seriousness.

Billy drove him in the red convertible to the airport. He helped him with his luggage. They shook hands. For a moment Billy stood at ease, with his hands hooked behind him. Then he waved and drove off.

Harold thought that his decision to go on having sex at all was either a stubborn sign of the life force or a mere habit, depending on one's interpretation. He smeared Androgel on his body every morning, a clear salve containing androgens, the sex-drive hormone. Without it he'd never feel a twitch of desire. His doctor had prescribed it: 'It'll give you some zest for life, improve your energy level. Appetite. Zest,' he repeated. He rather liked it when he forgot to use the hormone salve and felt no sex desire (though that included other desires as well). Without a sex drive people became depressed, it seemed. Were monks depressed?

Was he lacking in zest? For sex, yes. But for life? Yes, he thought. Whereas Billy had a survivor's instincts. He was determined that he and his family would survive.

Harold was so happy to be back with Tom, though he missed the dog, Roger. Tom was dating his girlfriend three nights a week now. Beth. Her name was Beth. A month after Harold came home, Tom said he was moving out.

'I'm going to try to make things work with Beth.'

'Really?

'You know how much I've always wanted children. A child. I only realized that after Roger died.'

'What?'

'Roger was our child. But when he died I thought how pathetic it was to heap so much tenderness on a poor, short-lived, dumb animal. I'd like a human child. Beth wants one, too.'

Harold didn't like Roger to be called 'poor'. He was so shaken that he didn't think much about Billy. Once or twice he showed Billy's spread in *Frisk* to his friends in Princeton. They said 'Wow' but they were humouring him. They obviously felt sorry for him. Did they think he was to blame for Tom's change of heart, of life?

One day, while researching an article on Woodrow Wilson at Princeton, Harold came across a remark Wilson had made twenty years after graduation, 'Plenty of people offer me their friendship; but partly because I am reserved and shy, and partly because I am fastidious and have a narrow, uncatholic taste in friends, I reject the offer in almost every case and then am dismayed to look about and see how few persons in the world stand near me and know me as I am.'

Six months later he called Sid in Key West just to chat.

'Say, did you know Billy is getting married?' Sid asked.

'No,' Harold said. 'For immigration reasons?'

'Apparently, it's a real romance. She's not even American. She's from South Africa.' Sid downshifted. 'I don't really get that, do you? Switch-hitting?' He didn't know about Tom and Beth. 'You know Billy danced at our annual party. We took everybody on Captain Bob's boat and Billy was the entertainment. If I hadn't talked with him I wouldn't have known how serious and intelligent he is. I mean, he's such a thoughtful guy and then boom! There he was, bumping and grinding.'

'Maybe Billy was never gay,' Harold said. 'Despite all appearances. I assumed he'd come to the States to enjoy sexual freedom, but now I think it was just to earn some quick money to relocate his family.'

After he hung up, he threw some pumpkin-stuffed ravioli into boiling water. He was unaccountably hungry, in spite of the clammy summer day. A small, peevish voice somewhere inside of him said, 'See? He was just using you and everyone else.' But then Harold smiled, pleased at the simplifying form things had taken. He wondered if his understanding of the people around him was becoming as occluded as his vision. Were there moral cataracts that one could remove? □

GRANTA

SEVERAL ANECDOTES ABOUT MY WIFE

Gary Shteyngart

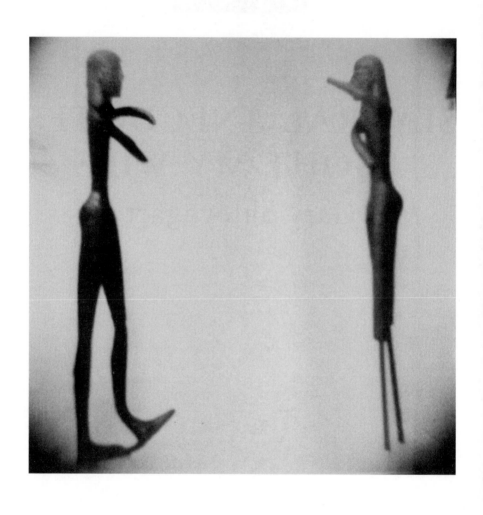

I am pleased to make her acquaintance

I met Pamela Tannehill at a conference in Midtown Manhattan. We were working for different non-profit agencies in New York. Her non-profit was known throughout the industry for its wavering commitment to social issues, mine for its slothful, dreamy staff. I was sitting in the front row discreetly doodling into my notebook how I would look if I were better-looking (a proud and aquiline nose pointing down to a well-formed, constructive chest; thick legs that could bear a rich man's weight) when I heard a tired, older voice—older, I say, but with some of the inflections of American youth ('Umm...')—asking about a difficult subject: the resettlement of Hmong tribesmen in Ulster County, New York.

I turned around and saw my wife-to-be, a pretty freckled face, parchment skin tautly drawn over two cheekbones, downcast grey eyes that for some reason flickered when she hit upon the hardest consonants (Z, K, R), and below that an angry little mouth that was steadily working itself into a frenzy over this Hmong business. Also, she had no chin.

Later, the conference broke up over lunch, and some of my colleagues, mostly social workers and public administration people, went outside to talk about their loneliness. I too felt suddenly bereft and ready for a solid good cry, when Pamela Tannehill touched my arm and told me she had heard of me from a co-worker, an American Jew named Joshie. Apparently, Joshie had said that I was one for witty remarks.

'Ooof,' I sighed, confused and, for some reason, rather hurt by this compliment. I suppose I like to think of myself as a serious and private person, one who can be amusing at parties but is basically *of a sadness*. 'Joshie likes to talk,' I muttered. 'But truthfully, I don't think I'm such a funny one.'

'Come again?' said Pamela Tannehill. She reached over and lightly slapped my fleshy chin, making me flinch. I had just turned twenty-nine and was already starting to fill out here and there. 'Did you just say *truthfully?*'

And she laughed at me.

We went to a pallid little Japanese restaurant where I further tried to play the comic type by waving my hands around a lot and smacking my lips after tasting the hot sake. I really wanted to please

CAROL MUNDER

her. But the real comedy was my scarf, which kept falling on the floor to the growing hilarity of two Japanese businessmen at the next table.

'You're such an idiot,' Pamela Tannehill said and smiled her kindest smile. She had thin Anglo lips and wispy eyebrows, a little nose and sad, old wrinkles around her eyes. There is some warmth here, I thought, as the sake clouded my chest and buffeted my groin. 'Tell me about yourself, you freak,' she said. 'Like, what's up with the accent?'

I explained to Pamela Tannehill what kind of a creature I was. My melancholy pedigree. I talked openly about how my family, the Abramovs, had come to America in 1979, along with the 50,000 other Soviet Jews who had taken to the air that year. I scrunched together a fistful of empty soybean shells to better demonstrate how we were pressed into so many Western jetliners, herded through the glorious transit points of Vienna and Rome finally to alight on these American shores, to fill Brighton Beach and other parts of Brooklyn and Queens with our stale, humid bodies. The tale ended at its logical terminus: the international arrivals building at JFK, where my family was greeted by our co-religionists, two older women named Hadassah and Berl, who gave us a booklet about the Ten Commandments, a ride to a dirty motel room in Queens, and some cheese.

Pamela Tannehill dispatched her grilled eel and cheerfully appraised my furry person. 'And your name is really Leonid?' she said. 'Like Leonid Brezhnev?'

'They call me Lionya,' I informed her, wiping my eyes with the cuff of my shirt. It had been years since my last good talk with a woman.

'Lit-tle, lit-tle Lio-nya,' she sang. 'Lit-tle, immigrant Lio-nya. Such a sad and lo-nely Lio-nya... Hey, little Lio-nya bear! Why don't you come home and paw me a bit? You have no idea just how neglected I've been...'

Pamela Tannehill makes love to me

She would seethe. Or perhaps hiss. I have never heard a woman create such a sound, which to my mind was a combination of the gentle American *ph* and the lusty Russian *sh,* both sounds sucked backward through her teeth, her face twisting into an unlikely grimace.

'*Phshhhhhh…*' Pamela Tannehill said as she mounted me a week after we had met at the non-profit conference. I was the victim of a horrible flu, lying in a puddle of my own sweat, wondering about the quality of my breath, a sick man's breath, which was gently blowing across her lock-jawed face. 'I'm going to eat you up,' she seethed. 'You little…'

'Oh, God,' I said. She was screwing me. Our first time in bed, after the conference, I had been too scared to take off my shirt, lest she spy how flabby and unfit I was for that sort of thing. But now I was completely naked and helpless beneath her, her healthy rural girl's body making a mockery of my own. 'I need to—' I said. 'Pamela, I need to—'

'Now *you* fuck *me*,' she said. She turned around and put her ass in my face.

'Please,' I said. I was looking for a tissue to blow my nose in, my moustache was wet with flu.

'Go ahead, little Lionya,' she said. 'Pound me!'

'I can't.'

'Pound me, you filthy immigrant bear!'

'Oh, honey.' I grabbed hold of this ass, which was the real Middle-American article I had once known in college, with a kind of pre-ass pouch between the back of the thighs and the ass proper, and then the two side-flaps that one pulled to give the woman extra pleasure.

'*Phshhhhhh,*' Pamela Tannehill hissed as I found a way inside her, wayward drops of my sweat and effluvia forming a distinct Cyrillic И on her back, which is similar in sound to the English *I*. 'Mmmumph!'

Later that night, after she had been kind enough to bring me a bowl of hot Udon noodles for my cold, she told me she had a boyfriend. 'It's not what you think,' she said. 'He won't make love to me any more. He's sick of me.' The term 'make love' was more surprising than the admission of a boyfriend. She smiled in apology and as she did I realized that she had not actually spent the last ten minutes crying silently, but rather that she had a constellation of beauty marks beneath her eyes which in the shallow half-light of her apartment—provided by a flickering plastic torchère in the kitchen and the green Brooklyn moon sinking into the Gowanus Canal—looked like mascara tears.

'Kevin will always be in my life,' she explained to me that night as I spooned her with my wet body on the futon. 'And there's nothing you can do about that, sweets.' She was speaking of Kevin Weisman, an aspiring young poet from Mahwah, New Jersey.

They met twelve years before we did, after Pamela, at the age of eighteen, had fled her family home with a black man. Ach, what can I say? An unfortunate life. As soon as my Pamela Tannehill was born in the easternmost part of Oregon state, her father left the family and she was poorly raised by an assortment of hicks, one of whom was her mother. Young Pamela had sex with black men when she was as young as twelve and her relatives would beat her for it, until the day she had had enough and bused herself across the country with her beau. In 1986, when I was taking my board exams and dreaming of a small Midwestern college thousands of miles away from my befuddled parents, Pamela arrived at the New York Port Authority with her lover, who, upon seeing with his own eyes just what kind of place New York really was, promptly left her as well. 'Men just lose interest in me after a while,' Pamela confessed to me that night, cradling her empty chest, 'so I'm very realistic about my prospects'.

She found Kevin Weisman after getting a job as an au pair in New Jersey. The patriarch of the family she worked for took time out of the Passover Seder to molest her in the solarium, and on the second night of the Jewish holiday she ran outside to find college-bound Kevin pruning an azalea in the backyard next door. They talked through a chain link fence separating the property of Pamela's master and Kevin's parents. I suppose when you're young in this country, and you're pretty—which Kevin and Pamela both were, ruggedly so in their youth—and you've been basting in the same cultural references and the same sense of entitlement and ennui, the differences of regionalism and class can be cut to pieces with, say, an inside joke about a television star who happens to be a midget, a sip from a common can of soda pop, a lonesome, furtive caress across the buttocks or genital area followed by a teenager's endless kiss.

Truthfully, this is just guesswork on my part, because when I was eighteen and growing up in a Long Island suburb under my parents' roof, it was not often that I had the chance to be alone and flirtatious with a beautiful American woman like Pamela Tannehill. But I have a feeling that my wife kissed Kevin Weisman that very night, that she even managed to swing herself over the chain link fence and let him go inside of her. And after they had satiated themselves amid the Weisman's garden, I imagine Kevin must have talked and talked in the loud, funny way of American Jews about the salient points of his life: his love of horticulture and poetry, his overarching need for the warmth of his mother, the films of Laurence Olivier (whose manners he adored), and his plans for building a truly inspiring birdhouse out of birch.

And she must have told him, in so many words, about her life, because the next day the Weismans bought her out from the neighbours next door, and she spent the next ten years under that family's downy wing. They showed her how to build a middle-class life—Olay protective cream for the face, summer drives to Jacob's Pillow in the family's AMC Eagle, the art of a raucous family fight in which everyone goes to bed with their sense of moral imperative intact. They even paid for her to attend the popular New York University, where she studied social work administration, the caring profession practised by the Weismans both.

'They are my family,' Pamela Tannehill told me. 'You never had to be reborn into another family, Lionya Bear, so you don't know anything. But if the Weismans ever found out about us... No, it's just impossible. You should know that right away.'

And that night, shaking from the chilly after-effects of flu and sex and my simple, rather uncultured hatred toward Pamela Tannehill and her New Jersey boyfriend Kevin, I agreed with her.

Lionya loves Pamela

Fully clothed, we looked like your average young Brooklyn couple, second-rate hipsters in retro garb hunting and pecking through a pancake brunch at Harvest or perusing the two dollar rack at the Community Book Store. Naked, on the other hand, we were a sight to behold—Pamela a giant blonde squirrel with her great bushy tail puffed up behind her and I a tiny, dark Semitic savage, genital in hand, standing glumly by her side in the mirror. To imagine that I could take her from behind or scale her pale supine bulk required unusual anthropological perspective, akin to imagining a love affair between a kangaroo and aardvark caged side-by-side at the municipal zoo.

But scale her I did. To mutual delight. Pamela, as she herself admitted, had been sexually neglected by Kevin for six months now (he needed his space, the bastard) and I had essentially been neglected for the past six years since breaking up with my college girlfriend. Thus, to borrow Pamela's words, our constant fucking 'filled a need'.

Not to say that Kevin Weisman was missing from our relationship.

Before Kevin I had been, loosely speaking, an animist. I worshipped a few memorable rocks and trees in Central Park, I worshipped the living spirits of my ancestors—my angry immigrant father, my nervous immigrant mother, crazy Grandma with one foot always in the grave—and I worshipped the spirit of the age, the sloppy fashions, the high-pitched political to-and-fro, the dubious drugs that had all but rewired my central nervous system. Kevin was my first brush with monotheism. He was my God. He was invisible to me, but His word was law.

His was the deep-timbred, phoney-English voice that I heard on Pamela's answering machine ('You have reached the residence of Kevin Weisman and Pamela; presently, neither of us is *in situ...*') His was the stern, all-knowing visage that surveyed our lovemaking from Pamela's bed stand, even while a slightly more bemused Kevin-god smiled at me from the bathroom wall, giving my mortal bladder an acute sense of shyness.

When Kevin called, and he called every few hours, I was exiled to the kitchen, my ear pressed to the negligible door as Pamela addressed Him in the quiet, obedient tone of a henpecked first-grader. 'Yes, of course, that's okay...What time is good for you? Do you think I look too fat in the green dress? How about I just wear black?' When Kevin wished to 'drop by' I had to scramble to get my clothes on, often dismounting Pamela in the process, getting in a few last humps before being zipped up and rushed out the door. I swear, in the moments before His arrival, Pamela exuded the smell of lilacs. She spontaneously smelled of spring.

On weekends, if the weather was clear and Kevin wasn't staying over, Pamela and I would saunter out of bed and go for long walks. As we left the confines of her minuscule studio apartment with its Kevin icons and constant collect phone calls from Mahwah, New Jersey, I felt my mind go empty and free, my lungs replenished by the unlikely perfume of industry and trees, that strange, sour Brooklyn air. Out amid the Greek revival houses, the fluted porch columns of her borough, I goosed her in the middle of the street with my wide-open greasy palm; I licked her freckled nose at the corner of Atlantic Avenue and Court Street; I begged her over and over to say 'I love you'. She refused, of course, but I liked hearing myself repeat those three ridiculous words to her. When you ask for something often enough, I learned, even a refusal can seem like an acceptance.

At times I would weep about Kevin, our jealous and vengeful God, and beg Pamela to choose me in his stead. Here were some of the things she said.

'Relax, cowboy.'

'No matter what I do, I'll end up hurting you. That's just a given.'

'Don't give me that I'm-too-delicate-for-your-worldly-ways bullshit... Coy little mother.'

'When it comes down to it, I'm all alone in the world.'

'I've cried a lot before and it doesn't interest me.'

'I don't want some stranger sifting through all the evidence and then condemning me.' [on the subject of seeing a psychiatrist]

'You're too hard on yourself. Why don't you just chill out, Lionya Bear.'

Pamela comes out into society

I decided to take her advice. Perhaps it was time to *stop being so hard on myself*, to, vernacularly speaking, *take it easy*. Now in my youth, I had attended a gentle, easy-going Midwestern college (its name would be familiar to many a reader) and as a consequence I had some friends who fitted a progressive portrait of America—two blacks, one Asian, an American Jew and an Anglo. Interestingly enough, all but the Anglo were women, as this gentle college was very woman-friendly (not to mention Lionya-friendly; oh, how well I had fared there!).

And so I decided to throw a little cocktail hour for my friends in the depressing Delancey Street hovel where I lived. It gave me something to do: I put on a pair of gloves and cleaned the toilet; I chased the dust bunnies out the door with a broken broom handle; I bought the latest compact disc featuring the Senegalese rapper MC Solaar plus five bottles of Vinho Verde and some sheep's milk cheese.

Gary Shteyngart

And I almost managed to convince Pamela that she was going to have a good time. 'As long as I don't have to play the loving girlfriend all night,' she said, pulling on the moth-eaten sweater that had accompanied her on the Greyhound bus from eastern Oregon. 'God knows, I'm through with that.'

'You just be yourself,' I said.

My apartment was, all told, no more than a queen-sized futon ringed by a couple of folding plastic chairs. A framed poster of the boyish-looking Soviet cosmonaut Yuri Gagarin took pride of place among my meagre possessions.

Pamela and I sat in the centre of the futon, my friend Kai-Ling, a freelance shopper for badly dressed technology executives, directly to my left, and Nancy and Christa, two slick, voluble Memphis natives just returned from a year in Paris, to my right. The Jewish woman and the Anglo were laughing it up in the kitchen, and we left them alone (alumni rumour had it they were going to marry each other, bring little pale babies into the world).

From the beginning, I had intimations of disaster. Pamela glared at the innocent Kai-Ling with a compressed fury that seemed to cast an orange glow across her corner of the futon, as if someone had introduced a lava lamp into the proceedings. She spent the first twenty minutes of our little party trying to burn a hole in Kai-Ling's combustible leather pants with her strange grey eyes. Finally, when I asked K. L. (who, on the occasion of my cocktail party, had sewn me a cute amoeba-shaped throw pillow), to pass the sheep's milk cheese, Pamela struck her lap with both fists and blurted out: *'Let him get it himself!'*

Near-silence. Nancy and Christa stopped their amiable French chatter in mid-bon. Even MC Solaar grew quiet and pensive on the compact disc player. 'I mean...' Pamela said, shaking her head at me, 'He just always...*wants*... He *wants* things... He *wants*...'

Now I had had many discussions with Kai-Ling, a fellow immigrant like myself (Guangdong Province to my Leningrad), about how we should face up to the authority of the native-born, but the brisk tone in Pamela's voice had stilled Kai-Ling's hand even as it skirted the edge of the cheese plate. My friend looked at me with simple social terror, while I desperately tried to fudge an expression of encouragement. 'Kai...' I said hopefully and lifted up one leg. In the hush of the room, we could hear Pamela's breathing.

And then, wordlessly, with a shudder of childhood fear still pulsing about her lower lip, Kai-Ling picked up the cheese plate and handed it to me.

'No trouble,' she whispered. 'Here you go, Lionya.'

We all exhaled.

In retaliation for the Passing of the Cheese Plate, Pamela drank six glasses of Vinho Verde in rapid succession and started to pal around with Nancy and Christa. She called them her 'sisters' and threatened they would have something called a 'throw-down'. The two black women, vaguely familiar with urban expressions, but more in tune with the Afro-French stylings of MC Solaar, smiled amiably and brushed back loose tendrils of their Paris-coiffed hair and tried to talk about Foucault's *Discipline and Punish*, a dog-eared copy of which was keeping my coffee table level.

'You *sistas* are all right by me!' Pamela said, scowling at Kai-Ling, who was quietly trying to explain to me the theory behind her amoeba pillow, a miracle of single-cell organic design. 'I dated lots of black guys in high school and, let me tell you, those boys *knew* how to treat a woman... They were like *for real*.'

'Excuse me,' Christa said. She put her drink down. 'What did you just say?'

'Nuthin', sweet pea,' Pamela giggled. And then she started kissing Nancy.

'Um,' Nancy said.

'You have such beautiful skin,' Pamela cooed as she sank her lips into Nancy's cheeks. 'It's like cocoa butter,' she said.

Nancy had always been something of the class clown—I still remember the weekly riots she instigated in our Zora Neale Hurston seminar—and so I expected from her some kind of delicate but appropriate joke, a mild rebuff, a playful slap across the backside.

But that night she just sat there, her lips pursed together defensively against Pamela's warm, inquisitive nose; one arm flailing in the air as if she was trying to hail a taxi. She was entirely at a loss. We were all stuck, in fact. Our gentle Midwestern college had always encouraged lesbianism in all its manifestations. What could Nancy do?

The kissing of Nancy probably took up no more than three minutes, but it was the centrepiece of the evening, the way films about the Titanic are memorable not for the obligatory love affair between the ill-fated cook and the thoughtful debutante but for the final scenes of the great ship rearing up its doomed prow over the Atlantic.

'*Bozhe moi,*' I whispered in Russian.

'*Mon Dieu!*' Christa seconded, clutching at her purse strings and jumping up from the futon, lest she be loved by my Pamela in turn.

'Honey,' Nancy finally said, pressing a restraining palm into Pamela's forehead, lifting her up a bit so that we could all share in the sight of an older woman's unhappy, lipstick-splotched face, the face that I loved. 'Please...'

'You don't know what it's been like for me,' Pamela was saying matter-of-factly. 'I have nothing. Nobody. My father gave me away. I'm all alone in the world, sister. I never even went to a fancy college like Lionya...'

I considered pointing out that Pamela had in fact been sent to the popular and expensive New York University by the caring Weismans, but as I was unhinging my dry mouth in preparation to speak, Pamela suddenly withdrew from the tender pleasures of Nancy's face and threw her wine glass against the refrigerator where it exploded in spectacular fashion. '*Why don't you just fuck her?*' she screamed at me, her hands shaking, her left eye shot through with the red tracery of a burst corpuscle. 'You think I don't see? Sitting there all cosy with your legs rubbing up... Why don't you fuck your little Kai-Ping in front of us? C'mon, sisters, let's all watch Lionya fuck his little whore. You want me to get a video camera?'

The smallness of my apartment ensured that Pamela was on her feet and out the door before Kai-Ling could say a word. I hastily pursued Pamela, just as the two lovers in the kitchen (the Anglo and Jew) were peeking out, turtle-like, at the unfolding drama, buttoning up each other's shirts, mouthing their happy dismay.

I ran down the stairs and into the rainy March night, following the slap-slap sound of Pamela's slippers against the wet pavement. Despite her fairly thick legs, she was an unusually fast runner (and a healthy woman all around, I'm pleased to say). Soon there was so much distance between us that I worried I would never catch her up, never comfort her in my hairy arms, never tell her there was nothing between Kai-Ling and myself, that we were essentially just good friends who had had an American college experience together.

Later that night Pamela returned to my apartment and begged for me to hit her. 'Smack me 'cross the face,' she hollered in some strange accent I could not place. 'Be a man, Lionya, and teach me something.'

I could not do as she asked.

We talked throughout the night about what had happened, as the remains of the sheep's milk cheese gurgled away on the coffee table (by the morning's light we threw it out altogether). This is what I learned from our long night together: apparently, seven years before, Kevin had had a brief affair with an Asian woman, an affair that had caused some serious damage in his relationship with Pamela. Thus, in Pamela's world view, women of Asian descent were not to be trusted. 'They come to this country with one thing in mind,' she said: 'Men. They come here to take our men, Lionya. That's all they're good for... Believe me, she'd throw you over as soon as someone more attractive came along. Or someone richer. Or more American. That's what happened with Kevin's little slut. He came right back to me with his tail between his legs. I'm just trying to save you some heartbreak, buckaroo.'

We both laughed at this, although it was hard to say why. I felt vaguely complicit in something I didn't like, but by this point I just wanted to get Pamela snug in bed and to get some sleep myself. Of course, I called Kai-Ling to apologize the next day, but, for various reasons, we managed to drift apart in the years to come.

Pamela Tannehill, my only friend

And yet, for the next seventy-two hours or so, I was a happy man. Pamela treated me to her best side. She was truly contrite. 'I'm sorry if I embarrassed you in front of your black friends,' she wrote to me in an electronic mail message. 'I really liked them. Especially that cute Nancy. Christa was kind of quiet, though. Shy, I guess.'

'Sorry to be such a shit to you,' she said, after saying some things to me at brunch. 'Self-pity is one of my favourite hobbies, in case you haven't noticed. What a bore I am, huh?'

'I hate that you feel so bad, sweetie,' she whispered to me over the phone, after I had been ejected by the second coming of Kevin. 'Wish I could come over and pet your black curls and kiss your sweet furry face.'

So, you see, she was coming around; trying to understand my

feelings; not such a difficult woman, after all; every relationship is troubled at first.

And then, of course, there was the time she comforted me. The time I had my episodic little breakdown on the subway.

We were taking the train to see a comic film about the difficulty of falling in love in a modern London neighbourhood. We were holding hands for some reason, when I heard, seated next to us, a Russian family speaking heatedly about cellular phones.

They were Soviet Jews of the least cultured kind, from Odessa perhaps, or one of the outlying Soviet Absurdistans where some of our people had settled for hard-to-understand reasons. They wore cheap leather jackets. The mother was a peroxide blonde in her fifties, whose heavy mouth articulated the careful, soothing sounds I know all Russian women are capable of (I'm thinking, in particular, of my mother during her best days). The son was a balding, oily Russian nerd of about twenty-two while his father, the patriarch, presented a more secure version of his son—fully rounded, his enormous nose bent at several junctures, the look of understood wealth in his eyes.

I winked to Pamela, trying to imply how evolved I was by comparison to my co-nationals, how I wore only the most fashionable Manhattan-style clothes, but she failed to notice.

Meanwhile, the post-Soviet cellular phone conversation was heating up. 'Six hundred minutes,' the son kept saying, anxiously waving his hands in the subway air. 'And the weekends are free! And that's long-distance too... You can call Izya in Los Angeles. We can each have a phone for thirty dollars a month!'

The family was caught up in these figures. Thirty dollars. Six hundred minutes. These figures cut and hurt, they tempted and teased, they somehow managed to bring out a hundred collective years of Soviet pain and ten collective years of American uncertainty. Finally, the patriarch put an end to the discussion. 'Sasha,' he said to his boy, 'The problem is, little son, you don't want to learn. *You have to learn.* You have to work part-time and go to Hunter College three days a week. Otherwise, how will you get a profession?'

The son started whining some more about his cellular plan, but then the mother switched out of her kind woman's voice and spoke conclusively: 'Don't compare what Americans get and what we get!'

she said. 'We are not like them! We are not like other people! How can you think we are like Americans? When will you grow up already, idiot?'

The forcefulness of this woman's voice made me tremble. I am not sure how memory works, but I do believe there are wispy force fields of desire and history that enfold Manhattan, a simple result of the number of foreigners that inhabit the island and cannot express themselves in their true language at any given moment.

Yes, unexpected memory. For just then, in the subway car, at the sound of the woman's voice, I stumbled upon the quiet image of my father consistently punching my face—first punch, lean back, watch my hand scramble to cover my face, find an unprotected space for the fist to lodge, left hand tight around my shirt collar, second punch. We lived then in our first American apartment—a garage sale assortment of bric-a-brac plus a coveted Romanian coffee table and a pair of lacquered footstools. I was a small, pale boy who stuttered in English and ate baloney sandwiches in the school bathroom to avoid my lunchroom colleagues, the throaty native-born boys who whispered things about me in their urban patois and tried to steal my beautiful sheepskin coat.

Father was punching my face for algebra problems I had failed to solve in school, while my mother's voice coloured the background with its insistent tone, the tone of the subway mother now before me. 'Don't hit the head!' my mother had pleaded to my father. 'Ai. Ai. Are you crazy? He has to earn money with his head... He'll have bruises! I beg you! Hit the stomach.' Also, the methodic, reasonable look of the subway patriarch reminded me of how my own father had approached his punching—soberly. With no outward malice in his eyes. For therein lies a major difference, I believe, between the kind of discipline I received and the kind doled out to my post-Soviet peers. *My father was never a drinker and so he did not punch my face when drunk.* His punching had a very specific purpose, grounded in cultural relativism, which was to make me a better student and a more conscientious person. In this way, I believe he had succeeded.

Pamela Tannehill didn't ask me why I was crying violently, hunched over on the subway floor, my beautiful polyester golf pants (a gift from Kai-Ling) smudged beyond repair. People were laughing. This must have been an unprecedented outburst for the genteel No. 6

train, and the Russians in particular were making some cutting remarks about my girlishness.

Pamela took me to her house and cancelled her evening date with Kevin, the first time she had done so and perhaps the last. I slept for three hours inside her embrace—she must have ignored the constant ringing of the phone, the thunderclap of her New Jersey God—and when I woke she gave me a slice of banana pie to eat. 'Tell me,' she said.

'What?' I said.

'Anything,' she said.

So I told her. She smiled and kissed my cheek. 'This is what our parents do,' she said. 'This is why neither of us will ever, ever, *ever* have children.'

'Mm-hm,' I lowed.

'But I thought your parents were educated,' she said. 'I thought educated folks didn't get physical. I thought everything they did was subtle and interior.'

Drowsy, bereft, dribbling banana pie on her bedspread (usually a punishable no-no), I explained to Pamela that my father, along with his dozen cousins, had been made fatherless by the Great Patriotic War, that they were raised by the men who had managed to avoid battle, the violent, dour, second-tier men their mothers had brought home with them out of loneliness. I brought up the familiar cycle of violence we hear so much about.

But Pamela wanted me to explain myself further, which was, in itself, a pleasant surprise (it wasn't often that we were talking about me).

And she was so lovely just then. So ready to listen to me and feed me.

She was, I thought, my girlfriend.

This is what I told her. The story of my father in America. The story of my papa and the girl we both loved.

Post-Soviet mutants on parade

To begin with, my father and his relatives were—as my mother would always remind me—of simple village stock and were quite keen on survival; that is to say, lessons could be learned from the way they prospered.

Only my father had gone to university, but the rest of his family did even better than he did. They ran gasoline excise tax schemes out in New Jersey, built fantastical European-grocery-and-bootleg-Russian-video empires in Forest Hills, cornered markets in improbable goods—man-sized containers of Riga sprats, coupon books promising the bearer free drinks in Belgian hotels, vials of horse tranquillizer bound for the Israeli market.

They set my father up with a tiny factory—light manufacturing, you could call it. Within this blighted space on an asphalted stretch of Nassau County three Caribbean women bound together the pages of wedding albums.

I worked at our family's wedding-album factory all through high school, answering phones in my struggling American accent, while my father ran around yelling at the poor Caribbeans and doing a passable impression of the harried immigrant male suffering a heart attack twenty-four hours a day.

'Getting married is a special time,' I found myself telling all sorts of amorous Long Islanders over the phone. 'There are many tender moments you'll want to preserve. I would definitely recommend the silk moire linings and genuine leather cameos.'

'Tell them about good screw!' my father would holler, sweating all over his desk.

'Oh, yes,' I said, 'I would be remiss if I didn't mention our special reinforced stainless steel screw, which, post binding, allows pages to lie flat.'

I don't think I ever sold an album to anyone.

The Caribbean women, all in their fifties, did their binding in complete silence, each bent over a portable fan (no talking or air conditioning was allowed). When not binding, they risked their lives running across the highway to fetch my father a never-ending supply of cigarettes and coffee. For twenty minutes a day, they clustered around a folding card table eating pigeon peas and rice. I could hear them muttering in low voices during their allotted break time and occasionally throwing a conspiratorial glance my way as if to prove to me they weren't entirely beaten.

One summer, a daughter, Lissette, replaced her mother for the season. She was a smart, handsome teenager, with a sweet lisp and a shy way of smiling that she was learning to use to her advantage.

After a month spent bearing the brunt of my father's seasonal anger (during July, the temperature in the factory approached 105 degrees Farenheit), I was shocked to hear Lissette ask him for a college reference. Equally shocked, Father demanded to know what she had read that summer. She softly lisped a couple of names.

'I have never heard of such person,' my father sneered. 'I am supposing this Achebe fellow is no Tolstoy. If you want to go to university, young girl, you should read Russian literature, *real* literature, not book by Chinese mandarin or Indian chief.' But eventually he relented and had me type up some of Lissette's better qualities—her punctuality and hygiene—on a Fordham University recommendation form.

'I bet that *obezyana* will get a full scholarship,' he told me later. 'This is simple socialism. How can she afford to wear such a fancy blouse when I pay her almost nothing? If only she would give me a foot massage with those long monkey fingers...'

August approached. My father and I started preparing ourselves for the IWPC, the International Wedding Photographers Convention in Cleveland, Ohio, an important annual event in our field. We put together our best album samples, hand-polished a dozen of our *specially reinforced stainless steel screws*, and worked on the logo for our booth.

'Big Memory Never Die,' my father suggested, 'If You Preserve Such Memory In Abramov Album.'

I was a fan of the word 'tender' and suggested 'Tender Memories Never Die'.

'Maybe *die* is too negative,' Lissette said, wiping sweat off her chest with a towel. Because of the equatorial heat in the factory, she had lost a lot of weight in two months and her body now had an erotically angular quality. I must confess that lying in my bed I would sometimes press my penis against the sheets imagining her sweet smile and sweaty chest next to me. 'How about "Tender Memories Live Forever",' she said.

'Yes!' my father said. 'I like the word "Live". It has positive connotation for marriage.' He smiled at Lissette, smiled with the crinkled-nose happiness he reserved for the rare occasion when something good happened to him in America. 'Yes!' he said. 'And you deliver slogan in clear, forceful manner! Maybe sometime you can talk to customer on the phone, because Lionya still has big Russia accent...'

I was a bit hurt by his comment about my accent and by having to share my phone duties with Lissette, but she did manage to sell thirty albums in one day (thirty more than I had ever sold), and when the time came for the IWPC in Cleveland my father surprised the entire factory by announcing that Lissette was coming along. 'A black girl is still an American girl,' he told me. 'She understands things that we cannot. Do not be afraid of her. If you want, I will put her in a separate hotel room so that there will be no strange problems.'

The convention was held in Cleveland's I-X Center, a kind of space-age barn near the airport which boasted the world's biggest indoor Ferris wheel. As in summers past, we had a lot of trouble setting up our booth and my father punched me several times on the neck and shoulders because I kept failing to do it right.

I wanted to do it right. My mother had told me that the convention was a time for me to support my father. He was scared of the other attendees, their perfect English, their easy, knowledgeable shop talk, the way their sports jackets settled around their shoulders just so. He got very drunk and sad during the complimentary IWPC stir-fry, a prime time to network with other suppliers, and I don't think we made any meaningful professional connections that year.

Lissette, on the other hand, was doing very well. While my father and I sat to one side of our booth, two dismal immigrants unhappily eyeing our own wares, our protégée drew in several of the younger specimens from the trade who flirted with her and came away with bundles of our rosy brochures. 'You've got to see our stainless steel screw,' Lissette crooned. 'It's specially reinforced! Check *this* out! The pages lie flat!'

My father and I stared at her silently. I think we were both attuned to the same aspect of Lissette, the way her deep dark eyes (a mythical attribute in Russian cosmology) would gaze into the middle distance and then lift up toward some imaginary horizon, as if measuring the distance between the warm, brutal islands on which she was born and the shores of Lake Erie where she now hawked wedding albums for a depressive Russian. I knew my father kept calculating similar distances himself. I knew he did not believe in his present life for a moment. His family, his home, his business—how could he account for any of it?

The IWPC was ending. My father stole two bottles of vodka from the farewell dinner and drank them down in our hotel room. 'We have had a very good convention,' he said, sprawling nakedly under the covers. 'This is a good industry to work in. You can meet nice people from all over the nation—California, Salt Lake City, Raleigh-Durham-Chapel Hill... Hey, you know what we should do now? We should go out and get some whores! We'll line them up and take our turns thrashing with them, father and son! We'll take them from the back.'

'Yes,' I said, non-committally. I could see my father's erection rising to form a significant tent under the covers. I remembered how we had once climbed a small cliff near Yalta, in the Crimea, a cliff that resembled an old man's face in profile. My father gave me a cardboard medal, the Order of Lenin for Socialist Mountain Climbing. He had drawn a crude picture of Lenin riding atop a mountain goat on it. I was maybe nine then.

'Let me ask you,' he said, 'Are you still a boy?' He threw down the covers and stuck out his hairy chest as if to show me what it meant to be a man.

'No, I have twice had an Italian girl from school,' I lied to him.

'A little Sophia Loren,' he sighed. He was not usually a drinker and I don't think he knew what to do with his drunkenness. 'Your mother and I thought you were only a boy,' he said. 'I'll tell you, the first thing I did when I became a man was hit my stepfather Valentin right across the face...' He laughed at this memory, picked up an empty vodka bottle and gave it a proper shake. It was still empty.

'I would never hit you...' I started to say.

'You know what?' my father said. 'I've been training Lissette. I've been giving her Chekhov stories to fill her mind. Sometimes I can't believe how kind I am to this poor black girl. Have you ever read the novel *Heart of Darkness*? It's by Joseph Conrad, a good writer of Polish descent... Ah, but what do you care about our stupid Lissette, when you've got your Gina Lollobrigida at school.'

But there was no such Italian girl, unfortunately. All I could think of was Lissette at the factory, her sweaty chest hovering over my hungry nostrils, her soft New World palms pressing into my shoulders when she passed by my desk. How I wanted her! Yes, her chest and her palms, and also her general non-Russian benevolence, her deep dark eyes gazing into the middle distance.

I was sixteen years old and growing tired of being a boy.

I turned off the lights and imagined our Lissette lowering herself on top of me. For about an hour I pressed my penis into the hotel mattress with Lissette's smooth, young body in my mind, and then I must have drifted off into sleep. I remember my dreams distinctly: we had scaled that small cliff in Yalta and my father was congratulating me for my manliness and bravery, my commitment to keeping the Soviet cliffs of Crimea safe from the Enemy. He was kissing my cheeks and calling me by the diminutives of my name that I have always loved: *Lionchik, Lionen'ka, Lionechka*. All those silly, tender Russian permutations.

When I opened my eyes it was early morning, and the casual Ohio sun was ascending to light up the forlorn cube of the Cleveland Hopkins Airport Marriott. I could hear my father's voice urgently whispering the diminutives of my name. I turned to him, my heart filled with a forgotten filial warmth. But his bed was empty.

After a brief period of dislocation, I realized that his voice was coming from the next room. My father was crying out my name. Only it wasn't my name...

Lissa! my father was whimpering. *Lissen'ka! Lissetochka!*

Half asleep, a somnambulist in a pair of stained white briefs, I stumbled out to the hallway. The door to Lissette's room was slightly ajar. Hesitantly, I gave it a slight push, and was straight away confronted with the unlikely sight of my own ass, an ass I knew well from the locker-room mirror at school, vigorously pressing down into a woman. There it was: the same caved-in posterior with a jaunty trail of thick, curly hair running up the middle, culminating in a spooky hollow at the base of the spine.

And there she was beneath him, Lissette, making a series of sounds, a pathetic *ukh, ukh*, almost Russian in timbre, that made me worry my father was hurting her, but also an emphatic *ah! ah!* that was unlike any sound I had ever heard.

I stood there. Not because of the sight of my father, but because I was entranced by the white bottoms of her feet hanging in the air, much whiter than I had suspected, bouncing up and down in tandem with my father's angry rhythm. Suddenly, I wanted to kiss those tiny white soles. I wanted Lissette to know who I was. I wanted her to shout my name and to cry out for me: *ah!*

If only my father had known the truth of the matter. The way I had watched her eat pigeon peas with a hand cupped beneath her spoon. How I had borrowed Toni Morrison's *The Bluest Eye* from the library. How I had requested an application form from Fordham University where she was applying. Lissette Townsend, kind and beautiful, the white bottoms of her feet making half-circles in the air, the room filled with her soft moans... All my life I had been waiting for her.

Pamela Tannehill, my wife

Now that Pamela Tannehill understood me, now that she knew we were fellow sufferers, I began to pressure her to cement our relationship at Kevin's expense. Two years after we first lay together, Pamela and I moved into a little walk-up tenement apartment in the Boerum Hill section of Brooklyn. I was so in love with her that often I could not look at the world around me without experiencing a joyous convulsion, a happy blurring of vision (later this was diagnosed as an anxiety disorder, and I was given pills to take). Each morning, I left the apartment for work a little earlier than she did, and walking down the stoop, passing the Jamaican cafe where we ate curried goat on the weekend, I felt a great proprietary peace, knowing that the woman I loved was still ensconced in the musty tangle of our bed sheets, her sleepy grey eyes ringed with my morning kisses.

We had it all worked out. Weekdays were spent in our apartment. After work, we'd cook up lamb and couscous, listen to the amiable droning of National Public Radio, read the more interesting parts of *Harper's* magazine, and make loud love on all fours before going to bed. It was a pleasant time and I could feel our affection for each other growing.

The weekends she would spend with the Weismans. I imagine there was a lot of embracing between her and Kevin, maybe a few smooches on the lips, some footsie under the dinner table, but no sex. Kevin slept on the floor of his room, and would scramble into bed with her when his parents knocked on the door to wake them up in the morning. I'm not sure what they did as a family (once she brought me seashells from the Jersey shore), but after I had called the Weisman house one weekend to tell Pamela how alone I felt, Kevin apparently said to her: 'I don't want that man calling this house ever again.'

This instigated a terrible row with Pamela. She was very honest about the situation. 'What can you give me?' she said, spitting into her palm, a vestigial gesture from her childhood years. 'Huh? Can you give me a family like the Weismans? They saved my life, you know. Are your freaky, fucked-up immigrant parents going to take care of me? Look what they did to you, Lionya Bear.'

I was surprised. We had once had brunch with my parents and I thought it went rather well. My mother held Pamela's hand and said: 'Pamela, it is very nice for you that you have such white skin.' (After my sojourn at the gentle Midwestern college, my mother for some reason believed that I was going to marry a black woman.)

And my father added: 'Yes, we could never imagine our Lionya with such a beautiful girl,' a remark so heartfelt that it made Pamela blush.

But at the end of the meal my father had performed his customary fumbling with the bill, whispering the amounts in his strange greenhorn dialect, while my mother, in her callous, Russian way, had implied that as a woman of thirty she had been prettier than Pamela and dating more successfully. 'One time, I went with head of Leningrad musical conservatory, another time with Sergei Sukharchik, famous alpinist!'

Come to think of it, Pamela had cried after the meal and, in one of her horrible attacks of low self-esteem, once again begged me to hit her. That was one of the last meals we ever shared with my parents. But this was also a time when our relationship continued to deepen. In fact, we were so into each other that even spending the weekends apart (her with the Weismans, me alone at home) often proved painful for us.

One day, after Pamela Tannehill had cried in my arms all night because she said that nobody cared for her—not me, not Kevin, not anyone else in the world—I had sent an electronic message to her workplace. *You should know, Pamela,* I wrote, *that I love you very much.*

My Little Lionya, she replied, *You are quite dear to me, but I am wary of the binding effect such tender statements can have on the parties involved. I'm not the slightest bit interested in hiding the truth from you or getting into some sort of ugly mess once again (story of my life, huh?). I hope these many qualifications do not diminish in any way your open-hearted declaration of love for me. Okay?*

I printed out that message on my office's best bond paper and carried it around with me for many months. Actually, I carry it with me still. I know that her many caveats are a little off-putting, but they simply reflect the careful way in which Pamela Tannehill considers matters of the heart. Someone with a history like hers cannot afford to be hurt again, the way Kevin Weisman hurt her when he refused to have sex with her after twelve years of intimacy. Still the message speaks for itself, I believe: *You are quite dear to me.*

Three months after I received this message, three years after we had met each other at the non-profit conference, I asked Pamela Tannehill to marry me. She took two weeks to consider my proposal and finally said she felt she had no choice but to accept (under the condition, of course, that her arrangement with the Weismans would continue in perpetuity). 'I don't want to lose you,' she sobbed. 'No one treats me like you do.'

We settled for a simple municipal ceremony. By this point I had lost all the friends I had made at the gentle Midwestern college and Pamela also could not come up with any friends of her own, so, somewhat idealistically, we decided to ask Kevin to be our witness.

After two years of loving Pamela, I finally met Kevin Weisman. I finally met my Maker. He was one of those five-and-a-half-foot Jewish-American men about whom everything is big—a bulbous nose twisted by schoolyard violence, a single hairy brow dripping with early-morning virility, enormous hands that hammered together birdhouses and could have easily ripped me apart as well. He spoke with the aplomb of Sir Laurence Olivier in one of his celebrated Shakespearean roles.

'There's no need for histrionics,' Prince Hamlet of Mahwah told me at our first meeting, after I had started raging about this triangular mess we had gotten ourselves into, about how my wife would never really be my wife. 'Pamela and I will be special friends

forever,' he said, 'because from the moment I declared her mine—
and rarely do I make such declarations—the gods decided it was so.
You should feel lucky that you'll never have to carry her weight alone
the way I did for twelve years. Aren't you a lucky fellow, now?'

'You fucking bastard,' I said. I wanted to speak brilliantly but was
terribly drunk and could not help sounding like a simple fool. 'You
fucking—'

'Now, now,' Kevin said, clearly delighted by the quality of his *tut,
tut* voice. 'No need to get nasty now, sport. I'm your best man, after
all.'

I had never hit a fellow before, so after I had lunged at Kevin
across the room, I found myself quite unsure of what to do with my
clenched fists. Kevin showed me. He beat my face for a good five
minutes—he seemed to excel at dispassionate beatings, like
my father—until, in a simple defensive measure, I bit one of his
hairy knuckles. 'Aw, shit,' Kevin said in a distinctly un-Shakespearean
turn.

After the City Hall ceremony, he bought us rotis and a pitcher of
wine at the Jamaican cafe and gave me as a wedding present Michel
Leiris's *Manhood: A Journey from Childhood into the Fierce Order
of Virility.* It was a warm June day and I thought Pamela looked
beautiful in her snappy velvet dress and a charming straw boater
threaded with one daisy. Kevin wore a polyester suit and rep tie. Only
I had opted for a traditional tuxedo.

We cried and fought all through our honeymoon at a Vermont
inn and after our return to the city Pamela opted to spend an entire
week with the Weismans. She came back happy and disdainful.
Apparently she and Kevin had done funny impressions of me during
the course of the week; in particular, they liked to dredge up the
remains of my Russian accent, the way the word 'attic' left my mouth
as 'addict', for example.

But for the next year or so, Pamela softened. She must have sensed
my singular sorrow at her teasing and cruelty and I was once again
reminded of the two things she had said in response to my wedding
proposal: 'I don't want to lose you' and 'No one treats me like you
do'.

Even Kevin, it turned out, felt bad about what had happened
between us and wanted to start a correspondence with me. He had

abandoned birdhouse-building as an occupation for the time being and wanted to concentrate on his poetry. To wit, he was highly influenced by the Polish Nobelist Czeslaw Milosz and wanted to see if I, as an Eastern European, had anything to offer him in terms of my own sadness and despair. I tried to oblige him, but our correspondence was tenuous at best. It was difficult to immerse myself in Kevin's poetry which was a kind of suburban updating of Greek myth, centring around Zeus's wife, the goddess Hera.

'Rising from the alfalfa-strewn lot/forty yards behind the Super-K-mart/Hylonome—female centaur lover/'browser of the woods'/ bow before the queen of heaven/protectress of children in childbirth/ spread my mother's legs/But know this, Hera/I will not come inside you/I will not clip the wings of moths.'

Finally, Pamela told me that Kevin had a new plan. As a poet, he needed to be around other poets, which was difficult to do at his parents' house in New Jersey. There was a little bar near Atlantic Avenue where some of Brooklyn's finest young poets gathered to exchange their verses and 'shoot the shit'. Wouldn't it be wonderful if instead of her going over to the Weismans, Kevin could come by on weekends and indulge himself in the life of the New York poet? Yes, it would be wonderful, I said, but how could he pursue this delicate kind of life with me puttering around the apartment all day, blasting Rachmaninov with my morning coffee, noisily lamenting the Week in Review section of the Sunday *Times*, and constantly coughing to clear my chest of phlegm (I was often sick)?

True, it would be difficult for him, she agreed. But what if I were to spend my weekends at my parents' house? It was clear to Pamela that our marriage was driving a wedge between me and my parents, and she didn't want to be responsible for a thing like that.

And so I left for my parents' Long Island estate. The Abramov manse was a nice, goofy, immigrant's house—mock-Tudor wedded to Dutch colonial with some Moorish influences thrown in as if to announce that the owners were real Americans, unencumbered by modesty or shame, who could damn well do as they pleased with their private property.

The first few weekends my parents were honestly shocked to see me, but soon enough they warmed to my presence and the opportunities it afforded for them to unbosom themselves to me. I learned in the course of four weekends that my parents were deeply unhappy people, that the cause of their unhappiness consisted of approximately thirty per cent Social and Cultural Dislocation Brought About By Immigration and seventy per cent Their Son's Failure to Be a Successful and Loving Son. They were at least relieved that I had managed to find an attractive wife on my yearly income of US $52,900, and they prayed each night to Yahweh that she would never leave me and that we would soon have babies.

One Sunday, after an afternoon spent on the patio watching my father glower at me from behind a stack of wedding-album samples, I decided to try to relieve some of my loneliness by going home three hours before I was due. All through the long ride on the Long Island Rail Road, I worried that coming home before I was expected was a kind of acting out, of invading the space of others. And my uneasiness was justified, for when I walked into our apartment, I immediately spied Kevin Weisman and my wife, the goddess Hera, lying together on the sweaty corner futon where she and I usually lay. At first, there was the usual range of unhelpful emotions: I was pained and debilitated, cut to the quick by their loud self-involvement, the unruly sight of two familiar bodies stuck together in the late summer heat, the stillness of the room punctuated by his whimpering and her pleading... But surprisingly, with the endurance of a Soviet citizen queuing in line for sausages, with the trembling resignation of my parents' son, I found myself oddly inspired by how hard they were working, both of them red-cheeked and winded, as they faced up to the difficulty of the task before them.

Before I could say a word of reproach (and what, really, can one say?), I had turned around and walked out the door, leaving them to themselves.

Pamela Tannehill's fierce order of virility

Shortly after Pamela Tannehill and the newly erect Kevin Weisman sued me for divorce, I found that I had no place to live, and so I decided to set up house with my parents for a few months (I was starting to see a therapist at this time, who, incidentally, found this idea perturbing). It wasn't so bad. Both my parents were working long hours, and I, having recently lost my job, was left to my own devices for most of the day.

The Abramov estate had a comforting effect on me. I had some pleasant memories of coming home to this house from the gentle Midwestern college and impressing my parents with my grades (my father actually kissed me on the mouth when I got a perfect average), and also of breaking a condom with my college girlfriend up in my bedroom, which had made me feel quite virile and long.

I remember the last time I introduced a woman to Casa Abramov, my honeymoon with Pamela Tannehill. We had borrowed my father's station wagon—the words ABRAMOV'S SUPERIOR WEDDING SYSTEMS stencilled on both sides, an unintended irony—and were going to return the car to Long Island and take the railroad back to Brooklyn. As mentioned, we'd been fighting all through our stay at the Vermont inn, Pamela accusing me of not being Kevin, of not knowing the things he knew, the names of North American trees and shrubs and marmots, or, more practically, how to drive a car or haggle over the room service bill with the proprietor of a humble country inn. She drank three stolen mini-bottles of Stoli on the drive down, and I think both of us were secretly hoping we would crash into one of the highway's formidable cement dividers, maybe take a little hospitalized breather from each other.

Speaking of breathers, as we pulled up to my parents' house, I found myself suddenly short of breath. 'I can't get through this,' I wheezed. 'I can't see my family right now.' Also, my eyes were red from crying and this would be unacceptable to my father. Gasping, I tried to explain the situation to Pamela.

'We'll be okay, bucko,' she said, stuffing her mouth with an entire container of breath mints. 'Just let me do the talking.' She winked at me, a clever, angry smile building in both corners of her mouth. '*And* the breathing,' she said. (Her joking often inspired me.)

My mother had set up a table of fishy Russian appetizers 'for the newly-weds,' and was decked out in her flashiest cosmetics and shoulder pads, looking exactly like the owner of a quasi-Moroccan-mock-Tudor-Dutch-colonial house. Sometimes it was hard for me to remember that she was essentially a small tired woman whose parents ate their share of horsemeat during the siege of Leningrad and whose hands still trembled when she handled a fifty-dollar bill.

My father was relegated to a lonely corner of the vast dining room table and allowed to speak only when spoken to. This was a few months after my mother found the letters from Lissette. Mother told me she was considering the financial ramifications of a divorce (too costly, said their accountant), and presented me with a bale of letters as evidence. The letters were actually quite beautiful. That strange young Lissette was taking a course on Tolstoy at the university and was comparing my father, quite improbably, to both the sweet-tempered nobleman Levin and the dashing Count Vronsky. 'Does that monkey think she's Anna Karenina now?' my mother spat at the delicate blue-lettered script. It turned out Lissette had been seeing my father for over three years.

On the day of our return from the honeymoon my father was glancing at me sullenly, motioning for me to pass the sardines and the vodka. My breathing problem was hardly easing and I was trying to reinvigorate my battered lungs with a bottle of chilled white wine. Pamela, meanwhile, was getting properly soused with whisky. 'So, Mr Abramov,' she said. 'What's up?'

My father grabbed at this rare opportunity to speak. 'My pretty new daughter,' he mumbled, a monumental green vein bulging across his forehead. 'I was just now thinking, Pamelachka... Do you know what it is, the meaning of your name?'

'My name?' said my wife, laughing. 'You mean *Pamela Tannehill*? Oh, it doesn't mean anything, Mr Abramov. I'm just white trash, that's all...'

'Ah,' my father said, although he had clearly not understood my wife's meaning. 'No, I was thinking, that, mm-hm, deh...'

'Speak English already!' my mother shouted at him, stabbing a sturgeon with her fork.

'I was only thinking,' my father said, 'that Pamela means in Greek "sweet like honey". See, Pamela, as a young man I was aspirant to the faculty of philology at Leningrad State University... Hmm... So, Lionya, when you are addressing your wife, you are saying to her that she is "sweet like honey".' He managed something like a laugh.

'Well, that's very nice of you to say,' Pamela told him. They briefly smiled at each other across the table. 'Sweet like honey,' Pamela whispered to herself, pleased. She finished her drink and poured another.

My mother decided to steer the conversation to her favourite topic, the lightness of Pamela's skin and hair. 'Now I was thinking,' she said to Pamela, 'that perhaps when you bear us children you will dilute some of Lionya's dark blood. Look at his black hair! Just look! He is like an Armenian. *Or worse.*' She stared balefully at my father, the acknowledged Master of Miscegenation, the betrayer of our sad, marmot-faced tribe.

'Oh, I like my Lionya just fine!' the generous Pamela declared, rocking from side to side.

'Really?' My mother was shocked. 'But our son is nothing! He makes nothing! I am embarrassed to discuss him with friends. I am only proud of his beautiful wife.'

'Don't say he's nothing!' Pamela suddenly shouted. 'He's my husband! How can you say he's nothing…' She lowered the neckline of her blouse and stuck out her neck, whereupon a giant black hickey glimmered for all to see. 'Look!' she shouted. 'Look how he ravished me last night! Is that nothing? Answer me!'

My parents did not have a ready answer to this question. We sat around the table, silently eating, Pamela giggling to herself and sipping more whisky. 'No, it is something,' my father finally said. 'It is really something.'

I let out a concerted wheeze.

Meanwhile, an important event was taking place. Pamela had abandoned her fork and was scrounging under the table with her right hand, a glass of whisky in the other. After she found what she was looking for, after my pants had been soundlessly unzipped, after I was partly naked under the table and fully cupped in her hand, I let go of my fork as well.

Recently, I have asked my therapist to reappraise the meaning of humiliation, to try to find something a little more favourable, a better fit, a more inclusive definition, at least as far as the post-Soviet immigrant male is concerned. For sitting at my parents' table back then, growing larger, my wife's hand massaging the organ that cinched us together, my cheated mother snorting into her fish, my disgraced father dreamily considering something in the folds of his cotton napkin—his forbidden Lissette?—I felt, oddly enough, in full possession of my lungs.

I take in a long breath, enjoying for a change the American smells of the house—the odour of burnt rubber and spent electricity that lingers over the enormous television console; the heady scent of lemon spray that keeps the kitchen sparkling with possibility; the aromatic, cloying discharge of newly cut grass that hangs over the back acre.

Believe me, I am home. □

BOOKFORUM

THE BOOK REVIEW FOR ART, FICTION, AND CULTURE

THIS SUMMER

Jonathan Lethem *on* Philip K. Dick

Dutch novelist Cees Nooteboom interviewed

Maggie Paley *on* Kathryn Harrison

Geoff Dyer *on* Robert Warshow

Andrew Solomon *on* Rick Moody's "Black Veil"

Luc Sante *on* John Cohen photographs

Curtis White *on* "Empire" after 9/11

Greil Marcus *on* Atomic America

ON NEWSSTANDS MAY 21

GRANTA

THE CHELSEA AFFECT

AFFECT

Arthur Miller

Arthur Miller, 1963

I decided to move to the Chelsea in 1960 for the privacy I was promised. It seemed a wonderfully out-of-the-way place, nearly a slum, where nobody would be likely to be looking for me. It was soon after Marilyn and I parted, and some of the press were still occasionally tracking me, looking for the dirt in a half-hearted way. A friend who I would later marry had done photos for a book on Venice by Mary McCarthy and Mary had recommended the Chelsea as a cheap but decent hotel. (Mary of course hated my work, but that's neither here nor there.) My friend, Inge Morath, who normally lived in Paris, had stayed there for short periods of work in America, and found it shabby but, to say the least, informal. 'Nobody will bother you there,' she assured me.

The owner, Mr Bard, showed me a newly redecorated sixth-floor apartment overlooking the parking lot (since covered by an apartment house) behind the hotel. The parking lot is important.

I did not know quite what to make of Mr Bard. A blue-eyed Hungarian Jew, short and with a rather clear, delighted round face, full of energy, he waved a hand over the room saying, 'Everything is perfect. All the furniture is brand new, new mattresses, drapes... Look in the bathroom.' As we walked to the bathroom I noticed a worn path down the middle of the carpet and what felt like coal dust crunching under my shoes. 'The carpet,' I started to say, but he cut me off. 'A new carpet is coming tomorrow,' he said with raised index finger, and one knew he had not thought of replacing the carpet until that very minute. He turned on both sink faucets and pointed proudly to the water pouring out. 'Brand new faucets, also in the shower. But be careful in the shower, the cold is hot and the hot is cold. Mr Katz,' he said. We returned to the living room and stood there.

'What about Mr Katz?' I asked.

'He does the plumbing. Sometimes, he...' Again he broke off and said, 'So what do you say?' Before I could answer, he continued, 'I guarantee you nobody will know you're living here. A maid comes every day. Some days when I feel down, maybe you'd like to join me, I go fishing in Croton Reservoir.' One almost knew what Mr Bard was talking about, but not quite. He began to remind me of a woman I knew in Coney Island who used go out at night and steal radiators from construction sites for a new upper storey she and her husband were illegally adding to her house. To her son's objections she would reply, 'But they have so many.' The way she said it seemed reasonable. Mr Bard had a similar talent for overriding probability, an emotional fluency which sent his thoughts on swallow loops from subject to subject, a progressive, enthusiastic view of life. In a word, anarchy. 'The furniture is all new.'

'You told me,' I said. In fact, it was raw, south-of-the-border furniture, Guatemalan maybe, or outer Queens, and I gingerly touched a bureau but thankfully the varnish was dry.

Within a week the gossip columns, as I half expected, were reporting my new abode, and friends in Europe noted the same great news in some Continental and British papers. 'That's too bad,' Mr Bard said when I confronted him, 'we did our best not to mention it. Everybody.'

'Everybody what?'

'Who we told not to mention it.'

'Including the newspapers.'

'Including the newspapers, what?'

'Who you told not to mention it.'

He thought that was funny and laughed. I laughed too. I was getting into the swing of things. I had heard a rumour that he had won the hotel in a high-stakes card game played in the New Yorker Hotel which had also changed hands a few times as a result of the game.

Despite parboiling myself in the shower a few times I began to like the hotel, or at least some of the residents, or denizens as some liked to call themselves. You could get high in the elevators on the residue of marijuana smoke. 'What smoke?' Mr Bard would ask indignantly. Allen Ginsberg was hawking his new *Fuck You* magazine in the lobby sometimes, Warhol was shooting film in one of the suites, and a young woman with eyes so crazy that one remembered them as being above one another, would show up in the lobby now and then, distributing a ream of mimeographed curses on male people whom she accused of destroying her life and everything good, and threatening to shoot a man one of these days. I had a serious talk, or what I took to be one, with Mr Bard and his son Stanley who was gradually taking over, but they pooh-poohed the idea of her doing anything rash. As I slowly learned, they were simply not interested in bad news of any kind. Of course she shot Warhol two days later as he was entering the lobby from 23rd

Street, aiming for his balls. But this only momentarily disturbed the even tenor of the Chelsea day, what with everything else going on.

Anyway, it was certainly more *gemütlich* than living in a real hotel. In the early Sixties truckers still took rooms without baths on the second floor and parked their immense rigs out front overnight, and the Automat was still on the corner of 7th. There I often had breakfast with Arthur C. Clarke, who in his dry Unitarian-minister manner tried to explain to me why whole new populations would soon be living in space. Feigning interest in this absurdity I wondered what the point of living in space would be. 'What was the point of Columbus wanting to cross the ocean?' I supposed he was right, but not really. Meantime at tables around us numerous street people were hugging their coffee mugs to delay ejection into rain and wind, and would ultimately drive the Automat out of the area with their unappetizing ear and nose-picking, quick fights, copious coughing fits and exhausted deep sleeps from which the manager could sometimes not awaken them. At the time I doubt that either Clarke or I registered the strange contrast between his cloudy space-talk and the grimy Automat reality. But unlike space it was the reality that would soon disappear from public view, tucked away in shelters for the homeless.

One could tell how bad the weather was by having a brief chat with a gaunt, six-and-a-half-foot tall minister, denomination unknown, who, in his perpetual ankle-long and droopy raincoat, seemed to appear in daylight only after it had been raining or snowing for several days. He had the exaggerated reactions of a man living alone with mice and one light bulb, leaping forward to grasp a proffered handshake with a simultaneous deep bow of obeisance. He always wore the same eviscerated black tie, whose lining hung loose, and harassed black suit, his pant cuffs flapping high above his bulbous shoes, and rose to his toes with each loping stride, a man of fifty or so, with a sympathetic if dour expression which fairly exploded with instant gratitude to anyone at all who addressed him. He carried a black doctor's satchel, not for thermometer and stethoscope but for a prayer book and a once-white, now yellowing, satin stole which he would drape over his shoulders for the funerals he specialized in presiding over, deprived as he was of a church or income. The worse the weather the more frequent the funerals, and after a week or two of freezing rains one came to expect a certain bright businesslike expression in his face. 'How's it coming?' I would ask as the clanking elevator rose.

'Oh, just fine, just fine,' he would intone.

'Tough weather.'

'Oh, yes, yes indeed,' he would reply, his contentment barely disguised, the water dripping off his black hat on to his brown grocery bag with its celebratory bulge.

Europeans soon began showing up, expecting God knows what adventures in this celebrity artists' hotel they'd read about, and some just as quickly fled in polite panic. One of these, a German businessman, told me, 'It's like a certain kind of hotel in Paris,' and added, 'in fact, a little too much like it.' But for many it met their expectations; it was thrilling to know that Virgil Thomson was writing his nasty music reviews on the top floor, and that those canvases hanging over the lobby were by Larry Rivers, no doubt as rent, and that the hollow-cheeked girl on the elevator was Viva and the hollow-eyed man with her was Warhol and that scent you caught was marijuana.

But more important for me was that my shoes were still grinding the grit in the carpet. Rose, the maid, came every day, as promised, and waved at things. She had a carpet sweeper but walked about the apartment pulling it behind her as she smoked. These things are never of importance until, as though from nowhere, a kind of pointless rage enters the mind and one finds oneself yelling into the phone, 'For Christ's sake, Stanley, don't you have a vacuum cleaner in the house!'

'Of course! We have lots of them.'

'Then why aren't they ever used?'

'They're not used?'

'Stanley! You know goddamned well they don't use them!'

'I never heard of such a thing! Why don't they use them?'

'You're asking *me* why they don't use them?'

'Well, you're the one who brought it up.'

'Look, just get a vacuum cleaner up here and let's forget this conversation.'

'Fine. How are you otherwise?'

'Truthfully, there is no otherwise—all I am is a man waiting desperately for a vacuum cleaner.' And he would laugh, grateful for another happy tenant.

A fateful, rather amazing delivery of a new roll of carpet was made one morning. It was left temporarily in the lobby where denizens stopped to stare at it as the first new object many of them had ever seen entering the Chelsea. Its size and heft being central to a grasp of the succeeding events, it may be described as about four feet in height and about a yard in diameter, its weight probably over 500 pounds. It was destined for the second-floor corridor and after some hours was deposited up there awaiting the installers who were to come the next day. Its arrival suggested a possible new reformist management attitude which had disturbing implications for some; for one thing, it might mean the building was to be fixed up. This would surely raise rents and send some unimproved tenants into the street.

But the new carpet roll was especially inspiring for Mendel Rubin, the building 'engineer', a bulky, benign, Jewish ex-Marine private, who dared hope now that some of the below-stairs equipment which he was forever nursing might also be replaced. Between bouts with his oil burners, Mendel would occasionally surface to help hang pictures in the lobby or strike up little time-passing artistic conversations with the guests. Learning of the astronomical sums Rivers got for his work, Mendel saw no reason not to begin scribbling designs of his own on leftover linoleum tiles he had found in the basement, splashing them with orange, green and black paint from leftover cans down there. These tiles he would display here and there in the lobby, and a lady visitor from Iceland, I think, or possibly New Zealand bought several, and paid him in money. He would never be the same. All his time now was spent on his tiles and he even managed to have a show in a downtown gallery. I never knew how or why he disappeared from the hotel, but before he did he confided in me a deep and abiding hatred of the house detective whom he was sure was a phoney, something which would turn out— as will shortly be explained—to have a profound connection with the new roll of carpet.

The Chelsea in the Sixties seemed to combine two atmospheres: a scary and optimistic chaos which predicted the hip future, and at the same time the feel of a massive, old-fashioned, sheltering family. That at least was the myth one nursed in one's mind, but like all myths it did not altogether stand inspection. The idea of family had limits. Unless one was drugged out, or spending one's days putting paint on canvas, words on paper, chisels on stone, or singing operatic arias at the piano, one found it difficult to hold Stanley's attention. In fact, I cannot recall a single real businessman-guest, although some of that type may have frequented the regular all-night card games, like the one which caused a bit of a rumble when two hold-up men stationed themselves outside the room and robbed the happy winners as they emerged into the hallway. But such mishaps were rare and would be denied by the management even though it gave the place a certain panache, or relief from real life's ordinary constraints. It was not, one thought, that Stanley cultivated weird people, potheaded layabouts and some extraordinary as well as morbidly futile artistic types, but simply that he seemed to think these dreamers were normal; it was the regular people who made him uneasy. In any case, it was a general rule that when something weird happened, nobody—not Stanley, not the desk man or the phone operator or Mendel—would ever really know quite what it was all about, and so a kind of fog of exhausted enquiry suffused the place.

What certainly did happen was Kleinsinger, who had moved into the Chelsea from a regulation suburban marriage, and got girls by keeping a fisheries exhibit in his room; in enormous glass tanks rising nearly to the ceiling strange South American fish floated, some of them armoured with pearly scales and wiry antennae waving up from their heads. In ample cages large snakes lounged, vipers plotted, weird Amazon turtles with long snouts stared motionlessly, speckled Patagonian lizards and an occasional small monkey made smells. Now and again a snake would escape and the whole hotel would be on its knees looking under beds. A blind couple in the rooms next to mine had to have Mendel Rubin scour their apartment, and not knowing how to call snakes he searched the closets calling 'Psss, pss' as to a lost cat.

Kleinsinger's pleasure was to excite his guests, particularly ladies, by opening his door for them with a fat cobra-like reptile draped over his shoulders. He composed music, mainly for documentaries now, although he had begun as a writer of concert pieces and in the far distant past, I think, Popular Front oratorios. Kleinsinger had a merry smile, a debonair manner and a racking smoker's cough. He had left the suburbs to live on the edge and the last time I saw him, shortly before he died, he was sprinting down 23rd Street in shorts and running shoes pursuing health and his youth, trailing heavy smoke from a long cigar and nodding pleasantly to neighbourhood acquaintances along the way.

The Chelsea, whatever else it was, was a house of infinite toleration. This was the Bards' genius, I thought, to have achieved an operating chaos which at the same time could be home to people who were not crazy. I wrote most of *After the Fall* there and our daughter had her first baths in the kitchen sink. Virgil Thomson offered lethal martinis to his occasional guests, and Arthur Clarke doggedly charted the next millennium in his room. There were also, tragically, people at the end of their rope wandering the corridors or the elevators at midday in pyjamas, one of whom, according to many of his peers, had been the finest designer of women's clothes America had ever produced, Charles James.

That he was deeply troubled was obvious, his helpless desperation written across his eyes. He was a broad-faced man in his sixties, still quite strong, I thought, and intelligent, but occasionally forgetful enough to start out into the street in his sleeping clothes. Kennedy had just been murdered when we happened on one another in a corridor, and he held on to my hand and said, 'Is this the beginning of the end?' and looked at me intently, as though the bullets had barely missed him.

The place, in fact, reminded me of Nevada in the early Sixties and still does. There was a similar kind of misfittedness about so many of the people who had either dropped out or never entered the normal ruts where most human traffic flows. Poor Brendan Behan was staying there for a couple of months at the point in his life when he seemed casually amused by death's closeness, no different in this than Charles Jackson's depressive sadness before he ended his life in his room (in 1968, twenty-four years after he published *The Lost Weekend*), or Dylan Thomas's gallant swim toward a private cataract of alcohol that would catch him at last and fling him down on the rocks below. But where there are artists there will be suicides. It had always stuck me as odd, how glamorous a number of writers thought New York was. For me, born on 112th Street and Third Avenue, the city was certainly the world's most interesting place but surely not a field of diamonds glittering under the moon, filled as it was with mere people rather than infinite possibilities. Behan seemed star-struck, putting in a lot of time in nightclubs wearing a proper suit and tie and uncorking Irish stories and one-liners that would be printed next morning in Leonard Lyons's column, even as he was dancing as fast as he could toward his dying. I came on him one afternoon standing outside on the sidewalk in brilliant sunshine, happily talking to some woman while an unnoticed trickle of vomit dropped from the corner of his mouth on to his tie right through his speech. One morning, surprisingly, he called to invite me up to the choreographer Pearl Primus's room for a spot of breakfast, and I found him sober then with lots of uneaten food in front of him. She, veritable black earth mother, was obviously trying to feed and repair this man whom she hardly knew but whose plays she had admired, attempting to tuck his napkin into his collar as with a mock-lordly wave of his hand toward her living room, he said, 'My second home!' Dylan likewise had ended here, helpless in the hands of an adoring woman. Behan (one is tempted to add 'God save him') seemed a rather patched-together personality of several colours by this time, I thought, what with his desperate, heedless lunging backwards toward a passing fame that required the image of the happy-go-lucky, late-rising, debonair Irishman, all on a sick stomach. Balancing himself like a bully boy on feet spaced apart and rapping out slang like a worker-chap, he was in actuality a son of middle-class Irish people. When I sat with him at breakfast that morning, he turned to me and said, apropos nothing in particular, 'You're a real playwright, but I'm not. I just scribbled some dialogue a couple of times...' and broke off with a surge of anguish which he deflected with, 'But we're all born and dead in a day, aren't we.' When I said I had been moved by his *Borstal Boy* and *The Hostage*, he brightened gratefully but waved it all away nonetheless. In his morning sobriety he seemed to cease concealing something crushed in his gut, the joking was gone, silence reigned within him and it seemed terrible that people were in effect encouraging him to drink and perform his cute Irish act with his salivating brogue which Americans adore.

Wherever he went in the evenings, there was a big Irish ha-ha-ha! But on that morning, in the light pouring on to him through the tall old windows from over 23rd Street, his fair skin was blotched, and the tremor noticeable in his remarkably small and delicate hands.

His hair was still wet and not so much combed as patted down and I supposed he had made a play at freshening up for my visit. If his condition called for pity, I still could not help recalling that his Irish friend and bodyguard, who stayed close to his side from morning till night, had gotten fed up with him starting bar fights which, the bodyguard claimed, he was left to finish. The man was most probably jealous of what he saw as Behan's undeserved literary fame, for he turned out to have a book of his own he was trying to get published, but in any case he had confided one evening at the bar downstairs that Brendan had a small child over in Jersey and was still bedding the mother even though he suspected that he had syphilis. Was this, I had to wonder, why he was so patently killing himself with drink? Or was it all a galloping nightmare he could no longer decipher, born of the painful irony of his notoriety in New York growing precisely when he knew he could not face writing a new play or anything else any more?

Leaving Behan that morning it seemed odd that it was here in the Chelsea, ten years before, that I had found myself commiserating with another self-destroying alcoholic Celt, Dylan Thomas. All Brendan could hope to do was perform a bit longer; he had slowed to a sodden halt. Dylan had been different, still pursued, so I thought, by the guilt of his own success when a beloved poet-father had failed to achieve any recognition for himself. When Dylan stood, still young, roundish and cherry-cheeked, before the worshipful audience in the school auditorium on Irving Place, one hand gripping the podium to steady himself, his lilting voice, a musical instrument, leading us all with unearthly assurance into his fields and dreams and village streets, one heard something very ancient and mysteriously grave. His was a voice echoing out of stone crypts and things buried, and he appeared to me a man chosen to carry some lost spirit back into the world rather than a mere writer scrounging for a word or theme. Hearing him I knew what a bard was, and that he was dying of no disease as he sang for coins and the pleasure of strangers was terrible and strange. The Chelsea's walls could tell a lot about the self-loathing of talented people.

'Move back! Rent free! I have a wonderful apartment for you!' It was Stanley Bard greeting me, years after we had ceased to live in the hotel. Every year or so I found myself dropping in when I was in the neighbourhood to chat with him and, I confess, sip again a little of the spirit of the place. But not too much.

'Why don't you want to live here?' he would demand more and more insistently as the years went by. Now he was a grey-haired middle-aged man and his father was long gone and his own son was beginning to take over, threatening to clean up the place and even remodel parts of it.

'Because I like surprises but not where I'm living,' I said. 'Like when that girl got shot on the seventh floor...'

'What girl?' He was genuinely flummoxed.

'The prostitute who got one eye and a finger shot off.'

'I never heard of such a thing!' he said, really and truly outraged but at the same time smiling emptily as though at a remark he really could not understand. Why did people continue telling such stories! Managing the Chelsea was like managing a forest where little fires kept breaking out.

'Well, it doesn't matter,' I said. 'What's happening these days?'

'Nothing. It's nice and quiet. And we're full.'

We were sitting in his office whose geography is indescribably complicated. Part of it is in one room and another part is as though in another room behind a glass partition which stands at one end but doesn't separate anything from anything else. And one dares not ask what the partition is for lest the explanation answers nothing and only distresses the mind. The furniture was late McKinley, a treasure trove of discarded dark oak desks and sunken-bottomed chairs and ancient heavy electric fans and wooden filing cabinets. For no reason I thought of James, the designer.

'Remember what's-his-name-James, the designer?'

'Sure. Wait a minute...' The phone had rung. I found an old *New York Times* on the floor and picked it up and began reading it. I could not remember any of this news, it was like a future newspaper telling of things that hadn't happened yet. Suddenly Stanley was shouting into the phone.

'Now just a minute, Ethel...no, wait now, I have something to say! You are not coming back. I don't care, we are not having that kind of business here and you know what I'm talking about...'

A beautifully dressed young woman walked in.

'Stanley...?'

'Please shut up a minute, darling,' he said to this new arrival, who indignantly threw up her head and stamped her foot with one fist pressing into her hip.

'You heard what I said, Ethel,' Stanley continued into the phone, 'this is final, I don't want you here any more, darling!' And hung up.

'Where is my money?' the beautiful young woman asked.

'Now listen to me, Bernice, I am not your father, I have no money for you till the first of the month!'

'The first of the *month*!' Bernice, wearing 3,000 dollars' worth of beige suit and matching boots and an enormous white beret, had an angelic, wealthy face with frightening green eyes that at the moment had murder in them.

'What am I supposed to *do*! I've got a twenty dollar bill to my name!' A little girl's plaint was in her voice now.

'First of the month, Bernice, that's all I can tell you. I have no money for you till then. Now please leave me alone.'

Bernice was in tears now, sobbing.

'I'm not listening,' Stanley said and turned to me. 'James, you mean?' he said. 'James died a couple of years ago.'

Bernice continued to stand there, weeping into an embroidered handkerchief.

'Pathetic man at the end,' I said, ignoring Bernice just as Stanley was doing, sensing as I did that while her anguish was real it was still a performance, repeated, no doubt, every few weeks. 'He used to complain about how you were treating him.'

'How I was treating him? Why? How did I treat him?' And he suddenly remembered something. 'Wait! I have a wonderful letter from him...' And he turned his swivel chair and faced the Chelsea filing system, a stack of yellowing paper rising at least four feet high from the top of his desk. 'It's right here someplace...' He peered at the hundreds of sheets piled up before him, raised his hand and with forefinger and thumb delicately drew out a sheet, glanced at it and handed it to me. 'Here it is. Read.'

Still impressed with his lightning retrieval system, much faster than any computerized one, I took the paper, a handwritten letter, as his phone rang again. Bernice had meanwhile wandered out into the lobby to howl. The phone continued ringing as he explained about her. 'They're a very well-to-do family, but she's on drugs, so I'm not supposed to give her money except on the first of the month.'

'You're in charge of her?'

'Not in charge, I just...' He shrugged at this, yet another unanswerable Chelsea question, not sure what his function was except that he was stuck with it. He picked up the phone, and while I read the letter he was now yelling into it, 'Ethel, you are bothering me!' And hung up again, his benign face neither blanched nor reddened by what must have been anger.

The letter from the late James was a frontal attack on Stanley for having demanded a rent rise when he knew that James could no longer earn very much and, from the sound of it, might have been on welfare. James mixed outrage with pathetic pleading, 'You are destroying me!' and so on.

The phone rang again and he picked it up and slammed it down. 'I can't stand crazy women,' he said. And pointing to the letter, with a benign smile spreading over his face, said, 'You see?'

'Have you read this letter, Stanley?' I asked.

His face clouded. 'Of course I read it. He loved it here. He'd been here years and years. It was the best hotel in the world, he used to say.'

'He says you were destroying him.'

Snatching the letter he said, 'Destroying him!' Clearly, he was remembering now as he glanced down at the handwriting. 'But look, see what he says down here?'

He held the letter in front of me, pointing down at the bottom of it, and read aloud, '"Very sincerely yours". You see?' And he slapped the letter lightly with the backs of his fingers, his case made. Now he sat back and smiled his old friendly smile; 'James loved it here. So listen, I'm serious. I'll give you the apartment rent free if you'll live here. At least look at it.'

'I couldn't live here again even if I had to pay rent,' I said, but he didn't get the joke. God knows why, but I soon found myself with him on one of the two elevators that was working that day and up we went to the seventh floor where painters were working in a large, high-ceilinged apartment.

'All the furniture is new, even the bathroom faucets...' Here I was again, over twenty years after the first demonstration I had attended with his late father, being invited to examine the bathroom faucets. Was this clan fated to go on forever reproducing itself and repeating the same things? A hundred years from now would a Bard be showing the brand new faucets to some hapless possible tenant? Depressed by these thoughts and their intimations of mortality, I had nevertheless to agree that it was indeed a lovely apartment although the porcelain had been rubbed off the refrigerator door, but I knew that there always had to be a certain remnant of shabbiness lest it turn into a real hotel that nobody would particularly care to live in. 'And look how quiet,' Stanley held up one hand as though conducting the silence.

'It's a terrific apartment, but...'

'Think about it is all I ask. You ever hear quiet like this in New York? You're in New York, would you believe it?' He cocked an ear.

I had to confess it was in fact extremely quiet, knowing as I did that the ancient walls were a couple of feet thick. We descended to the lobby, and stepping out of the elevator Stanley was continuing his peace and quiet theme, 'You could concentrate here, nobody would bother you...' My eye caught the strange sight of a deep pile of broken glass lying just inside the doorway to the street. Crossing the lobby we both realized that the glass doors were gone, collapsed into this pile at our feet. Stanley, his Buddhistic expression intact excepting for the panic drawing tight the edges of his eyes, called to the desk clerk who promptly came around and addressed him.

'I don't know what happened,' the clerk said. I couldn't be sure if the man was in still in shock or if he always looked so pale and hauntingly surprised.

'What do you mean you don't know what happened, the doors are gone!'

'Well, some guy stopped on the sidewalk and took out a pistol and shot them.'

'What do you mean, "shot them"? He shot the doors?'

'He shot the doors and they crumpled.'

'Why would he shoot the doors, for God's sake!' Stanley raised his voice, almost accusingly.

'How do I know? I seen him crossing on the sidewalk and he stops and takes out the gun and bang! And he walks away.'

Stanley, momentarily flummoxed, stood there shaking his head.

Another unanswerable Chelsea dilemma beyond the analytical reach of any mind. Outside on the sidewalk the blind couple had arrived and with their white walking sticks were feeling around in the broken glass which blocked the entrance. Stanley instantly stepped over the glass, and taking the woman's hand led her gently around the pile with the man following behind, telling them not to worry, everything was under control. Alone together again in his office, I said, 'This is what I mean, Stanley, it's too interesting here, I'd never get any work done.'

'Well, you always stayed in your room, you never hung out in the lobby; nothing's going to happen in your room. Will you think about it?'

'I will do nothing else for the next three months.' And he got the joke this time and laughed, albeit unhappily. His quick changes reminded me of his attractiveness for many people—he was a man of feeling, a passionate man. Along with some other qualities, but after all business is business.

A speck of dust fell into my eye. I hoped it wasn't glass and carefully working the eyelid tilted my head back, and up near the ceiling the good eye spied a foot-square white linoleum tile with red and blue squiggles painted on it. Mendel the Marine!

'Whatever happened to Mendel the Marine?' I asked.

Two immense cops walked in, no doubt to talk about the shooting of the glass doors, and I left a very nervous Stanley, obviously worried about some inevitably unfair publicity. Mendel's hatred for the house detective, back in the Sixties, surfaced in memory as I stood in the lobby waiting for two men to finish shovelling up the pile of glass. Bernice sat nearby, oblivious, under a Larry Rivers painting, doing a crossword puzzle on a folded newspaper resting on her thigh. I stared out to the street where, on a quiet Sunday morning in spring, the last before Kennedy was shot, I had managed to lock my car keys inside my Buick's trunk. The desk clerk had suggested I call upstairs to the house detective who, he said, 'had lots of keys'. He said this with a private little grin which I hadn't time or wit to evaluate.

At eight-thirty on a Sunday morning the detective's sleep-clotted voice sounded deeply controlled but furious. Apologizing, I told him my problem and he said he'd be down in half an hour or so, 'if you want to wait'. As though I could do anything else with my ignition key in the car trunk. I had seen this fellow once about a year earlier when, waiting to cross 23rd Street, I noticed a Saab with its roof so collapsed that a telephone pole might have come down on it. Its windshield was separated from the rest of the body leaving a gap through which snow was falling on to the driver's cap. His visor had about an inch of snow on it. Arriving at the hotel I saw the driver, who I later learned was the detective, unloading stuff from the car's trunk. One side window of the car was missing, which did not keep him from carefully locking its doors before going into the hotel; a man, I thought then, of deeply engraved locking habits. That was in winter. Now, on this lovely spring morning, he at last came down in his shirtsleeves carrying a steel ring about the diameter of a frisbee on which were hung about a hundred keys. As he tried one key after the other in the trunk's lock I kept silent with sinking heart, knowing that they were house keys and would never open a car lock. We ended the business by both of us removing the back of the rear seat, permitting me to reach into the trunk from inside the car. He was about thirty, a trim blonde man with a close military haircut and an unsmiling face even after I gave him ten dollars for his trouble. It had seemed odd to me then that a detective would not know that ordinary house keys were different from ignition keys, but again, at the Chelsea, the spirit of enquiry soon exhausted itself in answerless questions that trickled away like a brook in a desert—in this, come to think of it, the place was a lot like life.

Indeed, on the morning after the famous roll of new carpet was delivered and deposited on the second floor to await the installers, I emerged from the elevator to find three or four cops in the lobby, but they were not holding coffee containers. Instead they seemed to be working, quietly talking among themselves. Advised by my father at the age of seven to always stay away from crowds, I left, returning that afternoon to find Mendel the Marine selling a tile to some lady with a foreign accent, Alabama perhaps. Mendel caught up with me as I was awaiting one of the working elevators.

'Dja hear?'

'What.'

'They stole the carpet.'

That 500- or 800-pound roll of carpet gone? Disappeared overnight? The desk clerk would surely have seen it if it had gone out the lobby door. Or had he been in on it? No, impossible when he was hardly five feet tall, painfully timid and always exhausted. How then could so massive and heavy a thing have possibly left the building? Removing an object of that size and weight was about the equivalent of stealing a grand piano and moving it into the street without anybody noticing.

'Oh, it can be done,' said Mendel under his lip.

'How can it be done?'

With a glance left and right for interlopers, he gave me a head signal to follow him into one of the elevators, the one that was working.

In the second floor corridor Mendel indicated an enormous window at least ten feet high and perhaps six feet wide that looked down on the unlighted parking lot behind the hotel. 'This is removable, frame and all,' he indicated the window. 'Then you back up a truck down there and drop the roll on to it and you're in like Flynn.'

'But wouldn't somebody have heard? In fact...' I suddenly recalled that the house detective had walked up the stairs from the lobby rather than taking an elevator after my trunk key misadventure. 'I had some idea he lived on one of these lower floors.'

Mendel, straight-faced, raised a finger pointing at a door which displayed half a dozen locks just opposite the big window. 'The house detective lives right there.'

'Ah,' I said. 'You can say that again.'

'Maybe he wasn't home at the time.'

'That's right; maybe he wasn't. Maybe this isn't even Tuesday either.'

In the weeks that passed, or months—I no longer recall—the main drama of the period had been the steady disappearance from various rooms of typewriters, radios, air conditioners, televisions and even a few pieces of jewellery and a valuable watch or two. Police had come and gone with not a clue developing. One morning smoke began pouring out of the room next to the house detective's.

The fire department put out the fire in a few minutes, and following normal procedure asked Stanley for the key to the adjoining room, which happened to be the detective's, to be sure nothing was smouldering in there. Stanley, of course, had no key to the six locks on the detective's door and the sleuth was away at the time. The firemen, under Stanley's protests, broke down the door and entered the apartment. There facing them were shelves rising to the ceiling filled with a good selection of radios, typewriters, televisions, fur coats and other useful items. The police were awaiting the detective on his return and he received a medium sentence, it was said, since he was not at all violent. From then on until he disappeared, Mendel the Marine was nothing but smiles whenever we ran into one another, a happy man, I believe, for the rest of his life.

With all my misgivings about the Chelsea, I can never enter it without a certain quickening of my heartbeat. There is an indescribably homelike atmosphere which at the same time lacks a certain credibility. It is some kind of fictional place, I used to think. As in dreams things are out front that are concealed in other hotels, like the wooden bins in the corridors in which the garbage pails are kept, and for some unknowable reason this sort of candour seems so right that you smile whenever you pass the bins. It may simply be that nobody is urgently concerned about what is happening because nobody quite knows what is happening, or maybe there is a kind of freedom or severe disconnect with plain reality, or, as the saying goes, a sense that the inmates have long since taken over the asylum, which can be irritating but perhaps not altogether a bad thing, at least in the spiritual sense. It may in fact be as salutary a way as any of running a public place. But in recent months and years a new determination to update has begun to show. Stanley's son has come of age and there is a new carpet, wainscoting has been revealed from under its age-old coats of paint. The whole facade has been cleaned and restored to its long-obliterated Victorian elegance. On a recent visit there to Arnold Weinstein with whom I have collaborated on a libretto for a new opera based on *A View from the Bridge*, with music by William Bolcom, I found myself sinking back, psychologically speaking, into my original warm feelings toward the hotel as of my arrival there over forty years ago. And as we discussed some business in the total chaos of his living room, which is not so much furnished as littered with collectors' items suitable for a massive Salvation Army donation, the door to the corridor swung open and without a knock a powerful maid entered, her exuberant smile and glistening black skin all aglow with some sort of triumph. And raising up over her head four rolls of toilet paper, two spiked on the fingers of each hand, she called out at the top of her joyous contralto voice, 'I didn't forget you, Arnold!' And he rose from his wobbly chair and gratefully accepted her gift. And so I instantly knew that clean facade or not, refurbished lobby notwithstanding, I was back in the Chelsea again.   □

A Calendar of the Letters of Willa Cather

Edited by Janis P. Stout

An infamous clause in Willa Cather's will, forbidding publication of her letters and other papers, has long caused consternation among Cather scholars. Cather's letters will not come into public domain until the year 2017. Until then, even quotation, let alone publication in full, is prohibited.

Janis P. Stout has gathered over eighteen hundred of Cather's letters and provides a brief summary of each, as well as a biographical directory identifying correspondents and a multisection index of the widely scattered letters organized by location, by correspondent, and by names and titles mentioned. This book will be an essential resource for Cather scholars.

$60 cloth

Willa Cather and the American Southwest

Edited by John N. Swift and Joseph R. Urgo

The American Southwest was arguably as formative a landscape for Willa Cather's aesthetic vision as was her beloved Nebraska. Both landscapes elicited in her a sense of raw incompleteness. They seemed not so much finished places as things unassembled, more like countries "still waiting to be made into [a] landscape." The seemingly sterile indifference of the desert landscape posed a particular challenge to Cather's desire to find in all places evidence of human significance and cultural accomplishment. Here, historical cultural achievements were not immediately apparent and when found took Cather far from the European tradition that had formed her early works.

$40 cloth

NOTES ON CONTRIBUTORS

Rachel Cusk is the author of three novels. Her recent book about motherhood, *A Life's Work: On Becoming a Mother*, is published by Fourth Estate in the UK and Penguin USA.

Milan Kundera was born in Czechoslovakia in 1929. His novels include *The Joke, The Unbearable Lightness of Being* and *Immortality*. 'The Great Return' is taken from his novel, *Ignorance*, which will be published later this year (Faber/HarperCollins). He lives in France.

Adrian Leftwich teaches politics at the University of York.

Todd McEwen is the author of *Fisher's Hornpipe, McX* and *Arithmetic* (Vintage). 'The Little Plate of Childhood' is taken from a novel-in-progress. He lives in Edinburgh.

Jon McGregor was born in Bermuda in 1976. He grew up in Norfolk and now lives in Nottingham. His first novel, *If Nobody Speaks of Remarkable Things*, will be published later this year by Bloomsbury in the UK.

Arthur Miller's plays include *Death of a Salesman, The Crucible* and most recently, *Mr Peters' Connections*. His autobiography, *Timebends: A Life*, is published by Methuen in the UK and Penguin USA.

Deirdre O'Callaghan's photographs are taken from her forthcoming book, *Hide the Can*, which will be published by Trolley in September. They will also be part of a group exhibition, *Stepping In Stepping Out*, which opens at the Victoria & Albert Museum in London on September 3 this year.

Gary Shteyngart was born in Leningrad in 1972. His first novel, *The Russian Debutante's Handbook* is published in June by Riverhead Books in the US and by Bloomsbury in the UK in 2003. He lives in New York.

Rory Stewart served briefly in the British Army and then as a diplomat in Jakarta and Montenegro. In August 2000 he resigned from the Foreign Office and began walking from Turkey towards Vietnam. His book about the walk, *The Places In Between*, will be published by Picador in the UK.

Jonathan Tel is the author of *Arafat's Elephant*, a collection of stories set in and around Jerusalem (Counterpoint Press). He divides his time between New York, London and Jerusalem. He is currently working on a novel.

Olga Tokarczuk was born in Poland in 1962. 'Marek Marek' is taken from her novel, *House of the Day, House of the Night* (Granta Books). Her short story, 'The Hotel Capital', appeared in *Granta* 72.

Edmund White's most recent books are *The Flâneur* (Bloomsbury)—an essay on Paris—and a novel, *The Married Man* (Chatto/Knopf). He is currently working on a historical novel about Frances Wright. He lives in New York.